# Outlaw's Bride

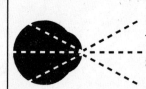

This Large Print Book carries the
Seal of Approval of N.A.V.H.

# OUTLAW'S BRIDE

## LORI COPELAND

**THORNDIKE PRESS**
*A part of Gale, Cengage Learning*

GALE
CENGAGE Learning

Detroit • New York • San Francisco • New Haven, Conn • Waterville, Maine • London

GALE
CENGAGE Learning™

Copyright © 1999 by Lori Copeland.
The Western Sky Series #1.
Scripture quotations from the King James Version of the Bible.
Thorndike Press, a part of Gale, Cengage Learning.

Thorndike Press® Large Print Christian Historical Fiction.
The text of this Large Print edition is unabridged.
Other aspects of the book may vary from the original edition.
Set in 16 pt. Plantin.

LIBRARY OF CONGRESS CATALOGING-IN-PUBLICATION DATA

Copeland, Lori.
   Outlaw's bride / by Lori Copeland.
      p. cm. — (Thorndike Press large print Christian historical fiction) (The western sky series ; no. 1)
   ISBN-13: 978-1-4104-2618-5 (alk. paper)
   ISBN-10: 1-4104-2618-1 (alk. paper)
   1. Large type books. I. Title.
PS3553.O6336B75 2010
813'.54—dc22                                    2010005067

Published in 2010 by arrangement with Books and Such Literary Agency, Inc.

Printed in the United States of America
1 2 3 4 5 6 7 14 13 12 11 10

# OUTLAW'S BRIDE

# PROLOGUE

*Barren Flats — formerly Paradise, California*
*July 1876*

Ragan Ramsey watched the trail of dust disappear, and then she let the curtain drop into place. "Thank goodness that one's gone."

Judge Proctor McMann, known to most as "Procky," chuckled and drew deeply on his pipe, the scent of cherry tobacco filling the parlor. "I have to admit that was a test of endurance."

With a sigh Ragan started for the kitchen, where breakfast dishes awaited her. She'd been the judge's housekeeper for three years, and she loved Procky like a father, but why she'd ever let him talk her into writing a book titled *Rehabilitation for the Unlovable* failed her. The past two years they had taken in one criminal after another, old and young. These were men who had shown the propensity for change, and Procky had hopes of gaining the inner workings of the troubled mind. However, sixteen-year-old Max Rutherford had returned to jail this morning after a brief but angst-filled stay. *Good riddance,* thought Ragan. None of their subjects had lasted more than a few months, and she didn't know why the judge insisted that they complete the book.

Procky patted his knee and Kitty bounded into his lap. "Things should settle down for a while."

"For a good long while, I'd hope." Ragan was still complaining when she entered the kitchen. "You promised, Procky. No more 'subjects' for a while." Her patience was stretched thin by hoodlums, miscreants, and the just plain mean. "You have to make it clear to Judge Leonard that we can't handle one more case for the time being."

When Ragan had taken the housekeeping job she'd known the path wouldn't be easy. With an ailing father and three younger sisters at home to feed, she would have her hands full. And true, when Judge McMann first talked about writing the book it all sounded exciting, helping criminals to become upstanding citizens, until she'd gotten down to the hard work. She wasn't a quitter, but she did have enough sense to know when enough was enough.

The judge's tone turned cajoling. "You were all for this project when we began the book."

"That was before I met the subjects." Ragan reached for the tea kettle and poured hot water into the dish pan.

Chuckling, the judge rolled his wheelchair into the kitchen. "You're all spit and fire right now, but I know your heart, Ragan Ramsey. When called upon, you'll report for duty."

Ragan dunked plates in the sudsy water. "Not this time, Procky. You promised. Give us at least six months to recuperate." Papa would be ashamed of her lack of compassion, but a body could only do so much.

"I'm not getting any younger, little lady. The good Lord could call me home any-time. What if I don't have six months to complete the book?"

Shaking her head, she scrubbed a dish. "I don't presume to know God's timing, but I do know you're as healthy as a horse."

He looked down at his wheelchair. "Then what am I doing in this contraption?"

"Admittedly, you're a little tottery."

"I can stand up, but I can't walk!"

She brushed his words aside. The judge, other than the normal complaints of an eighty-eight-year-old man, was fine, unlike her father, a much younger man who was in the last stages of senility. Papa had lost his mind; he was an empty shell. Procky was still as sharp as a tack.

Rinsing a cup, she set it on the counter. "Just promise we'll halt the program for a few months, at least long enough for me to regain my sanity. What with all these gangs riding through, shooting up everything, and having a sheriff who's not only lost his hearing but won't step aside —"

"Who in their right mind would take his place?"

She couldn't think of a soul. Not in this town or anywhere near. Though the gangs stole their cattle, livestock, and anything else not nailed down, the men in town were spineless, terrified for their lives and their families. Not a one would organize against the marauders.

"All right, you win. I'll write and tell Judge Leonard not to send any more subjects for a while." He yawned. "If I don't forget."

"I'll have pen and paper on your desk this afternoon."

He winked and rolled to the doorway, heading for his morning nap. "Still doesn't mean I'll remember it. And you know the mail system. Can't depend on a letter getting to the judge anytime soon —"

Ragan turned from the sink and pinpointed him with an icy stare.

"Okay. I'll write the letter." He rolled into the living room, mumbling under his breath. "Females. Can't live with 'em and can't manage without 'em."

# CHAPTER ONE

Trouble is like an ill-fitting shoe: You pay a high price for a poor choice, and you can't wait to get out of it.

Johnny McAllister stood before Judge Robert Leonard and waited for the ax to fall. He'd been tried for a crime he didn't commit in front of a jury that found him guilty, and he didn't have a way in the world to prove his innocence. When the judge raised his gavel, Johnny braced for the worst.

"Johnny McAllister, you stand accused of robbery of the First Territorial Bank of California." The judge peered solemnly over the rims of his spectacles. "And for kidnapping my daughter, Mary Beth, and scaring the waddin' right out of her. Restate your plea."

Johnny glanced at the young girl sitting on the front bench, smirking. If he had known Mary Beth was the judge's daughter, he would have run the other way. *"Not guilty,* your honor."

The judge pointed his gavel at the accused. "You plead not guilty. However, the jury finds you guilty and requests that you be hanged by your neck until dead."

*Hanged.* The word ricocheted in Johnny's ears. He'd never find Bledso. He'd never avenge his family's death. That stung more than the sentence.

Judge Leonard's shock of snow-white hair made him look like an insightful old owl. "You present quite a problem for me, Mr. McAllister. To be honest, I don't know what to do with you. For the life of me, I can't find any way that you appear to be associated with the gang of thugs you're accused of consorting with. The Puet bunch is as mean as they come, and they've ridden together for some time. It doesn't stand to reason that they'd accept a drifter like you in their ranks. You don't fit their profile."

He studied Johnny with owl-like eyes. "But I have my duty. Therefore, it is the decision of this court that you, Johnny McAllister, be remanded to the custody of Judge Proctor McMann in Paradise, California, for a period of no less than one year, and no longer than two years. The exact amount of time served will be determined by Judge McMann."

The convicted's knees threatened to buckle in relief. He wasn't going to hang. One or two years — he could do anything for a couple of years. He could do three if he had to, and still keep an eye out for Bledso.

Johnny waited as the judge shuffled a stack of papers.

Peering over the rims of his spectacles again, the magistrate said quietly, "You're wondering why I'm going so easy on you."

"Yes, sir, I am." In most counties, he'd be a dead man and he knew it.

"Well, I'm not necessarily convinced that you did rob the bank, if that's any comfort. You could be pulling the wool over my eyes, I'll allow for that, but you saved my daughter from certain harm, and I owe you a debt of gratitude."

His features softened. "Judge McMann is an old friend and trusted colleague. He and I have been working together for the past two years on a program that I will permit him to explain. But foremost, I sense something in you I don't find in most of the men who stand before this court."

Johnny couldn't imagine what that would be, but he wasn't going to argue.

"I may never be certain whether you did or did not rob the bank — and we're talking about my money too. You understand that, don't you, young man?"

"Yes, sir."

"I'm giving you a second chance. Do you know what it means to get a second chance from the law, Mr. McAllister?"

"I do, Judge."

"Good, because not everyone gets a reprieve in this court. I hope, even pray, Mr. McAllister, that you make the best of yours. It isn't likely you'll get another."

Johnny nodded. The judge could save his prayers. No one, including God, had ever given him a break, so he recognized what the judge had done.

"At the time of your arrest, you carried a handgun." The judge motioned to the bailiff, who laid the pistol in front of him. "It's a fine firearm."

"It belonged to my grandfather."

"Then it must hold a great deal of sentimental value to you."

"Yes, sir, it does." Gazing at the gun, he could feel Grandpa's arms tighten around him and steady his hands as he sighted the pistol for the first time. The old man's gentle voice brushed his cheek and quieted his turmoil. He'd give up almost anything he owned before parting with that gun.

It was Grandpa who took him in after his

parents died and quieted his nightmares when he woke screaming during the night. The old man had instilled in him a deep respect of right versus wrong. Grandpa was the only one he had after the murders. Johnny felt his presence now as surely as if he stood beside him.

"Your gun will be returned to you at the successful completion of your time with Judge McMann. At that time you will also receive a just and fair price, along with accrued interest, for the sale of your horse, which will be sold immediately at auction." He paused, and then he said quietly, "If a year or two in the custody of Proctor McMann doesn't mold you into a God-fearing, productive citizen, then may God rest your soul, because money or firearms won't do you any good. In the event you fail to serve your sentence, proceeds from the sale of your pistol and horse will go to compensate bank patrons for money lost during the robbery, and you will once again stand before me for sentencing. Do you have any questions, Mr. McAllister?"

"No, sir."

"Are the terms of the punishment clear?"

Johnny nodded. Serve the sentence without incident, and he'd go free. Violate the rules, and he'd hang.

# CHAPTER TWO

*Barren Flats, California*

Ragan Ramsey parted the judge's parlor curtains, her eyes widening as she got her first glimpse of the prisoner. Swallowing, she bit her lower lip. Procky had promised. No more subjects for six months. Now this one shows up. He came into town handcuffed inside a buckboard, dressed in black, looking meaner than sin and three times as evil.

*"Blessed are the meek: for they shall inherit the earth." Papa's favorite beatitude.*

Somehow, she didn't feel especially blessed this morning.

The buckboard rattled to a halt in front of the house. Two men with badges, rifles, and holstered firearms climbed down, knocking dust off their clothing. One moved to the back of the wagon and unlocked the prisoner's foot shackles, then he nudged him out of the wagon bed with the rifle butt.

Ragan stepped onto the porch, wiping her hands on her apron. *Make the best of it, Ragan. You won't leave the judge — you know that, though you're so angry with him about this you could spit nails.* He'd sent the letter. She'd mailed it herself, but apparently Judge Leonard had not received it in time to prevent this "subject" from arriving.

The man got out of the wagon slowly, his bitter gaze fixed on the officer. Motioning toward the house, the lawman shoved the prisoner through the gate and followed him up the walk lined with blooming marigolds.

Obvious resentment burned hot in the bound man's gaze. His scruffy appearance couldn't hide the pride and defiance of his stance. He looked as if he hadn't slept in days; purplish-blue circles ringed his dark eyes, eyes that lifted to confront hers without apology or shame.

She swallowed against the sudden dryness in her throat and shivered against a premonition that this man was going to be more — much more than she'd so far encountered. Thick road grime layered his clothes, and his hair hung limp and dirty beneath a black hat. Her gaze fixed on the broad set of his shoulders, the muscular, unyielding stance, and the square chin that jutted defiantly upward.

*Father, help us.*

One guard paused in front of the steps and touched the brim of his hat. "Afternoon, ma'am."

Ragan's gaze focused on the prisoner's handcuffs and shackles. It took a moment for her to force her eyes away. "Would you care for a cool drink?" The men were covered in dust and obviously trail worn.

The officer curtly shook his head. "Much obliged, but we'll be movin' along as soon as our business here is completed."

She stepped aside, allowing room for them on the porch. Digging the barrel of the rifle into the man's side, the lawman moved the prisoner slowly up the stairs.

Ragan's gaze took in the criminal's soiled boots. Old, scuffed, and in bad need of new heels. Her eyes lifted to his face, and she shook off a feeling of impending doom. It would take a lot more than a new pair of boots to improve this man's disposition.

Maybe all her years of sitting under Papa's sermons about love and patience helped her to feel his humiliation. He and others like him had ruined her town. She should feel nothing but revulsion. Instead, she felt pity. Pity that the young man hidden beneath all that grime would throw his life away for a few moments of excitement and a bag of bank money. Maybe Procky was right to care for him and others like him, but lately she had had to work at compassion a little harder.

He glanced her way, and she stepped back. Then again, maybe Procky was a fool, as he'd often been told, to try and rehabilitate men like this.

The guards paused before the screen door. "Where would you like him, ma'am?" one asked.

The judge, in his wheelchair, appeared in the doorway, his face flushed from an afternoon nap. His thatch of gray hair stood on end. "Bring him into the parlor, officer." He opened the screen, and the aroma of frying chicken penetrated the air. Judge McMann smiled. "Come in, son. It's hot out there."

The three men stepped inside, and an officer unlocked the handcuffs. Straightening, he tipped his hat. "I'd watch this one, Judge. He's a hardhead."

The judge nodded. "Thank you, gentlemen. Sure you won't stay to supper?"

As he chatted with the sheriff's men, Ragan stepped into the foyer with the prisoner, flicking at imaginary dust on the hall table. She supposed she was uncomfortable because this prisoner was near her own

21

age. The others had been either younger or older. She avoided his bitter gaze.

The man stood quietly, hands folded in front of him. His stance made it clear he wasn't inviting conversation, so she didn't have to worry about social niceties.

*Well, this is plain silly,* she told herself when she felt perspiration begin to dampen her back. They couldn't stand in this strained silence all day. The judge was a talker, and her chicken needed to be turned. The prisoner was here, so she would make the best of it.

"Would you like a glass of tea?"

The man shook his head, his dark eyes now avoiding hers.

"Procky does tend to go on at times. I'll show you to your room."

Judge Leonard had said the prisoner wasn't considered unduly dangerous. Bank robbery. He wasn't to be locked behind bars, but his whereabouts were to be known by Ragan or Judge McMann at all times until they felt comfortable giving him more freedom. Ragan didn't care for the idea of trusting a prisoner with any freedom, especially as the last two adult cases had proved Judge Leonard's judgment erroneous.

She climbed the stairs leading to the second landing, motioning for the prisoner to follow. He picked up a worn brown satchel and followed. *Pity that a man's whole life can be carried in one insignificant bag.*

Opening the door to the east bedroom, Ragan said, "I think you'll be comfortable here." The room was her favorite of the guest rooms. Sunny in the morning, shaded during the hot afternoons. Maddy McMann had stitched together the pretty wedding ring quilt the year she died. The walls were wallpapered blue, and the rosebush beneath the open window perfumed the room with its heavenly scent.

The prisoner's gaze traveled the quarters dispassionately. She couldn't tell if the room suited him or not. She supposed it didn't matter; he had no choice. It would be his home for the next twelve to twenty-four months, if he made it that long.

"You'll need a pitcher of water for the washbowl," she said. "I'll get it for you."

He nodded, setting the valise on the floor. She turned and hurried to the door.

"Is that it?"

She turned. "Breakfast is at six, dinner at noon, and supper at five o'clock sharp. Please try to be prompt. Procky gets cranky if he doesn't eat on time."

He lifted a questioning brow.

"Procky — Judge Proctor McMann. His

friends call him Procky." She supposed he wouldn't find that information all that useful, though whether or not the prisoner knew it, Procky would be his friend. "And one other thing: no profane language. Ever. Liquor is forbidden as well as tobacco."

"And I suppose church every Sunday."

"No. You are welcome to accompany us to services when we're able to have them, but unfortunately our church is not fit for worship at this time. We hold services in our homes. You are invited to join the Judge for Bible study anytime you want, but he feels you can't make a man come to the Lord. It must be of his free will."

His gaze roamed the room, coming to rest on the open window. "Are you the judge's daughter?"

"No. His housekeeper. I leave after the supper dishes are done and return in the morning to fix breakfast and clean."

His eyes came back to meet hers briefly. Goose bumps rose on her arms as his dark gaze boldly assessed her. "That's all that's expected of me? Show up for meals on time?"

"Don't curse, drink, or use tobacco and attend daily research sessions."

He gave her a hard look. "Every day?"

"Monday through Friday." Did he think

this was a guest ranch? "You rest up from your trip and eat your supper. If you need anything, please inform me."

He turned and walked to the window. Pushing the curtain aside, he looked out. "I'm not hungry."

"You'll have to sit at the table anyway." Prisoners attended meals, hungry or not.

He slowly turned to face her, his eyes locking with hers. "Why is this town shot to pieces?"

She thought about the chicken frying in the skillet. "There'll be time for chitchat later." She turned toward the door. "I'll get that water for you."

"Don't bother. I can wait on myself."

Kitty shot through the door, darting between the man's legs. He looked down as the cat purred, rubbing her whiskers against his scuffed boot.

Ragan's eyes acknowledged the pet. "Kitty, the judge's pride and joy. If she bothers you tonight just push her off the bed. She'll likely end up trying to sleep with you."

The man's expression said the cat wouldn't be sleeping with him.

Not tonight.

Not ever.

# CHAPTER THREE

Leaving the room, Ragan pulled the door closed behind her. Her legs felt a bit shaky as she descended the stairs, thinking about the coming months. How would she ever manage this man? Judge Leonard expected Procky and her to set his scuffed boots on a righteous path?

She couldn't be sure she'd convinced him to come downstairs for supper.

Well, the judge couldn't fault her. She'd warned him the subjects were getting increasingly worrisome. From the moment Everett delivered the wire from Judge Leonard, she'd made her protests vocal.

"Want me to get that?" the judge asked when the knock had sounded at the door.

"No, stay where you are." Ragan wiped her hands on her apron and went to answer it. When she opened the door, she found Everett Pidgin trying to catch his breath. The lanky

27

telegraph operator panted as though he had run all the way from the telegraph station. His breath came in ragged jerks. He eyed Ragan, flushing four shades of red before he could state his purpose. "Afternoon, Miss . . . Miss Ragan."

"Hello, Everett."

"Tele . . . telegraph just came in for the judge. I came as soon as I could."

He looked for the entire world like a puppy that wanted his owner's approval for retrieving a thrown stick. Ragan had to squelch the urge to say, "Good boy."

"Telegraph for me?" The judge made his way to the door to join them. "Now, who could be sending me a telegraph?"

Everett grinned, his eyes fixed on Ragan. "Robert Leonard in Barrow County."

"Robert?" Judge McMann quickly scanned the missive.

"Procky," Ragan warned. A telegram from Judge Leonard usually meant trouble. She returned Everett's smile. "It's warm out there today. Would you like to come in for a glass of lemonade?"

The besotted young man took a step backward and promptly dropped off the front of the porch. He landed in the rosebush at the side of the steps, his spindly legs floundering in the air.

Ragan hurried to assist him. "Are you hurt?"

The red-faced messenger thwarted her efforts. Arms flailing, he rolled to his feet, flushing a deeper hue. "Not hurt, thank you. Just a misstep. Could have happened to anybody."

Ragan reached to brush off a clump of leaves, but Everett backed away.

Jerking his suit jacket into place, he stalked off, opened the whitewashed gate, and then latched it carefully. Striding toward the telegraph office, he kept his chin held high. She probably should have told him about the rose branch dangling from the back of his jacket, but it would only mortify him further.

"Poor man's got it bad," the judge chuckled when Ragan came back into the house.

"I know, and I wish he wouldn't think of me in a romantic vein. He's had his share of rejection, and I don't want to hurt him too."

After Sunday services, Everett followed Ragan around like a lovesick fool. During the week, he waited outside the mercantile to carry her parcels.

If the sun was too hot, he was there with a parasol to shade her. If it rained, he held an umbrella over her head.

It was a wonder he found time to run the telegraph office. He smothered her, yet she couldn't and wouldn't hurt his feelings. Though he was a wonderfully kind young man, Ragan had no romantic feelings for him. His infatuation with her made him the laughingstock of Barren Flats. He had been in love with her since he was in the first grade and she was in the fifth. He refused to accept the fact that she didn't love him back. She'd tried, desperately tried, to center his interests elsewhere, but he only had eyes for her.

"Well, well." The judge refolded the message, following Ragan into the kitchen. "Seems we're about to have company again."

She whirled to face him. "Procky! You promised."

"I know I did, and I wrote the letter, but apparently it didn't reach Robert in time. Don't get your skirts in a bunch. We'll manage."

Who was Judge Leonard sending now? Hopefully it wasn't another sixteen-year-old. Last time Max almost did them both in.

"This particular fellow is a little older than you," the judge mused. "Says here he's twenty-eight."

Ragan's heart dropped. "After Max, Robert promised to send only older subjects, Judge."

"I know, but Robert must feel this case is an exception. We do need the documentation, you know. Why, the book's only half done."

"Wire Robert back and tell him we can't accept this man, and make it stick this time. We agreed. At least six months of rest."

30

"I know you're upset, but there's not much we can do about it now," the judge said. "The prisoner is already on his way."

Ragan groaned.

"One last try," the judge soothed. "If this one doesn't pan out, then you have my promise that we will quit the program and complete the book as is." The old man chuckled. "If Robert knew about all the trouble we're having with gangs here, he wouldn't have sent us another case." The judge poured cream into a saucer and set it on the floor for Kitty. "He'd insist that I move."

Ragan cracked an egg into a bowl. "If we had the sense God gave a goose, we'd all move."

"And where would we go, missy?"

"I don't know. Anywhere but here." Ragan added salt and then began to knead the dough. "A town with a perfectly lovely name, Paradise, forced to change its name to Barren Flats because of gangs. Disgraceful."

"I'm not going anywhere. This is my home." The judge's faded eyes roamed the kitchen, pausing on the cracked floor covering, walls begging for paint, and cabinets needing repair. The old house was falling down around his ears, but that obviously wasn't important to him.

"This is where I brought Maddy the day I

married her. This is where my three children were born, where two died of smallpox in infancy. Maddy drew her last breath there on the parlor sofa." His tone wavered as it always did when he reminisced about Maddy and the twins, and he blinked to clear the mist from his eyes.

"I'm an old man. I'm not leaving the only home I've ever known. Paradise is where I was born, and it's where I'll die. No matter how bad it gets, I'll stay right here. They'll bury me right out there next to Maddy and my babies. No-good hoodlums aren't going to run me off."

Covering the bowl with a cloth, Ragan set it on the counter to allow the dough to rise. The judge was lonely. His only living child was his son, Blake, who lived in Colorado. They were seldom able to see each other. The judge had never made the trip to Denver.

She sighed. "When will the new prisoner be arriving?"

"The wire didn't say. I'd guess soon, if I know Robert. He insists on swift justice. He'll either hang a man or dole out suitable punishment. He won't keep a man guessing."

Ragan shook herself free from her thoughts when she walked into the kitchen and smelled the chicken burning. Jerking off the skillet lid, she turned the scorched pieces, her mind now fixed on supper.

# Chapter Four

*So this is Paradise.*

Johnny's eyes roamed the room again. Someone needed to buy Judge Leonard a dictionary. Johnny didn't know much about spiritual things other than what Grandpa had taught him, but he'd gotten the impression that Paradise — or heaven, if there were such a thing — didn't look a thing like this town. He stood up and walked to the window to part the curtains. God. He mentally scoffed. It had been a long time since he'd thought about his Maker.

Main Street stretched north to south. He'd noticed a livery and blacksmith shop as they came into town. Then they'd passed a general store, telegraph office, bank, the sheriff's office, saloon, surveyor's office, and title office. Didn't look like a place where there would be much buying and selling going on. The buildings were peppered with bullet holes, and he'd noticed more than one buckshot-riddled windowpane. The town looked like a battlefield.

At the south end sat a steepled white building that looked to be in bad shape. He hadn't seen a cow, goat, or steer in the area.

Johnny let the curtain drop back into place, his mind going back to the ill-fated day two weeks earlier that had brought him here.

After stepping down from his saddle, Johnny climbed the three wooden steps to the First Territorial Bank of California and scanned the row of weathered wanted posters flapping in the hot breeze for information on outlaw Dirk Bledso. Two smiling women emerged from the land title office. He touched the brim of his hat. "Morning, ladies."

They eyed his trail-worn appearance and ragged shoulder-length hair. Chins tilting upward, they pointedly looked in the opposite direction. One raised a dainty lace handkerchief to her nose and sniffed as she passed.

And a good morning to you. He wasn't surprised by their lack of civility. A lot of folks didn't cotton to drifters.

His gaze shifted back to the posters. No telling how old these things were. He smoothed a torn fragment, holding it down with his palm. Outlaw Jack Brooks, wanted for thieving horses. He'd been hanged two years back, in seventy-four, for his crimes.

A gust of hot wind ruffled the tattered flyers, and Johnny reached to steady one. Nothing posted about the Bledso gang, in particular Dirk, the yellow-bellied coward who had consumed Johnny's life since the day he shot and killed the McAllister family. Bledso, known in some circles as the Viper, always seemed to be one county ahead of him. Then, about two years ago, all news of the Bledso brothers had dried up. They seemed to have vanished from the face of the earth.

The slaughter drilled through Johnny's mind as it had hundreds of times in the past sixteen years — Mama's screams, her pleas that the children be spared. Baby Elly's frightened whimpers while little Lara slept, never knowing the terror she faced. Johnny's hand tightened into a fist. Pa's angry shouts, in his struggle to save his family, still rang in his ears. The images cut through his soul like a knife.

Memories tightened Johnny's stomach, and the acrid taste of sun-dried hay choked him. Sweat had rolled down his temples into his shirt collar as he huddled in the barn loft, terrified for his life. No twelve-year-old should have to witness such carnage. No one of any age should have to see those horrors.

A ruckus inside the bank jerked Johnny back to the present. Raised voices barked orders, growing persistently louder. He stepped toward the open door as three masked men burst through in a hail of bullets. Two aimed their pistols over their shoulders, returning fire.

A big man with a bushy red beard encircled the waist of a young, screaming girl with one arm while he shot with the other. Fighting to break free, she kicked and struggled.

Johnny dodged another round of bullets. Instinctively, his hand flew to his holster. Before he could pull his pistol, the frantic girl latched onto his hand. His fingers reflexively clamped around her arm and he pulled, trying to break her assailant's grip.

The outlaw held on.

"Let her go!" Johnny shouted.

The bearded man tightened his hold, trying to drag his squirming hostage toward a waiting horse.

Diving in headfirst, Johnny knocked the man to the ground. They scuffled, each trying to gain control of the hysterical girl.

The young woman kicked and clawed. Her skirt flipped over her bonneted head and Johnny blindly grappled with a sea of frilly petticoats. Bystanders stood rooted to their spots, eyes wide and mouths agape.

A fourth man backed out of the bank, guns blazing. Two doors away, the sheriff and a deputy spilled from their office, weapons drawn. Bullets zinged and ricocheted in rapid-fire volleys.

Johnny finally gained control of the female. He tucked her close, and in a split-second decision, he made a break for his horse, shielding her with his body. The girl fought like a wildcat, flailing and squealing, pounding his chest as he forced her across the porch, keeping low.

She dug her toes into the boards. "Let go of me this instant!"

Clamping his arm tighter around her waist, he grasped the saddle horn and his foot found the stirrup. Something heavy slammed into his chest and wedged itself between him and the girl. He glanced down to see a bank bag. Teetering in the stirrup, he strained to balance, and then he swung into the leather, positioning her protectively in front of him. His spurs dug into the horse's sides.

The riders disappeared in a hail of bullets, hightailing it out of town.

Dust rose in red plumes as the sheriff and his deputy returned fire toward the disappearing cloud.

"Put me down! Let me go!" The girl twisted and gave Johnny a hard uppercut to the jaw.

His teeth rattled and stars floated overhead. He fought to stay astride, biting back the metallic taste of blood spreading through his mouth. She could have knocked out his teeth with that blow! He did an inventory — uppers, then lowers — all there. The only casualty was his tongue.

Tightening his grip on her, he warned, "Don't do that again, young lady." He grasped her wrists, pinning them against the saddle horn. The big sorrel galloped headlong down the road behind the gang.

"You put me down this minute!" She thrashed, striking out until her heel connected with his shin.

"I'll be only too glad to do that as soon as you're out of danger." He glanced at the bank bag, spurring the horse harder. At least the money had been saved.

Lawmen pounded behind them, firing their weapons. Whipping the sorrel faster, he kept the retreating bank outlaws in sight. Far ahead, the four gunmen cut off the road and ducked into a creosote thicket.

The girl twisted in the saddle and looked back at Johnny, her face contorted. Johnny hitched her tighter. "Don't you start crying on me. You're all right."

"Are you going to hurt me?" she whimpered. Her body quaked against his chest.

"Why would I hurt you?" He was trying to save her from harm. "Just calm down. This will all be over in a few minutes."

He slowed enough to trail the robbers but stay out of the range of their gunfire. With the girl in front, he couldn't take a chance on her taking a bullet. The sheriff and his posse were closing in. Soon the thieves would be apprehended, the girl could be safely returned, and the money safe. He cut his horse through the thicket and up a steep embankment.

A bullet zipped by his ear. He bent lower in the saddle, glaring back at the posse. Why didn't they hold their fire? The robbers were out of range.

"My daddy's going to be very unhappy," the girl promised in a voice jolting with each hoofbeat.

Her daddy would be unhappy? What about him? One minute he was minding his own business reading the wanted posters, and the next he was in the middle of a bank robbery, trying to save her hide. And she was complaining? He ducked another round of posse fire.

She started sobbing, great, anguished wails, and Johnny finally had enough. Forget the robbers. Let the lawmen do their jobs without his help. Slowing his horse, he awkwardly patted the young woman's heaving back. "Okay, okay. It's over. I'm not going after them. Dry your tears. You're safe."

She shook her head, sobbing louder. "You're horrible . . . and . . . and you're mean! You robbed our bank, and kidnapped me. You are in so much trouble!" She glared at him, then her lip quivered, and the corners of her mouth dipped downward.

"Robbed your bank? Do you think I was a part of that?" The irony of the situation hit him. That's exactly what she thought. Why wouldn't she? He did a quick take at the fast-approaching posse. Did they think he was part of the gang? "Young lady, I didn't rob that bank."

"Oh, yes you did." She sniffed. "I saw you."

Shifting her to the side, he set her on the ground. He was getting out of here. "Stay right there. The posse will take you home. I'm out of this. They don't need me anymore."

She gazed up at him, tears spilling from her big brown eyes.

"Look, I know what you think, but I'm not one of them."

She sniffed again. "If you're not a bank robber, what do you have in that bank bag?"

He glanced down, and his stomach pitched. The bank bag. He quickly rammed the bag into his saddlebag, fumbling with the strap.

A shot whizzed by his ear, and his horse lunged forward. He let the animal have his head, turning for a final glance at the girl, who stood, hands on her hips, in the middle of the road.

"You can't just leave me here!" she wailed, stomping her foot. She hopped up and down, stomping and yelling.

Whipping his horse, Johnny flew down a ravine. The sorrel's hooves pounded the brush, and then slid on loose rock. The posse was on his heels now.

# CHAPTER FIVE

Grimacing, Johnny snapped back to the present. He turned, his eyes roaming the small bedroom. Time and love had gone into the furnishings. He touched the spread pattern, running his rough fingertips along the intricate stitching.

Grandma had made quilts. On summer evenings she sat on the front porch, a basket of outgrown clothing by her side. She cut and sewed for hours, patiently explaining the history behind each scrap of fabric, weaving stories and spinning tales as she sewed. Assuring him that God loved him and that he'd always look after him. Right.

Little Elly loved the pink remnant of her baby blanket, and Lara always pointed a chubby, dimpled finger at the flower print of Ma's work dress. Winters, Grandma sat by the fireplace, her needle flashing as she tackled her piecework with a vengeance. That seemed a lifetime ago. He turned from the window.

He moved to the side of the bed and sat down, careful not to muss anything. Sitting up straighter, he bounced once, testing the old mattress. It had been a long time since he'd slept in a real bed. Months — maybe a year.

He lifted a pillow and smelled soap, sunshine, and fresh air, a far cry from his sleeping bag. Arranging the feather tick carefully back in place, he glanced around him. Now what? Instead of searching for Dirk Bledso, he was stuck in a blue-flowered prison with a quilt made from scraps of a shirt an old man wore fifty years ago. He could walk away. He'd thought of nothing more for the past week, but in the end he'd be a fool. He'd serve his time, and then he would resume his search. Grandma was right. God had sure looked after Bledso. He had given him another year or two to live.

A light tap sounded at the door, and he waited. A few seconds later the knock sounded again, followed by a woman's voice. "I have your water."

She was stubborn. He'd told her he'd get it himself. It had been a long time since he'd had a pitcher of water in his bedroom. It had been a long time since he'd had a bedroom. "Leave it in the hall."

The bowl clanked as she set it down. "Mr. McAllister?"

"Yes?"

"I cannot overemphasize how the judge likes his meals on time. Supper is at five." Johnny glanced at the clock over the bedstead. It was ten of five.

When he didn't answer, she rapped soundly. "Did you hear me?"

"I heard. I'm not hungry." Or deaf.

"Are you coming?"

"Pretty soon."

He wasn't about to sit at a stranger's table and make polite conversation. He had nothing to say. Nothing these folks cared to hear.

Her tone firmed on the other side of the door. "Judge McMann hates cold food. Unpack your clothes. Supper won't be on the table for another few minutes." Her footsteps sounded as she went back downstairs.

Johnny rolled off the bed and walked to the dresser. How long would it take to unpack an extra pair of pants, a shirt, and a change of long johns? There were three large drawers in the chest. One for pants, one for shirts, and one for underwear. He found an extra blanket in the bottom drawer. He'd need an extra blanket in this desert town about as much as he needed that woman firing orders at him.

Stretching, he moved to the north window. Leaning out the sill, he watched the lazy activity below. Not much stirring this time of day.

Scents drifted up the stairway, and he turned and stared at the closed door. Something smelled mighty good. His stomach growled. Maybe he would go down to supper. No, he was a prisoner. Weren't they supposed to bring his meals to him?

He sat back down on the side of the bed. He'd be so docile they'd think they were babysitting the archangel Gabriel himself. He'd keep his nose clean and his eyes open for word of Dirk Bledso. Maybe he'd get lucky, and Bledso and his no-good cutthroat, yellow-bellied, baby-murdering gang would save him the trouble of tracking them down. Lying back on his pillow, he closed his eyes. Maybe, with a little luck, they'd pay him a visit right here in "Paradise." The grudge he was carrying was a little heavy after sixteen years.

And when they did, he would shoot them. One by one, he'd put a hole through each of their black hearts, and then he would kick dust in their faces before he walked away.

Grandpa's voice echoed in his mind.

*Johnny boy, the Lord will avenge the enemy.*

*But he hasn't avenged mine. Bledso is still alive.* His stomach rumbled. That chicken smelled mighty good.

The sun sank lower. Johnny lay across the bed, careful not to muss the quilt. The hands on the clock crept past five, then five thirty. Six. Quarter to seven. He could hear the judge's voice, and what did she say her name was? Ragan. Colonel Ragan.

Seven o'clock and not a hint of a breeze came through the open window. His eyes fell on the slop jar. There was no way he was using one of those, so he opened the door and quietly descended the staircase, heading for the outhouse. Muffled voices floated up from the first floor.

Pausing on the landing, he glanced toward the dining room and did a double take when he saw the woman and the judge sitting at the table. Their plates were clean, napkins folded carefully at the side, the silverware untouched on each napkin. A third place was set opposite the woman.

The judge spotted him and smiled. "There you are. Take your seat, Mr. McAllister. Supper is getting cold."

Ragan gave him a dark look and rose to pour him a glass of tea. Platters of food that had been hot two hours ago sat stone cold in the middle of the table. She motioned to the chair. "I'll get the burnt biscuits out of the warming oven."

Johnny edged through the doorway and sat down, his eyes trained on the judge. What was this? Some sort of joke?

When Ragan returned, Judge McMann waited until she sat down, and then he bowed his head. "Blessed Lord, allow this food to the nourishment of our bodies. Thank you for blessing us with the presence of yet another of your children at our table. Let us be a light unto his path and a lamp unto his feet. Amen."

He looked up pleasantly. "Mr. McAllister, I hope you like fried chicken and biscuits. Please, help yourself."

Johnny shook his head. He'd been sentenced to a loony bin. "I'm not hungry."

"Nonsense. A man has to eat." The judge picked up a bowl of greens and dished up a healthy serving onto his plate. "We've found if we keep our meals on time, the day runs more smoothly. Breakfast is at six, dinner at noon, and supper at five." He handed Johnny the bowl of greens. "And we do appreciate our guests being on time. Try to remember that."

Johnny was about to pass the greens along untouched, but Ragan patiently ladled a serving onto his plate. "Do you like sorghum with your biscuits, Mr. McAllister? Or do you prefer butter?"

Two fat biscuits plopped onto his plate before he could protest.

"Butter . . . I guess."

The biscuits weren't burnt, but the chicken was cold and so was the gravy, yet it was the best cold gravy and chicken he'd ever eaten. Before he realized it, he was putting food away like a half-starved animal. When apple pie was served, he downed two pieces, feeling ashamed of himself. He hadn't tasted food this good since Grandma died.

Judge McMann rolled his wheelchair back from the table, a merry twinkle in his eyes. "I like to see a man with a healthy appetite. Another slice of pie, Mr. McAllister?"

"No. Like I said, I wasn't hungry." Johnny pushed his empty plate aside. He met Ragan's mocking eyes — eyes as blue as the ocean — and then looked away.

The judge chuckled. "My dear old mother used to say she'd rather feed a hungry man any day of the week than one who wasn't hungry — saved on food. Better reconsider that other piece of pie. You'll need your strength. You're doing the dishes tonight. Supper's run late, and Ragan needs to be getting on home."

Dishes! He'd rinsed out his coffee cup for years, and he had washed a skillet in a stream occasionally. He'd never washed a whole pan of dishes.

The judge pulled a pipe out of his pocket. "We all take our turn at the sink."

Ragan picked up their plates and the food bowls, disappeared into the kitchen, and came back in a few moments untying her apron.

"Before I go home, I want to take a piece of pie to the reverend." She moved aside as the judge wheeled by her and into the parlor.

"Be careful walking home."

"I always am." She turned back to Johnny, who still sat at the table, uncertain as to what he should do. She seemed to read his thoughts, and he didn't like it. His thoughts were his own; the law couldn't take those away from him. She sighed. "You'll find hot water on the stove. Clean dishcloths and towels are in the top drawer to the right side of the sink."

They were serious. They expected him to wash dishes! He'd anticipated man's work. Since when did a man wash dishes?

"Any questions?"

"What's the chance of an early parole?"

"None. Be sure to rinse the dishes twice with scalding water."

# CHAPTER SIX

Johnny rinsed the soap off the last dish and laid it on a clean towel to drain. He glanced up when the judge wheeled into the kitchen.

"Looks like you found what you needed." Johnny nodded and hoped his sentence didn't include keeping the old man company.

"Hmm," Judge McMann murmured, pulling on his pipe and sending a plume of smoke toward the ceiling. "Not much of a talker, are you?"

"Don't have a lot to say."

The judge chuckled. "The world might be a better place if more folks thought that way. Well, no matter. We have plenty of time to get acquainted."

Johnny picked up a dish and dried it. That was an understatement. Two years in this tea parlor wasn't going to be easy.

Judge McMann drew on his pipe thoughtfully. "Tasty chicken; Ragan's a good cook.

She's a fine woman. All the Ramsey girls are. It's surprising Ragan's not been snatched up by some young man, but the girls have their hands full with their father."

"Yes, sir." Johnny wasn't sure what he was expected to say, but he was sure the judge spoke the truth. Ragan was a fine-looking woman. Bossy, but fine looking.

"Fulton Ramsey's well thought of in this town, and we don't make light of his problems. He pastored our flock for thirty years." Judge McMann leaned forward, knocking the ashes of his pipe onto a plate. He repacked the pipe bowl and lit it. "He led many a man to God in his day. Now that his mind's taken leave of his body, folks look after him. He spends his time whittling and telling rambling stories to children. I feel real sorry for the Ramsey girls. They lost their mama early on. Now they have a hard row to hoe."

Johnny dried a skillet and set it aside. Ragan Ramsey's problems weren't his concern. Sticking his nose in other folk's business had landed him here, and he wasn't about to repeat the mistake.

Ragan came into the kitchen carrying a wicker basket. "Reverend was appreciative of the pie. He sends his best, Procky. I need to be getting on home now."

"Hold on a minute, missy. I want to talk to the two of you while I've got you both in one place."

Johnny mentally groaned, hoping a lecture wasn't coming. He'd had about all of this cockamamy sentence he could take today.

The judge motioned him toward a chair. "Sit down, son."

Glancing at Ragan, Johnny lay the dishcloth aside and took a seat. Ragan sat across the table from him, looking uneasy.

"Mr. McAllister, I suppose you're wondering what's expected of you," the judge began.

Johnny's eyes shifted to Ragan. "She told me."

"She did?"

Ragan shrugged. "I told him no profane language, no liquor or tobacco, daily sessions, and that you like your meals on time. Nothing more."

"I understand the rules," Johnny snapped. "I'm a prisoner; not a moron."

The air in the room charged as the young couple faced off.

Sitting up straighter, Ragan met his stare. "Mr. McAllister, I'm getting a little weary of your attitude. I have been trying my best to be civil to you. I offered hot water and invited you to supper, and you refused both courtesies."

"I don't like fried chicken."

"You ate *four* pieces."

His eyes narrowed. "I was *hungry.*"

She glared back at him. "You said you *weren't.*"

"Get off my back, lady. I don't need a mother hen clucking over me. I can take care of myself." His eyes shifted to the window.

"Obviously you haven't," she muttered.

He snapped back to confront her. "Where do *you* get off telling me how to run my life?"

"Where do *you* get off talking to me like a —"

"Children!" The judge threw up his hands. "We're having a civil conversation. Let's not turn this into an all-out war."

Crossing his arms, Johnny refused to meet Ragan's eyes. He didn't have to put up with her — or did he?

Judge McMann cleared his throat. "I'm sure Judge Leonard explained our program —"

"He didn't."

"Well, then permit me. Robert and I have been working closely on a plan designed to rehabilitate prisoners, men whom we judge to be worthy of a second chance. Robert has obviously seen something in you he feels is worth saving. Ragan and I are writing a book on the project, and you will be one of our subjects, perhaps the last one. I'm sad to say the program doesn't seem to be working out. Now, we're not hard to get along with, Mr. McAllister. You're at liberty to move about freely, but you're not to be out of our sight without permission. Weekdays we will spend about an hour talking with you. Your thoughts, what's led you to a life of crime? That sort of thing. And once you prove that you can be trusted, you will be permitted more freedom. I ask very little: my meals on time, Ragan treated with the utmost respect, and that you keep yourself out of trouble."

Johnny sent a sour glance in Ragan's direction. Her fiery stare returned the sentiment.

"Are there any questions?"

"She's in charge of me?"

"No one's 'in charge' of you, Mr. McAllister. You'll be judged on how you take responsibility for yourself while helping others, but Ragan will generally be supervising your efforts. My advancing age keeps me close to my chair and the couch, I'm afraid."

Johnny wanted to tell him what he thought of the so-called program, but he wasn't a fool. He'd do what he was told. All he had to do was survive for two years. Maybe less if he behaved.

"So, do we understand each other?"

Johnny nodded and kept his eyes trained on the wall opposite the table.

"Good." The judge gave a wide yawn. "Well, it's this old man's bedtime. If you'll turn out the lamp when you're finished, I'd appreciate it." He rolled to the doorway and then looked back over his shoulder. "Ragan has breakfast on the table at six."

*And dinner at noon and supper at five. Got it.* "Yes, sir."

Ragan got up from the table, looping the basket over her arm. Brushing past him on her way out, she said, "You can make this as hard or as easy as you want, Mr. McAllister. I'm willing to make this arrangement amicable, but it's entirely up to you."

"Don't press your luck, lady."

Lifting her chin, she proceeded to the back door and left. He winced when the slamming door rattled the kitchen window.

He might have to be under her wing for the next couple of years, but he didn't have to like it.

Chuckling, the judge rolled to the doorway. "My, my, Mr. McAllister. I do believe

# CHAPTER SEVEN

Johnny woke at daylight to the sound of a rooster crowing. The smell of frying sausage drifted up to him as he shaved.

Shots broke out. He jumped, muttering an expletive when his shaving mug crashed to the floor and his razor dropped into the water. Whirling, he stepped to the window. Chickens squawked, dogs barked, and a bullet hit the side of the house. Yells and whoops and the sound of galloping horses jolted the early morning silence.

He saw two riders hightailing it northward, firing toward one house and then another. The riders paused to reload, and then they spurred their horses on down Main Street.

A movement in the side yard caught Johnny's eye. Ragan ducked, hurrying across the grass and onto the back porch. He heard the screen door flap shut as she let herself in. Turning from the window, he walked back to the shaving bowl and picked up the pieces of broken glass. *Breakfast at six,* he reminded himself.

Raids weren't his problem. Dishes were his problem.

Judge McMann took his seat at the breakfast table, smiling. "Good morning, Mr. McAllister. Did you sleep well?"

"Yes, sir."

"Gunshots startle you?"

"No, sir."

Ragan sailed through the kitchen door, carrying a plate of eggs and biscuits. Johnny's eyes followed her movements.

"Well, they certainly scared the wits out of me. I almost broke the eggs I'd just gathered." She turned to address Johnny, obviously taking the judge's warning about civility last night to heart. "Alvin Lutz, our town sheriff, is getting up in years, and he's as deaf as a fence post. He needs a successor, but no one will take the job. And nobody, including Alvin, will stand up to those thugs."

The judge nodded, buttering a stack of flapjacks. "We have to do something. We won't have any dishes to eat off of if it doesn't stop soon. Maddy's entire cherry blossom pattern is almost gone. Bounced right off the shelves with all the commotion and noise. She loved those plates."

"It's not safe for little ones to be on the street," Ragan agreed. "And everything but our milk cows and chickens has been stolen."

"They took the Tilsons' old heifer the other night."

"Oh, dear. I hadn't heard. I'll take them some fresh milk and butter."

Images flashed through Johnny's mind. Elly's screams, little Lara's terrified cries.

Sweat beaded his forehead, and he set his knife aside, his appetite gone. Would he ever be rid of the nightmare? Could he ever see a little girl again without feeling pain?

Ragan reached to pour his coffee. A shock coursed through him as her arm brushed him and her rosewater scent filled his senses. "Holly and Jo have learned to avoid the raiders," she said. "Everyone avoids the main road."

Johnny was still aware of the spot she'd touched after she moved on.

"Holly, Jo, and Rebecca are my sisters, Mr. McAllister. Holly's engaged to Tom Winters, and they plan to marry in the fall, if finances work out. I don't know what I'll do without her when she leaves. Jo, who's fourteen, and Becca, who's nine, help with the housework and cooking, but much of the responsibility of our home falls on Holly's shoulders. More biscuits?"

He took a couple more.

"Jo's a dear girl, but she's still young in many ways. It's not easy to grow up in such difficult times, with Papa and all."

Done serving breakfast to both men, she sat down to fill her own plate.

He didn't care, he reminded himself. He didn't care about this town, about these people, or about her. Being here only delayed him from tracking down his family's murderers.


"Mr. McAllister?"

Johnny stiffened when he heard Ragan call his name three days later. She marched toward him like a woman about to beat a rug.

If she was looking for him, it meant one thing. She wanted him to do more demeaning housework. What did she want now, mattress stuffing? Polishing the stair railing?

He pretended to be interested in the porch step he was repairing. "Need something?"

"Actually, I do."

It figured. "What?"

"I need your help in the kitchen. The ladies' auxiliary is having their annual library bake sale, and I've promised to contribute nine dozen sugar cookies."

"So?"

"So, I need your help."

He turned to stare at her. "Baking cookies?" She wasn't serious. He could barely boil water without burning it.

"It won't take that long. If you'll just roll out the dough and cut them out, I'll get them in the oven." Her brow lifted combatively when he gave her a cool look. "I need help. I'm way behind on my chores and have to get these cookies baked."

*Work my foot.* It was just another thing to harass him. During the daily meeting with the judge, he was forced to talk about his private life, though he told very little. Hang the judge's research. He wasn't a criminal, and his private life was his, nobody else's. He resented the sentence more every day. Hanging might have been more merciful. Tossing the hammer aside, he stood up.

"You'll do it?"

"Do I have a choice?"

"Of course you have a choice. You can go back to jail. We are not ogres, Mr. McAllister."

He trailed her into the kitchen and spotted a large bowl of dough sitting on the table. A rolling pin, with flour sprinkled on top, rested beside it.

"The ladies' auxiliary is small — just Minnie, Pearl, and Roberta, when Roberta's not busy at the millinery — but they manage to have a lovely bake sale every year." She stopped and assessed him. "I assume you've never baked cookies before?"

"No, ma'am."

"Call me Ragan," she tossed. "I am not here to torture you, Mr. McAllister." Tying an apron around her waist, she added, "We'll make this as painless as possible. Do you want an apron?"

He stiffened and muttered an expletive. "No, I don't want an apron."

Stepping around him, she admonished, "Language, Mr. McAllister. You are in a lady's presence, and I do not tolerate that sort of talk." She picked up the sifter and dusted a generous amount of flour onto a large, white cloth. "Do you have a favorite cookie?"

Images of Ma making oatmeal cookies surfaced in his mind. She'd blend rich yellow butter, sugar, eggs, oatmeal, and flour, allowing him to lick the spoon when she'd finished. The memory curled around his heart as warm and sweet as the treat itself.

"Pie's more to my liking."

She glanced up, her face flushed from the kitchen heat. For a moment it was hard for

64

him to take his eyes off of her. "That's a shame. Personally, I favor molasses cookies."

Molasses gave him a bellyache.

Reaching for a mound of dough, she laid half of it on the floured cloth and then picked up the rolling pin. "Roll the dough very thin, and then use this water glass rim to form a shape."

She rolled the dough smooth, pressed the glass on it, and a second later laid a perfect round on the pan.

Johnny studied the glass rim.

"Now, let's put you to work rolling out more dough. Do you want to stand or sit?"

"Stand."

She brushed by him, trailing her flowery scent. What was it? Lemon? No, rose. Definitely a rosebush today. Handing him the rolling pin, she said. "Let's see what you can do."

His first attempt was pathetic, even to his untrained eye. The dough wadded into a sticky ball and clung to the rolling pin. Lifting the tool, he looked at her helplessly. "What's the problem here?"

"Inexperience." She took the pin away from him and cleaned it. "You need lots of flour, but not too much or the cookies will be dry."

Lots, but not too much. What was that supposed to mean? A bushel or a teaspoon?

Moving around him, she looped her hands around his waist and steadied the pin, rolling the dough to a delicate consistency. His fingers moved over the wood to capture hers. He'd see if he was in the presence of a *lady.*

The pin paused, and she eyed his hand.

"Mr. McAllister."

"Yes?" Running his fingers lightly over the satiny texture of her skin, he deliberately invited a response.

"You're touching my fingers."

He looked down. "So I am."

"Are you trying to gain my attention?"

"Could be."

She removed the roller from his hand and smacked his fingers. He winced and drew back, smile fading.

She picked up a glass. "We have nine dozen cookies to bake, mister. You'd best get busy."

# CHAPTER EIGHT

Johnny was in the kitchen two days later washing the breakfast dishes when raiders came through again. He paid them no mind until he heard footsteps rushing up the back porch steps. Ragan slammed inside with a choked, "Oh my goodness!"

Johnny dropped the cup he was washing and whirled to face her.

"What's wrong?"

"The . . . the . . ."

She was so upset she couldn't get the words out. Had she been shot? Had one of those roughnecks accosted her? He looked her over briefly, and she seemed to be unhurt.

He wiped his soapy hands on his denims and crossed to the screen door to look out. "Does the judge need a gun?" Proctor would have one somewhere.

She shook her head, biting her lower lip between small, even white teeth. "They shot all of our chickens!"

He frowned. "They shot what?"

"The chickens." She wrung her hands, tears spilling from her eyes. "They shot the judge's *chickens!*" She burst into tears.

Stunned, he awkwardly moved to calm her. For a moment he was so near even he knew she would object. She was hysterical over chickens? It just meant sixteen fewer beaks to feed.

His hand came up to stroke her hair, and then dropped away. "It's not the end of the world. You can get more chickens."

She lifted her head, sniffling. "You don't understand. What am I going to do with *sixteen* dead hens?"

His smile waned, and then he groaned. He hadn't thought about that. Sixteen chickens were a lot of birds to pluck.

That afternoon, the Honorable Proctor Mc-Mann dropped the notes he and Ragan were going over and dove under the dining room table as bullets again ricocheted through the front parlor. "The cat, Ragan! Get the cat!"

Johnny dropped out of his chair, dodging the hail of gunfire.

More shots and then Kitty yelped.

Procky turned white. "She's been hit,

Ragan!"

"Here, Kitty. Here, Kitty, Kitty." Ragan crawled along in front of the sofa, groping underneath for the wounded pet. Her eyes focused on a tuft of black fur quaking beneath the round lamp table. "There you are." Reaching for the feline, she gently tugged. The cat dug into the wool rug, refusing to budge.

"Kitty!" Judge McMann yelled. "How bad is it, Ragan?" His voice hinged on panic.

Ragan gently extracted the pet and examined the superficial wound. "She's all right, Procky. She's just nicked." Ragan ducked as more shots pinged through the room, shaking her head in resignation as a pillow on the sofa exploded. The picture of a young Maddy McMann, which had been hanging over the mantel, spun across the floor like a toy top.

Ragan tucked the yowling animal safely under her arm and crawled under the table to join the judge. Motioning for Johnny to join them, she made room for him in the cramped shelter.

Judge McMann reached for his pet, tenderness shining in his eyes. "That was a close one. When the shooting stops I'll clean that wound — nothing at all to be concerned about." His lined features shown with pain. "So far we've lost livestock, but never people or pets."

Kitty nuzzled the judge's chest, purring loudly.

*Ping!*

Another bullet bounced off the porch.

The judge sat stroking Kitty as a crystal chandelier swung overhead, its dangling bangles tinkling and sending tiny flashes of light bouncing from wall to wall. One moment they'd been having their meeting, the next the place was exploding.

Horsemen galloped down the block before turning to make another pass by the judge's house.

Johnny flinched as a bullet took a hunk out of the table leg. "*Why* do you people put up with this?"

"Because we don't know how to stop it," the judge said. "If we shoot 'em, then more come. What's a body to do?"

"We've tried," Ragan added.

"I suppose that's what started our interest on doing a book on gangs and criminals," the judge noted. "I can't imagine what would make a man or woman enjoy a life of crime."

Ragan glanced at Johnny. "It used to be a quiet town. Then the gangs started coming across the border once they were liquored up. Last month the citizens voted to change the town's name from Paradise to Barren Flats." She sighed as hot lead shattered a windowpane. "If only we knew how to stop this."

"Well, your father tried," the judge muttered, still peering at Kitty's wound.

"Yes, and look where it got him."

# CHAPTER NINE

Fulton Ramsey, Ragan's father, was once a community leader. He'd pastored Paradise's only church and cared deeply about his flock. He had tried to stand up to the gangs and was burned out, his cattle shot, and the church torched and burned to the ground. The death of his only son, Jacob, was the final straw.

Ragan still hurt when she thought about her young brother. The boy had died racing his horse home to warn them that raiders were coming again. The horse stumbled, and Jacob was thrown in the lane leading to the Ramsey house. He died where he fell.

Papa finally succumbed to despair over his losses. His anguish was so deep, so irreversible, that he'd retreated into a world that no one, not even his daughters, were able to penetrate.

He now sat silently for hours either whittling toy animal figures or staring into space, a broken man. Once Fulton Ramsey had been looked upon as a charismatic man of God; now the townsfolk merely looked upon him with pity.

If Ragan could just hold the family together until Jo and Becca were raised, she'd be grateful.

Procky was getting on in years and Papa — well, there was no telling how long Papa would live. His body was healthy, even though his mind was not.

Once her responsibilities were fulfilled, she wanted to leave this raucous town and attend school. Perhaps, if Procky had his way, she would study for the bar. There would be enormous sacrifices if she decided to do so. She'd have to move far away from her sisters because it was mostly Midwestern schools that admitted women for law degrees. Then she'd have to fight to prove that as a lawyer she could handle cases as well as a man. Most women took over practices begun by their fathers or husbands, but she would have to prove her own worth.

The judge had already told her he would provide funds for her tuition, and she could go anytime that she wanted. But right now that was impossible — too many people in Barren Flats were dependent on her.

# CHAPTER TEN

By that evening the commotion had died away, Kitty's wound was cleaned and dressed, and supper was over. The judge settled on the open porch where a cool breeze relieved the day's heat. Ragan handed the men bowls of blackberry cobbler with a generous portion of thick cream over the top. Leaning back, Procky stroked his pet. "These raids are getting more and more violent. Kitty could have been killed today. It's nothing short of a miracle that someone hasn't been shot during the raids. It's time to call a town meeting." He focused on Johnny. "Son, I'm curious. What would you do about this problem?"

A muscle tightened in Johnny's jaw. "It's none of my concern."

Disappointment lined the judge's features. "Any suggestion would be welcome at this point. I would assume you are not a stranger to the problem. You'd have a fresh outlook on it."

Pouring coffee, Ragan said softly, "Mr. McAllister, if you have any ideas —"

"I don't." He didn't know a thing about gangs, and he resented the inference that he did. He'd been convicted for a crime he didn't commit. He was merely in the wrong place at the wrong time. Otherwise, he'd kept to himself. He wasn't a criminal. At least, not yet.

Ragan glanced at the judge. They both shook their heads.

She finished pouring coffee and set the pot aside, and then she sat in a wicker chair beside the judge. "Shooting the chickens and wounding Kitty are really the last straw. I'm glad you suggested the town meeting, Procky. Surely someone can come up with a plan this time."

"What did you do with all those chickens?" the judge asked.

"I had Mr. McAllister deliver them about town. I figured they shouldn't go to waste."

"No . . . certainly not."

"I'll make posters tonight for a town meeting and hang them in the morning." Ragan glanced at Johnny. "You can help, Mr. McAllister."

Johnny spooned a bite of cobbler in his mouth. Of course. He would have bet on it.

"If only there were enough able-bodied men in town . . ." The judge gazed contemplatively at the sunset. "But most are older. They don't have the health or the gumption to get involved, even when their family's safety is in jeopardy."

Early the next morning, Ragan and Johnny tacked up posters about the town meeting that night. Curious crowds gathered around trees and storefronts to read the circulars.

"Count on the Southerns being there," Frankie called to Ragan. His wife, Kensil, nodded.

"See you tonight," Timothy Seeden promised as he left the bank.

"We'll be there with bells on," Minnie Rayles said. "I'm sick to death of all this violence!"

"Shooting chickens, the very notion!"

"I'll shore nuff be there," Rudolf Miller called, laying aside his hammer and anvil and waving.

Handing Johnny the last notice, Ragan stepped back to watch him post it. "Isn't this exciting?"

"Thrilling." He missed the nail and walloped his thumb instead. A bad word followed.

"No profanity, Mr. McAllister." She

picked up her skirt and moved on.

The Oasis Saloon, the largest establishment in town, served as a border watering hole and town meeting hall. The proprietors, Florence and Hubie Banks, took orders for lemonade and coffee as people made their way into the establishment a little after five. By five thirty all the seats were filled, with people lining the walls. Judge McMann left the group he was chatting with and rolled to the front of the room. He raised his hand for attention and gradually a hush fell over the crowd.

"Folks, I'm glad to see you here. Appreciate your concern. Now, we've called this meeting to make some decisions. This raid problem is out of hand and we can't ignore it any longer. But first, Reverend Pillton has something to say." He waved toward the black-frocked minister sitting near the back of the room. "Reverend."

Samuel Pillton stood and a hush fell over the crowd. "I don't know what to do about the violence, but it's time we repair our place of worship. I don't think it makes a lot of difference to God where we say our prayers, but we need to take a stand and show these hooligans what's important in our lives. Why, Kitty was wounded in this

77

last raid, and the next thing we know it'll be one of us. It's time we put our full faith in God and take a stand." His voice was soft, but as with his sermons, everyone understood his message.

There was silence, and then a mounting buzz. It wasn't long before it was decided to begin restoring the church come Saturday. Work assignments were handed out.

"Now, let's address the best way to deal with the main problem at hand," the judge said above the noisy clatter.

"The chicken killers!" Rudolph shouted. "Any man who'd shoot our chickens is just plain mean. We got to do somethin'!"

"What are you goin' to do about 'em, Judge?" someone called.

"That's what we're here to decide. What are we going to do about them?"

Johnny looked at Ragan, who was sitting in the second row. Three younger girls sat with her. They were undoubtedly the sisters she talked about; the girls bore a marked resemblance to each other. His eyes effortlessly slid over Ragan's slender frame, noticing the way her nose tilted slightly, just enough to be interesting.

"We gotta do something, Procky! There's not going to be anything left of the town if we don't!"

The judge lifted his hand again for quiet. "It seems to me we're going to have to take action or face the risk of getting burned out."

"I think we should move the entire town," Maggie Anglo volunteered. "Get farther from the border. These hoodlums ride through, go into Mexico and get liquored up, and then here they come, riding back through shooting up again. Barren Flats is straight in their path."

A man in the back stood up. "Maggie's right. If we move the town ten miles farther north, we wouldn't be in their way."

The old sheriff held his hand to his ear. "You going to pack that big two-story house of yours onto the back of a horse and move it?"

"Yeah, and how about the bank, the sheriff's office, the stores, and all the other buildings? You going to give 'em all to the gangs?" Rudolph Miller called out. "We can't run away from our trouble. We have to face it, and face it now!"

Alvin Lutz got to his feet. "As sheriff of this town, I'm doin' the best I can. There are at least a dozen different gangs that I've counted riding through here. Some have as many as fifteen riders."

Jewell Scott twisted a lace handkerchief

and seemed on the verge of tears. "Oh, my. Alvin's right. I've counted at least that many. It's very disturbing. I'm thinking about moving clean out of the county. I don't feel safe in my own home anymore."

Several women, some openly crying, spoke fervently of their fear for their children and their frustration with having to clean up after every raid.

"Plaster sifts down from the ceiling when they ride through. There are so many bullet holes, Clifford can't get them repaired." Sylvia Kincaid shot her husband a frustrated glance. "The mister was taking a nap in the parlor yesterday when they passed through. When he woke up, he had so much plaster on his face he looked like a ghost." When her neighbors laughed, she blushed. "Well, he did!"

A man rose to his feet near the back. "I say we build a new road around the town. Make 'em change their course!"

Heads turned at the suggestion.

"Frank, a new road wouldn't stop 'em, and that could be bad for business." Shorty Lynch frowned. "Real bad. I get a lot of drifters coming through here for groceries, and there's always a few with horses that need reshoeing."

"Shorty, neither you nor Rudy do business with the gangs. What business would you lose?"

"Well, there could be some lost with a new road."

"Be a lot of trouble to build a new road, wouldn't it?"

"Yes, it would. We'd have to put it a mile or so to the west —"

Austin Plummer jumped to his feet. "Now, hold on there. That'd cut up my land. I just got my fence back up from a raid a week or two back." The farmer's face flushed and his fists balled. "We'd have to make that new road to the east of town."

A second man stood and appeared ready to fight anyone who agreed with Austin. "Wait just a minute! I can't split up my homestead, and I don't want those bandits riding through my property. Don't be planning any road through my land!"

Fans waved in front of faces and handkerchiefs mopped foreheads.

The judge shook his head. "Listen to yourselves. Can't anyone agree on anything? We got to do something, people. And now!"

Johnny sat quietly, listening to the exclamations and declarations break out around him. It was amazing how far grown men would go to avoid trouble.

Minnie Rayles shot to her feet. "I say we

hire a shootist!"

A hush fell over the room. The citizens of Barren Flats looked at one another and then murmured back and forth. A shootist? What shootist?

"What are you talking about, Minnie?" The banker's wife turned around in her seat to stare at her.

"A shootist." Minnie sat back down in her chair and straightened her hat.

"Good grief, Minnie." Her husband, Carl, filled the stunned silence. "Where are we gonna get a shootist?"

"Right here, that's where." Minnie fished in her reticule and came up with an article from a journal. "Says here that Sulphur Springs was having the same trouble as us. They hired them a shootist, Lars Mercer. He cleaned that town up slick as a whistle. He could do the same thing here. The paper says he's still up there."

Johnny sat up straighter. Lars Mercer? The legendary gunslinger?

Carl took the piece of paper from his wife, his eyes scanning the article.

"A shootist?" Alvin Lutz got slowly to his feet, his hand cupped to his ear. "How much would something like that cost?"

Minnie frowned. "Don't rightly know, but we could wire Mercer and ask."

Everett lifted his hand. "I could send the wire off first thing tomorrow morning."

"Now, hold on," the pastor objected. "We can't hire to have someone killed! We're God-fearing folk!"

"Kill or be killed," Carl said. "We don't have a choice."

A buzz went up as the crowd warmed to the idea. Johnny couldn't believe what he was hearing. They were willing to hire a shootist to do their dirty work?

Judge McMann cleared his throat. "It seems to me that we should be able to confront this problem without outside interference." He eyed the audience. "We have plenty of men right here in Barren Flats."

"Who can't do a thing to stop these gangs," Lillian Hubbard said. She looked at her daughters. "When will our children be safe again? I say hire this shootist! Pay him anything he wants! We want our town back!"

An outcry went up. "Get the shootist!"

"Get our town back!"

"Pass the hat. I'll put in five dollars," one man said.

"Five dollars — now hold on here," his wife cautioned.

"Money isn't the issue. Getting our town

back is, and you can't put a price on freedom! It's worth whatever the cost," someone else shouted.

Ragan's eyes met Johnny's as the uproar continued. It wasn't hard to read her silent plea. Did he have a suggestion? He calmly looked away.

Judge McMann rapped the bar for order. "All right! We'll take a vote. Those in favor of sending for a shootist, raise your hand."

Twenty hands shot up.

"Those opposed?"

Johnny counted sixteen.

"The yeas have it." The judge banged his gavel. "Everett, send a wire inviting Mercer to come in and clean up the town."

As everyone got up to leave, Johnny shook his head. These people had spit for brains. Mercer wouldn't hang around forever, and then the gangs would return. But stupid plan or not, Johnny supposed they all went home thinking they would have fresh eggs for breakfast tomorrow morning.

# CHAPTER ELEVEN

"Stick the needle through the hole, and pull the thread tight."

Tongue wedged between his teeth, Johnny concentrated on spearing the eyes of the button.

"That's it, nice and easy. You're quite good at sewing buttons."

"I'd rather shoe a horse."

"Judge McMann believes sewing builds character." That wasn't exactly true. Actually, Procky said the busier a man was, the more likely he was to stay out of trouble, and Ragan was running out of things to keep Mr. McAllister busy. He'd beaten rugs, hoed the garden, whitewashed the fence, and helped Mrs. Curbow with her garden. The afternoon loomed ahead when Ragan spotted the basket of sewing.

Johnny swore as the tip of the needle pricked him for the third time.

"Mr. McAllister . . ." Ragan reminded.

"Shoot!"

"Let your nays be nays and yeas be yeas," Ragan reminded.

"What's that supposed to mean?"

"Don't curse." She glanced at his work. "You sew as if you're branding cattle. Think: lightly, carefully." She selected a button and effortlessly attached it to a shirt. Johnny eyed the exhibition with cool detachment, but his jaw tightened and she heard his teeth grind.

Demoralizing him wasn't her intention. Indeed, she was starting to be amused by his fumbling attempts to serve his sentence. Though he didn't talk a lot, she did glimpse an occasional smile, tempting her to think that he was warming, if not to his sentence, then at least to his surroundings.

Lately, her thoughts were plain worrisome. Like noticing how nice his hair looked after a bath, all soft and touchable in long, brown waves. Or when he nicked himself on the chin while shaving. She found herself wanting to wet a cloth and wipe the tiny flecks of dried blood away. She glanced at him and then back at her handwork. *He is a criminal, Ragan.* But she *had* been taught to love one another. Papa had drummed the Lord's commandment into his family's heads day after day when he'd been younger.

But after three weeks Johnny had finished most of the house repairs along with other sundry chores, and now she simply did not have the resources to keep him busy other than the daily session with the judge. It had been easy enough to send Max Rutherford outside to play stickball when his work was finished. He'd spent many idle hours honing his batting skill. She even played catch with the boy a few times.

She held the repaired shirt up for inspection. "See? Good as new."

Johnny glanced at her and then the shirt. "Sewing's woman's work."

Ragan set a pile of mending in front of him. No matter how the Lord softened her heart toward this man, it would be nice if he would cooperate with a more willing spirit because, for now, they were stuck with each another.

"By the time you've worked your way through that pile of mending, you'll be able to sew on buttons as well as or better than any woman." She smiled sweetly. "In case you ever wish to take up tailoring."

He grunted something, and yanked thread through a buttonhole.

Untying her apron, she slipped it over her head. Sewing wasn't her favorite chore either. "I'll be back to check on you in a few minutes."

The needle drew blood again. "Sweet Hilda!" he muttered under his breath. He gave her a look black enough to sour milk.

"Lightly, carefully," she repeated over her shoulder. Closing the door behind her, she released a sigh.

Soon she was bent over the woodpile, chopping kindling. The sharp ax bit into the fine wood, causing chips to fly. The sun was warm, but she didn't mind. She enjoyed outdoor chores far more than indoor ones. She picked out a few pieces for her father and laid them aside. He was prone to leave the house to search for wood when his basket was empty.

Absorbed in her work, she didn't hear approaching footsteps. A shadow fell over the woodpile as she raised the ax above her head to swing. A hand shot out to clasp her wrist. Startled, she stared into John McAllister's unsmiling face. Her heart flew to her throat, and her hand automatically tightened around the ax handle.

His eyes darkened to a black hue at her response. "Afraid of me, Miss Ramsey?"

If she were, he would never know it. Her gaze met his steadily. "Are you through with the mending?" He couldn't be. There were enough missing buttons to keep him busy all afternoon.

His eyes shifted back to the woodpile. "I'll swap chores with you."

Shaking off his hand, she raised the ax and swung it. Kindling flew. "No, thank you. I'd just as soon chop wood." She'd just as soon do about anything other than mend.

He took a step back to avoid being hit. "Women sew. Men chop wood."

She took another mighty swing, splitting a log in half. "Not in Barren Flats." He stared at the two pieces and then at her.

They'd had the same argument this morning when he wanted to paint the eaves instead of beat rugs. She refused to humor him. He would never learn discipline if she caved in every time he disagreed with her instructions.

Reaching for another log, she jerked back when a green garter snake slithered from under the pile. Dropping the ax, she hopped aside. Try as she would, she couldn't overcome her snake jitters. The little reptile darted her way, and she whirled, colliding with a wall of solid chest muscle. Her eyes locked with McAllister's, and a ridge of goose bumps broke out on her arms. She'd never been this close to a man.

Swallowing hard, she tried to keep her voice even. "Would you please pick it up and carry it to the garden?"

Johnny cocked his head and frowned. "It? You mean the kindling?" He bent to pick up the wood she had just split.

She gritted her teeth. "No, Mr. McAllister. The snake."

A slow grin started at the corners of his mouth and spread across his face. Her cheeks grew hot and her heart sank. This was his moment of triumph. That snake could dart straight up her skirt and he wouldn't lift a hand to prevent it.

"Oh, *it*. The snake." His innocent eyes held hers. "Sorry. I have buttons to sew on." He turned and sauntered back to the house.

She glared at his retreating back. Where was a good-size rock when you needed one? Well, all right! The battle lines were drawn. By cracker, she was through being pleasant to this man!

Keeping one eye on the snake and the other on McAllister's retreating back, Ragan picked up the ax and prodded the slithering creature toward the garden with the handle. Just let McAllister ask her for help with the dishes — or mending — or rug beating — or anything else!

The screen door slammed shut.

She fanned her face.

*Rogue.*

When she returned to the kitchen a short while later, the judge was up from his nap. The two men sat at the table, sorting buttons. Kitty was perched in the middle of the activity, batting at strays. Dumping an armload of wood into the kindling box, Ragan gave Johnny a sinister look as she reached for a match. "Up from your nap so early, Procky?"

The judge frowned, placing a blue button on a pile. "I couldn't sleep. Came to the kitchen for a glass of buttermilk, and John looked like he could use my help."

Ragan closed her eyes. Procky was too softhearted to deal with prisoners. If only he would realize that his sympathy with his subjects made her job that much harder.

Her gaze touched briefly on Johnny's hands. They looked like raw meat where he'd pricked himself with the needle. A pile of mending was still in front of him. Her heart turned over.

Johnny avoided meeting her eyes.

The judge frowned, reaching for another button. "Are all those potatoes for us? Are we feeding an army this evening?"

"No. I fixed extra so I could take some home to Papa tonight."

"Your sisters don't know how to mash potatoes?"

"Of course they do, but Papa seems to think mine are special."

"Well, I'd have to agree with Fulton on that one." He smiled at Johnny. "Guess you've noticed she's a dandy cook."

"The grub's edible."

Ragan struck a match and threw it in the stove. *Edible. He sure eats my apple pies without complaint.* The kindling caught, and she shoved the iron lid into place. Shooing Kitty off the table, she moved to the cabinet.

The judge dropped another button on the pile and began as he did every day about this time. "You know, John, you've been mighty quiet since you got here. Tell us a little more about yourself."

Ragan pretended interest in what she was doing, but her ear was tuned to the conversation. She'd like to know something about him. Where he came from, how he came to be in his present situation. Anything but those stone-cold eyes — she knew them far too well.

Johnny focused on his task. "There's nothing of interest to tell, Judge."

Cutting through the underbrush, Johnny rode a dry riverbed through a canyon. The horse was winded, but he pushed the animal harder, up and down ravines, in and out of

92

thickets. He turned up a steep incline. When they burst out of the brush, the sorrel's head jerked up, and the animal shied nervously.

Johnny found himself staring down the barrels of a half-dozen rifles.

Crows cawed overhead. Heat bore down as the posse leisurely rode toward him, forming a circle, their rifles centered on the middle of his chest.

"Throw down your gun," the sheriff ordered. Johnny shifted in the saddle. "Look. I know how this seems —"

"Throw it down, boy!"

Johnny's hands were already in the air. He gingerly lifted the pistol from its holster and let it drop into the dirt.

The sheriff swung off his horse and walked toward him. The man was big and stocky, and he had thirty pounds on Johnny. There was no way to take him, and even if there was, he couldn't take on six men.

"Where's the money?"

"Left saddlebag."

"Get off your horse."

Johnny dismounted and stood beside his horse, hands above his head.

The sheriff rummaged through the bag. "Ain't here. Where is it?"

Johnny took a step toward the horse to search. A gun clicked.

"Stay where you are, mister," one of the men said. "I don't relish dragging a corpse back to town."

Johnny lifted his hands higher. "I don't relish that either."

The sheriff wasn't amused. "Where's the money?"

"I put the bag in my saddle pouch."

"Ain't no money here." The leather saddle-bag landed at Johnny's feet.

He grabbed it and shook it upside down. His heart sank as the contents spilled to the ground. The bank pouch wasn't there. He studied the men. Not an eye blinked as they stonily returned his look.

"I must have lost it on the trail."

Heads swiveled to stare back at the way they'd come.

Straightening his shoulders, the sheriff leveled the barrel of his rifle at Johnny. "Get back on your horse, son."

# CHAPTER TWELVE

Judge McMann assembled a pile of red buttons as the mantle clock ticked. "I find it hard to believe that you'd have nothing to tell. Every man has something interesting to speak about. How did you come to be involved in a bank robbery?"

"I didn't." Another button hit the pile. "I'm innocent of the crime."

"So you've said." The judge continued sorting. "Well, there must be something you'd like to tell us about yourself. How do you feel about God?"

Johnny shook his head. "If you're asking if I believe in God, yes. If you're asking if we're on friendly terms, no."

Drawing on his pipe, the judge nodded. "I understand. There have been a few times I've been a little put out with God, but eventually he brought me around to seeing things his way. What about family? You have parents, don't you?"

"No, sir."

"Family? Brothers? Sisters?"

"No. No brothers or sisters. No parents."

Johnny's tone was guarded now, evasive. The judge had struck a nerve. *What was he hiding?* He didn't just materialize out of thin air. Was he being stubborn? Was he ashamed of his behavior and trying to protect his parents' identity? Ragan studied the prisoner's dark good looks as she dumped flour into a bowl. At least he wasn't a heathen, yet what set a man like him on the path of self-destruction? He made it plain that he was a loner, a man with a chip on his shoulder, daring her or anyone else to befriend him. She gasped as the flour spilled over.

"Been on your own for some time, huh?"

"A long time, Judge."

Ragan swallowed the sudden lump in her throat. Vulnerability in his voice was the last thing she'd expected to hear. *He's a criminal,* she reminded herself, shoving sentimentality aside.

He was as uncaring as the men who terrorized Barren Flats. She detested them all for the misery they caused innocent people, and Johnny McAllister was no better than any of them. At least that's what the law said. If Judge Leonard hadn't shown this particular hoodlum leniency, he would have hanged by now.

Judge McMann changed the subject. "You attended the meeting yesterday, John. Think hiring Mercer is a smart move?"

Annoyance flooded Ragan. The town didn't need a shootist. What they needed was less talk and more action on their part.

"Well?" The judge prompted when Johnny didn't answer.

"Perhaps Mr. McAllister doesn't care to offer his advice." Ragan set a stack of plates on the table. The prisoner had made that clear when Procky broached the subject earlier.

Judge McMann glanced up. "Is that true, Mr. McAllister? I don't want to bother you. I just thought that now you'd had a spell to think about the problem, you might have advice that might help some fellow or someone on down the line. You know, 'Do unto others.' "

Johnny reached for another button. "Clean out of advice, Judge."

The older man cleared his throat and shifted in his chair. "I understand the circumstances of your involvement in the bank robbery are questionable."

Silence dominated the room. Then, "I told you. I'm innocent. I didn't commit that robbery."

Judge McMann glanced at Ragan and continued. "You can be honest with us. We're all in this situation together, and you might as well reconcile yourself to the fact that you're going to be here a while, sure as the sun comes up in the east. Now, Ragan and I, we're bound to this project by endless hours of research and writing. I must say, I still harbor the hope that the program will work and will be of benefit to future generations. I'd say you'd better lower your guard and make the most of your situation."

It was as close to a lecture as Ragan had ever heard from Procky.

The judge leaned forward and patted Kitty. "Isn't that what you'd say, old girl?"

Kitty merely rubbed against McAllister's leg. Her wound was barely discernible now. Back and forth she moved, gracefully arching her back and purring loudly. Johnny moved his foot to the side. The cat followed, rubbing against his boot.

He met the judge's gaze evenly. "Judge Leonard has my grandfather's pistol. I intend to get that pistol back."

"And you will, as long as you serve your sentence with no trouble. Break your word, and the matter is out of my hands. We're not going to ride shotgun on you. You have access to tools of destruction — such as the ax for chopping wood. What you choose to do is your responsibility. The idea of the program is to allow a convicted man to prove his say. Have you had your say, Mr. McAllister?"

Johnny reached for another shirt. "I won't give you any trouble." He gave the cat a slight nudge with his boot. She moved back to sit beside the judge.

"I'm glad to hear it. We should get along fine." Judge McMann wheeled his chair from the table. Patting his knee, he invited Kitty to join him. She leaped gracefully to his lap, and he chuckled when her nose nudged his ruddy cheek. "Yes, old girl, I love you too."

His eyes met Johnny's look over the cat's head.

Ragan reached for the shirt, taking it out of his hand. "I'll finish the mending. There's another pile of wood to be split."

Johnny was on his feet before she completed the sentence. The judge reached to steady the table.

"Supper's in a half hour," Ragan called as he disappeared out the screen door. She slid a pan of cornbread into the oven, avoiding the judge's gaze. "I believe he'd rather do men's work than sew on buttons."

Judge chuckled. "That's the impression I get."

"I'm not sure about the wisdom of handing an ax to a prisoner."

"In some cases I'd say no, but I don't believe McAllister's a threat. I'm surprised you've kept him inside as much as you have."

She brushed a wisp of hair out of her eyes. "He's just not responding. He has a chip on his shoulder and refuses to warm to anyone."

"Now, missy." She always knew the judge disagreed with her when he called her "missy." "All of our guests have begun their time with a chip on their shoulders. That's a part of the process. Our success is measured by the wearing down of that chip. Sometimes it wears away fast, but others . . . well, others have to be whittled away a little at a time. It depends, to a degree, on how the chip was formed in the first place. Did it come a little at a time through years of abuse, or did it fall across his shoulders like a tree felled in the forest?"

He pulled a folded paper from his shirt pocket. "I think there's more to John McAllister than meets the eye. There's something about this man . . ." He smoothed the paper and pushed it toward Ragan. "Here's the message I received from Robert this morning. He contends his suspicions at the time of the trial were strongly in favor of Johnny's innocence. There's no concrete proof that McAllister is a member of the Puet gang. None at all."

Ragan stood at the window and watched the mystifying man chop wood. Powerful muscles played across his back as he swung the ax with a vengeance. She sighed. Whoever he was, he didn't intend to let anyone — most of all her — near him.

"Come away from the window, Ragan. We need to work on the book."

Heat seared her cheeks as she quickly turned away.

# CHAPTER THIRTEEN

After supper Ragan packed a large crock of mashed potatoes and a pot roast into a basket and closed the lid. She handed a bowl of green beans to Johnny and picked up the basket before she stepped to the parlor doorway. "Goodnight, Procky. Mr. McAllister is helping me carry food home tonight. He won't be gone long."

The judge waved back from his spot in front of the window where he was reading. "See you in the morning."

She held the screen open for Johnny. Carrying the bowl of green beans, he preceded her to the porch. The judge's earlier words rang in her head. He didn't believe McAllister was a violent man, but they didn't know that for certain. And here she'd just asked that he accompany her home. The Lord surely must watch over fools.

"Let me carry the basket. You carry the beans."

"Thank you, but it's not that heavy. Be careful, Mr. McAllister. The beans are still hot."

As they reached the gate the sound of galloping horses caught their attention. Riders came into sight. Banditos, holding liquor bottles in the air, shouted drunken obscenities and spurred their mounts faster, heading straight for the house.

Grabbing Ragan's hand, Johnny pulled her the few steps back and dove for the porch floor, shielding her body with his. Her heart slammed against her ribs as he curled around her, putting himself between her and the riders.

Glass shattered, and green beans spilled down the wooden steps. The judge's petunia patch exploded in a barrage of gunfire. Bullets ricocheted off rooftops, accompanied by derisive shouts and ribald laughter.

Together Johnny and Ragan scrambled under the porch swing, ducking as gunfire riddled the house.

"Keep down," he warned, crawling on his belly across the painted wood toward the screen door. "Judge?" he shouted.

Judge McMann's muffled voice came back. "I'm all right. Kitty and I are in the hall closet."

The riders fired into the air, their horses

toppling a section of picket fence. Weaving back and forth, they shot out windows, and bullets pinged against the weather vane on top of the judge's house.

Trampling the lawn, they fired aimlessly, their merriment filling the once peaceful early evening.

Then, as quickly as they appeared, they galloped off. Johnny crawled from behind a wicker settee and helped Ragan to her feet. Green beans and bits of purple and white petunias littered the porch floor.

Ragan surveyed the damage, outraged. "The hoodlums!"

She was about to thank Johnny for protecting her when she noticed how his dark eyes followed the riders' trail of disappearing dust. She frowned when she saw his features harden.

"Mr. McAllister?"

His eyes remained on the fading riders.

"There . . . is there something you'd like to say?" Perhaps now that he'd almost been killed, he would drop his guard and offer a solution to this horrendous problem.

His gaze went to the littered porch floor. "Green beans are getting cold."

# CHAPTER FOURTEEN

Shaken to the core, Ragan checked on the judge a second time and refilled the bowl with beans before they set off again. The evening was calm, the sinking sun a fiery glow in the west. Rattled though she was, Ragan tried to relax.

"I meant to put salve on your hands," she apologized as they walked to the Ramsey homestead. "Those pricked fingers will be sore by morning." She bit back a grin. Needles could be painful when used incorrectly.

"I don't need any salve."

"Too girley, huh?"

"I don't use salve."

She glanced at him impatiently. He never thought he needed anything, much less attention. He was being obstinate again and for no reason. If he didn't need salve for the nicks, then why had he flinched every time she passed him a bowl during supper? You'd

105

think a man could accept a little concern without feeling threatened.

"How long have the raids been going on?"

Ragan was so surprised he'd initiated a conversation that it took her a moment to organize her thoughts. "Um . . . years. They had lessened for a while, but all of a sudden they're back in full force."

"And the reason the town does nothing to stop it is?"

"Not enough able-bodied men to fight them off." Ragan shook her head. "We've tried, but there are too many different gangs and the men fear that if they're shot their families will have no one to look after them. Folks have simply lost the will to fight. We're all terrified they'll burn the town down. Most of us have to live and work here. We can't afford to lose everything."

"A shootist isn't going to solve your problem."

She glanced at him. "Do you have a better idea?"

"It's not my place to have an idea."

"Saying a shootist isn't going to help is having an opinion."

"Having an opinion is not the same as having an answer."

Conversation ceased, and they walked in silence until they turned the bend in the lane leading to the Ramsey place.

"What you said about having no family —
is that true?" The smell of honeysuckle hung
sweet along the path in the fading twilight.

He was quiet for so long she wondered if
he would answer. Finally, he said, "Does it
matter? I'm the one serving time, not my
family."

"No, it doesn't matter. I just wondered
who you are. Family's important to me. Is
your family here in California?"

"You could say that."

She could say that and still know nothing
about him, and it wasn't likely she ever
would. Still, she knew she had no right to
pry. Even a man serving time was entitled
to his privacy.

"Papa pastored the church here in town
until a couple of years ago." He didn't
respond, but she went on anyway. "The
gangs burned his church, and then our
house and barns. We were able to build the
house back, but they just torched it again.
Then my brother died, and after seeing
everything go up in smoke a third time,
Papa broke. He just couldn't take any
more."

She didn't know why she was telling him
about her problems. He clearly wasn't
interested, but talking made her feel better.

She didn't need him to say a word, just listen. Once again, the town had chipped in and built the house back, only smaller this time.

"Mama died ten years ago, so with Jacob gone, it's just me and my sisters. The money I earn working for the judge isn't much, but it's enough to keep food on the table and clothes on our backs. Holly and Jo take in sewing, and I put up a large garden every year. We get by."

"The town's foolish to waste money on a shootist."

She turned to look at him. He hadn't heard a word she'd said. "We have to do something."

A young man on horseback stopped at the end of the lane and waved at Ragan.

She returned the greeting. "Everett Pidgin," she said under her breath. She realized she made the name sound like a curse. Thank goodness he headed on and didn't approach to talk as he usually did.

Johnny glanced in Everett's direction, but he didn't offer a response. They turned at the fork and proceeded up the rutted path leading to the Ramsey house. The lid on the green bean bowl rattled as they covered the uneven ground.

"Everett lives on a farm south of the

dynamite shack." She gestured toward the direction in which the young man was headed. "Papa owns the town's only deep well. Folks pay us what they can afford for water, but mostly they catch the rains when they come. You've seen the dynamite shack out near Muriel Davidson's place?"

He shook his head.

"It's back behind the rise, southeast of the church."

"Why do you wear that hat? That's a man's hat."

Ragan touched the brim of her high-crowned felt hat. "Because the sun's hot, and I like it."

"Women should wear bonnets. Little frilly things with ribbons and bows."

"You might not have an opinion on much, but you sure have a preconceived notion about women."

He grinned. "Women. Not females who chop wood and wear men's hats."

As they approached a simple wood-framed house, a young girl ran out to meet them. Racing down the lane, her long blond hair flew out behind her, a flashing smile lighting her face.

Ragan caught her sister, laughing. "Hello, Jo!"

Jo hugged Ragan's neck, holding on

109

tightly. "I've been watching for you." Her eyes traveled to Johnny, her smile wavering.

"Jo, this is Mr. McAllister."

Jo nodded solemnly. "The bank robber. I saw him at the town meeting yesterday."

"Jo!" Ragan reprimanded softly. She'd spoken the truth, but . . .

The girl graciously extended her hand. "Good evening, Mr. McAllister. My name is Jo — short for Josephina. I hate Josephina, so please call me Jo." She paused, her blue eyes sparkling with mischief. "What's your given name?"

"John."

She cocked her head. "John or Johnny?"

Ragan was surprised to see a smile soften the corners of his mouth. "I answer to either one."

"I will call you Johnny."

Jo was young and sometimes talked too much. Ragan said, "Run along, and tell Papa I'm bringing mashed potatoes."

"He'll be dee-lighted." Giving Johnny a smile, she skipped off, calling ahead, "Papa, Ragan's here, and she's bringing mashed potatoes!"

"I could have yelled to him myself."

They climbed the back steps and Ragan walked into the kitchen. Closing her eyes, she drew a deep breath. "Mmm — cinnamon cookies."

A dark-haired girl stepped away from the stove, grinning. "I knew you'd appreciate them. Where have you been? I was beginning to worry about you." Her eyes shifted to the stranger.

"Holly, this is John McAllister. Mr. McAllister, my sister, Holly."

"Nice to finally meet you, Mr. McAllister."

Setting the beans on the table, Johnny nodded. "Holly." He shook the hand she extended to him.

Holly turned back to the stove. "I thought you and the judge might be working late on the book."

Ragan bit into a warm cookie and offered the plate to Johnny. He shook his head.

"No, but we finished chapter seven this morning."

"Seven? You're coming right along."

"I'm sorry I worried you. We were delayed a few minutes."

"We heard the shooting."

Ragan nodded. "Another gang rode through."

"Well, the shootist will be here any day now. I talked with Minnie at the mercantile this morning. She said Everett sent the wire, and Mr. Mercer has already replied. Perhaps his presence can keep the gangs away."

"With the Lord's mercy, we'll pray that it's so. It can't be soon enough. I thought you'd be with Tom this evening." Ragan lifted the basket to the cabinet.

"No, Tom's putting up hay. I don't expect to see him all week."

Ragan gave her sister a quick hug. "How's Papa tonight?"

Holly sobered, shaking her head. "He's been very quiet all day."

Ragan stepped to the parlor door and peeked in. A thin, stooped man sat in a rocking chair before an open window. Although the growing dusk was warm, a heavy blanket rested around his shoulders. Nine-year-old Rebecca read from the Twenty-first Psalm. She looked up, smiling when she saw the visitors.

"Hi, Becca."

"Hi, Ragan."

Closing the door, Ragan said quietly, "I'll ask Marta to stop by tomorrow."

Sighing, Holly stepped to the stove and removed another batch of cookies from the oven. "Wish the town could afford a real doctor."

"Marta's as smart as any doctor . . . you know that." She turned toward Johnny to explain. "She's an old Cherokee woman who's nursed the whole town at one time or another."

Holly frowned. "Is there enough money — ?"

"Marta will settle for canned goods. We can spare a few jars of peaches, can't we?" Ragan handed a cookie to Johnny before biting into another one. What man didn't like hot cookies? Unless he was being obstinate.

"We can, if necessary," Holly murmured.

Johnny handed the cookie back to Ragan. "If you're through with me, Miss Ramsey, I'll be going."

Becca burst through the kitchen doorway, almost bowling Johnny over. "Papa refuses to eat. He says he isn't the least bit hungry. He wants me to keep reading to him." She took a moment to catch her breath. "Oh, hello. You must be Mr. McAllister."

Johnny nodded.

"I'm Becca. It's very nice to meet you."

Ragan reached in the cabinet and took out a plate. "I'll see if I can tempt Papa with my mashed potatoes."

"May I walk Mr. McAllister to the end of the lane?" Jo asked.

Ragan set the plate down with a bang. "No!" She carefully tempered her voice at Johnny's quick look. Although he had so far proved himself trustworthy, she could not allow Jo to be alone with him. "No, Jo. It's getting dark. It isn't safe — not with the renewed gang activity."

Jo's face fell.

Johnny stoically met Ragan's gaze. "Your sister's right. A young lady shouldn't be out after dark."

The girl left the kitchen with an unhappy sideways glance at Ragan. Smiling her apology, Holly excused herself and followed her sister.

One look at Johnny's dark features and Ragan felt compelled to explain her refusal. Resentment burned deep in his eyes. "Mr. McAllister —"

He cut her off coldly, brushing past her. "Judge McMann is expecting me back."

Ragan trailed him outside and watched as he stepped off the porch and started off down the lane. She kept an eye on his tall frame until it faded into the darkness. Leaning against the porch column, she wondered if she'd hurt his feelings. Well, of course she had; she couldn't miss the offense in his eyes. Perhaps he'd keep on walking. He wouldn't go back to Procky's . . . no, he wanted his gun back. Somehow, Ragan knew that gun meant more to John than freedom at this point.

Resting her head against the post, she gazed at the darkened sky. It was a beautiful night. Millions of stars shone overhead, and fireflies flickered in the field. She didn't want to cause anyone unhappiness. With the exception of a sour disposition, Mr. McAllister had stayed in line. Yet it was better to hurt his feelings than endanger Jo.

She made a mental note to speak to her sisters, to warn them to stay away from Johnny McAllister. He was young, good looking, and brash. Her heartbeat quickened at the memory of his body shielding hers. She wondered what Papa would say . . .

This man was a convicted felon. How did these strange feelings she was having make sense? Emotions tugged at her heart, and yet she felt a sense of restraint.

She was surprised how often she had to remind herself of that, and at fourteen Jo was much more impressionable. Johnny McAllister could easily steal a young woman's heart.

Best she remember that fact, and often.

# CHAPTER FIFTEEN

The sounds of hammers and saws filled the air on Saturday morning. The town had assembled in full force to work on restoring the church. Johnny, Ragan, and Judge McMann arrived a little before nine o'clock.

"It will be nice to have Sunday services again." Ragan shaded her eyes from the sun to watch the activity. Men crawled around on the rooftop, assessing the damage.

"Indeed it will. Before the day's over, the church will be a fitting place of worship." The judge twisted in his wheelchair to address Johnny. "Don't you agree, son?"

Johnny shrugged. Ragan smothered a spark of irritation. She'd like to shake the indifference out of him. But it wasn't his town, and it wasn't his problem. She had grudgingly conceded that point. If circumstances were reversed, and she was the detained and he the keeper, she would be feeling a bit constricted.

"We could use a hand over here!" Austin Plummer called from the roof. He and two of his older boys were already soaked with perspiration.

"I'll be glad to help!" Judge McMann called back.

Plummer grinned good-naturedly. "Come on up!"

Proctor swiveled his chair to join the effort, but a large, iron hand reached out to block him.

Johnny shook his head solemnly. "Maybe you ought to hand up nails."

The judge's face fell. "Oh, fiddle-faddle." He feigned disappointment, but still, Ragan thought Proctor seemed downright smug over what he'd just accomplished. He'd gotten Johnny McAllister to respond in a positive manner.

The judge sighed. "I suppose you're right."

Johnny rolled the chair to rest in the shade of the building. As he handed the judge a fistful of nails, Ragan overheard him say, "Your Miss Ramsey gets upset easily. Let's not ruffle her feathers by having you climb up and down those ladders."

Judge McMann chuckled. "You've noticed she flies off the handle once in a while, have you?"

The very idea! Ragan felt her cheeks grow hot. Procky would be climbing up and down ladders and all over the roof if he had his way. Then, if he didn't kill himself by falling, she'd have to listen to him moan and groan for a week about his joints.

"Hey, McAllister!"

Johnny straightened to look up when Austin shouted his name.

The sun-browned Swede with twinkling blue eyes grinned. "Got enough work for everyone!"

Ragan joined the other women setting up long rows of food tables, but her eyes refused to leave Johnny as he scaled the ladder. The slight breeze ruffled his hair and made him look boyish. Her gaze fastened to the back of his sweat-soaked shirt, stretched over powerful shoulders. She swallowed hard. Had Johnny McAllister ever needed anyone?

On top of the roof the men gathered, hands on hips, and took stock of the damage. It was a mess, all right. It would take more than a day to repair this kind of destruction.

"The last fire took most of the old roof," Rudolf Miller said. "The gangs have about finished it off." He tested a section with his foot, kicking aside some broken shingles.

Miller's fourteen-year-old son, Clayton, frowned. "Not much sense fixin' the old thing if it's only gonna be shot up again, Pa."

"Well, the reverend thinks it bears fixin', son, so we'll repair it. Could be it'll hold until we can afford a new one. Besides, Mercer is going to rid us of the problem." He glanced at Johnny. "Ever hear of Lars, McAllister?"

"I've heard of him."

"What do you think? Can he do the job?"

"His reputation says he can, if killing is what you're looking for."

"Don't hold with killing. The Good Book says 'thou shalt not kill,' but unless we hire Mercer, we will *be* killed."

"Yes," Austin agreed with a solemn nod. "Hate the thought of violence, vile as those gangs are, but we have to protect our women and children."

When Ragan realized others were watching her shamelessly gawk, she quickly averted her gaze, surprised at how giddy the sun made her feel. She should have worn her hat, as the judge suggested.

A tall, thin, intense-looking man joined the conversation. "Roberta's all the time talkin' about calling the town Paradise again. That sure would be nice. It would do us a world of good to take back our rightful name."

The men readily agreed. Johnny McAllister contributed nothing except another nail.

Ragan could hear the men's banter as she set dishes of food on the long, cloth-covered tables. Crisp fried chicken, biscuits, and jars of pickles, corn relish, and spiced peaches scented the thick air. Nearly every able-bodied soul in Barren Flats had turned out to help with the reconstruction.

The workers set upon the repairs as if with personal vendettas. Children worked diligently grooming the grounds. They piled debris to be burned later, and even the smallest tikes picked up tinder and hauled it away.

The clock hands inched slowly toward noon. Finally, Mazilea Lynch reached for the dinner bell and swung it in a wide arch, and the workers quickly laid down their hammers and saws and migrated toward the food area. Children scrambled toward the tables and were taken in tow by their parents.

Ragan poured lemonade and watched Johnny, who was helping the judge fill his plate. Procky seemed to be unusually picky about his food today, and she realized with a sinking feeling that he was actually enjoying Johnny's attention.

For a moment she struggled with a disturbing thought. Procky's only son lived hundreds of miles from Barren Flats and rarely got home for a visit. The judge missed him terribly, and she prayed Procky wasn't beginning to see Johnny as a substitute for Blake. That would only complicate matters and end up hurting Procky. She stole another glance at Johnny — whose thick, soft-looking hair gleamed in the sun — and realized she was the one in danger, not the judge. Their weeks together had mellowed her, and she had begun to look forward to her duties, to working with this man. She knew him well enough now to feel that when he said he wasn't guilty of the bank robbery that he was telling the truth. Either that or he was a skillful fraud.

But when Johnny's time was up, he'd be gone, and neither she nor the judge would ever hear from him again.

*Remember that, Ragan, and don't make me keep repeating the warning.*

# CHAPTER SIXTEEN

Johnny finished the last of his potato salad and leaned back against the tree trunk. Tipping his hat over his eyes, he dozed during the temporary respite. The sun was hot, and his belly was full. His mind wandered back to the day of his trial.

The crowd was tight outside the building, and they booed when Johnny came through the doorway.

"Clear the way," the sheriff yelled, pushing bystanders aside.

A burly onlooker pressed closer as Johnny was led from the courtroom.

"McAllister."

Johnny turned at the harsh whisper, and a man stepped in close. His eyes narrowed, and a set of rotting teeth flashed beneath a bushy red beard. An evil smile widened on the man's ruddy features.

"You're a dead man, McAllister."

Puet. The man who robbed the bank. Johnny halted and turned to say something to the deputy, but the officer shoved him ahead.

"Get on," he ordered.

Johnny stumbled and righted himself. Turning to look over his shoulder, he searched the spectators for the outlaw.

There wasn't a person who looked remotely like him in the crowd.

Johnny shook his head. If Puet wanted him, he'd have to come to Paradise to get him.

"More lemonade, Mr. McAllister?" Johnny cracked an eye to find Jo Ramsey standing over him, a pitcher in her hand.

He checked a smile. He didn't know what it was about Jo, but Ragan's younger sister reminded him of his sister, Lara. She'd have been a few years older than Jo now. And like Jo, Lara'd be so pretty she'd steal every boy's heart that looked her way. Pain twisted his gut, and he looked away. "I've had enough, thank you, Jo."

She set the pitcher aside and smiled shyly. "Mind if I join you?"

Johnny glanced in Ragan's direction. That probably wasn't a good idea; he didn't want her riled at him today. He'd rather have her smiles than those looks she could give him.

"I'll be going back to work shortly."

The young girl's face fell. "But not for a while."

She looked so disappointed he didn't have the heart to refuse her. What could a few minutes hurt? He nodded.

Flashing a quick smile, she sat down beside him. "Did you enjoy your dinner?"

"Too much," he conceded. It would be real easy to get used to this lifestyle. Good food, clean sheets, a good-looking woman looking after him. Sweet-smelling Ragan, serving him breakfast every morning. He clamped down on that thought, hard.

His mind wandered to the one time he'd seriously thought about marrying. Her folks owned a spread next to Grandpa's. She was young, pretty, and mad as a hornet when he rode away without asking for her hand. At the time he knew it was the right thing to do. He might have loved her. He'd at least been mighty attracted to her. Maybe he should have married her, started a family . . . But the shadow of Dirk Bledso covered him.

"Don't you think, Mr. McAllister?" Jo's question brought him back to the present. He lifted his head to meet her questioning eyes.

"Sorry, did you say something?"

"Don't you think that a girl has the right to tell a boy that she likes him?" Morning glory blue eyes gazed adoringly at him. "Ragan says —"

"Jo!"

A flushed Ragan stood over them, her eyes snapping, a wooden spoon clutched tightly in her hand. Jo looked up at her sister expectantly. "Yes?"

"Roberta needs your help cutting desserts."

"Yes, ma'am." The girl obediently got up, brushing dried grass off the back of her dress. She turned and gave Johnny a smile that would melt the devil's heart. "Thank you, Mr. McAllister. It's been nice visiting with you."

Ragan's left foot tapped impatiently. "Hurry along, Jo."

Johnny waited until the girl joined Roberta at the dessert table and was out of earshot before he turned to confront Ragan, his features taut. "I'm not going to hurt your sister."

Crimson burned her cheeks as she thrust a plate toward him. "I brought you a piece of pecan pie."

"No, thanks." He thrust it back, his earlier good mood gone. She sure knew how to take the fun out of a picnic.

Expelling a deep breath, she extended the pie again, insistent that he take it. "Minnie's real proud of her pies. Just because you don't like me doesn't mean you need to hurt her feelings." She motioned toward the row of tables. "She's watching to see if you eat it."

Johnny mentally groaned when he saw the mayor's wife wave at him. He didn't have to appease Minnie Rayles by eating her pie; he was sentenced to monotony, not gluttony. He halfheartedly waved back before turning back to face Ragan. "Who said I didn't like you?"

"You." She sat down, setting the pie plate on his chest. She was still upset, but she never stayed mad long, just long enough to pin his ears back. A grin played at the corners of his mouth.

The smell of pecan pie drifted to him, and he sat up. He'd eat the pie. He didn't want accusing female eyes on him all day.

"Exactly when did I say I didn't like you?" He bit into the tender crust. How could a woman take flour and lard and nuts and come up with something that tasted so good?

"You haven't ever specifically said it, but I know you don't." Ragan pushed a damp strand of wheat-colored hair out of her eyes.

He forgot the pie.

Clearly she believed what she was saying, and why wouldn't she? He'd given her a hard time from the moment he got here. He supposed he was blaming her for his troubles, troubles she had no part in.

She sighed, her tone softer now. "I don't blame you for being resentful. I know what you're going through is hard, but you should understand that what I'm doing isn't personal, it's the program. When I caution Jo to stay away from you, I'm only concerned about her welfare. Surely you're aware it isn't proper for a young woman her age to —"

"Associate with the likes of me?" He took another bite of pie. "So you keep reminding me."

"I never said that," she contended.

His features tightened. "Yes, you have." She said it every day in her tone, in the way she looked at him, in the suspicion in her eyes when he caught her staring. She didn't have to say it. Her opinion of him came through loud and clear.

She shook her head. "When did I ever say such a hateful thing?"

He cut off another bite of pie. "You say it all the time without words."

"Then I apologize. I don't disapprove of

you, Mr. McAllister. I disapprove of your ways, but I'm trying very hard to give you the benefit of the doubt."

"That's real big of you." It puzzled him why her respect mattered, but it did. These were good people, and he didn't like them thinking he was a criminal. "If this is a dressing down, Miss Ramsey, I'm not getting the point. Be specific. What do you want me to do?"

"Try harder. You do what you're told without complaint, but your heart isn't in it."

"You want me to like my circumstances? That will be a cold day in . . ."

"No," she interrupted hastily. "I don't expect you to like your punishment. I just want you to be more accepting of it. A year is a long time to carry a grudge against the judge and me. We're trying to make your sentence go as smoothly — and briefly — as possible. It will make it easier for everyone if you cooperate."

Polishing off the last of the pie, he settled back against the tree again and rested the empty plate on his chest. She was right. So why was he resisting? These people didn't ask for him to be here, and they'd been decent to him from the start. Other than being kept busy and staying in Barren Flats for the confines of his sentence, he had a reasonable amount of freedom. A lot more than the grave offered.

"All right." From now on he would attempt to make the best of the situation. And he would discourage Jo's interest in him, even though her presence brought Lara back, if only for a few minutes.

She shot him a skeptical glance. "All right, what?"

"You're right about me not liking you. You're headstrong, bossy, and opinionated, and you get on my nerves like a new blister." He paused, waiting for a reaction from her.

If possible, she got even prettier when she was angry. When her chin jutted upward, he added, "But you're only doing your job. I suppose I could try harder to get along."

To her credit, she took the character assassination in stride, only giving him a distant smile. "Well, I'm sorry you feel that way. At first I didn't like you either. Your annoying refusal to get involved here makes me want to slap you silly." Color rose to her cheeks, and she took a deep breath. "But you don't seem to be the violent sort, and you can be almost nice when you set your mind to it." Their eyes met, and he couldn't quite swallow his grin.

She hurriedly added, "The judge likes

you. You must know that."

"And that burns you."

"No, but I think it could pose a problem. Procky misses his son terribly. Blake lives in Denver, and I'm afraid he doesn't get home often."

"You're afraid the judge will start to think of me as Blake."

She opened her mouth to reply and then closed it. Well, at least she knew when to stop. She looked thankful that he let it pass. He wasn't blind; he knew the judge was lonely. Who wasn't?

"Set your pretty head to rest, Miss Ramsey." He closed his eyes. "I'll make sure Judge McMann doesn't confuse me for his son."

"Thank you." The relief in her voice was so blatant that it rubbed him the wrong way.

"And don't you forget on occasion that I'm a criminal, a vile man."

She gasped, but immediately she said snippily, "See. You're not even trying."

He wickedly grinned as she watched the activity going on around her. The silence stretched. He reached and pulled his hat over his face to shade the sun. "You ever get a good look at the gangs who ride through here?"

"Not often. We're usually in the hall closet or under a table. Why?"

"Ever hear of Dirk Bledso?" The outlaw was notorious. If he and his murdering brothers had ever ridden through Barren Flats, someone would have noticed.

"It sounds familiar, but there are so many who ride through." Ragan settled herself against the tree trunk, her brow creased in concentration. "Dirk Bledso. Isn't he also known as the Viper?"

"That's the one."

"I do recall a wanted poster bearing that name. He rides with his brothers, doesn't he?"

"Yes. How long ago did you see the poster?"

"Three — maybe four years. I remember because Papa and I talked about how vile the brothers looked."

"Vile" didn't begin to cover it.

Raylene Plummer fastened the ties of her apron and called to Ragan. "We could use your help, dear!"

Ragan sighed softly as though reluctant to leave.

"Thanks for the pie," he murmured. He listened for the rustle of her skirt as Ragan stood. A moment later he felt her fingers brush against his chest as she picked up his empty plate and fork.

Tilting his hat back slightly, Johnny studied her swaying skirts as she walked away.

# CHAPTER SEVENTEEN

A few days later, the hot summer morning was charged with excitement as townsfolk milled around the stage station, ears tuned to the north. Children balanced on the boardwalk railing and scampered back and forth across the road under the watchful eyes of their parents.

Voices hummed as the clock hands inched past two o'clock. Of all days, the stage was late.

The town band warmed up on a carefully erected platform covered in blue-and-white bunting. Their instruments clogged the air with disjoined harmony. Decked out in his Sunday best, Mayor Rayles paced in front of the dais, lips silently moving as he rehearsed his speech. In his left front pocket a town proclamation awaited the notorious gunslinger, Lars Mercer.

Lowell Homer stepped out of the mercantile, patting his ample stomach. "Fine day,

Mayor."

"Couldn't be better!" Carl Rayles indicated the elderly man by his side. "Sheriff Lutz is looking forward to this more than anybody. Right, Alvin?"

The sheriff looked blank. "Eh?"

"You're looking forward to gettin' rid of the gangs!"

Alvin nodded. "Yep. If Mercer cleans up the town, maybe I can get some rest." He tapped the badge on his shirt.

"Maybe," Lowell agreed. "Nervous?" he asked the mayor.

"Me?" Mayor Rayles laughed. "Looking forward to the excitement. How about you, Shorty?"

"Can't wait." Shorty Lynch stepped out of the store with Mazilea and locked up. "Coming to the picnic afterward, Carl?"

"Wouldn't miss it! I imagine our guest of honor has many a fascinatin' story to tell."

"Stage is comin'!"

A shout went up, and the band struck up a spirited rendition of "The Star-Spangled Banner." Folks craned their necks to see Mercer roll into town. Long minutes passed before they realized the speck of dust they thought was the stage was actually Austin and Raylene Plummer, with their sons, coming to greet the stage. The music died away,

134

and the townsfolk resumed chatting.

"How we gonna know it's him?" Florence Banks asked. "Nobody's ever actually seen this Mercer."

"No one has to see him. We'll know," Hubie assured his wife. "Can't miss a legend like Mercer."

"Anyone know what he looks like?" someone else called out.

No one did.

"He's mean."

"Mean, and so fast on the draw not a single man's ever lived to tell about meeting him."

"That's why no one knows what he looks like," a voice declared.

The hum rose and fell as anticipation mounted. The suspense was murder, but it wouldn't be long now.

Austin Plummer walked up to join the conversation. "Has to be a big guy. Swede, I'll bet."

"No doubt. Big man for a big job."

"Wonder if Mercer wears an eye patch? Seems I read somewhere he does."

"Probably. He's in a risky business. Could lose an eye real easy."

It was generally agreed the shootist was big, mean, fast, of Swedish descent, and probably missing an eye.

The town had put their money to good use.

"I see the stage!"

The band started up, and heads turned. Tubas and horns filled the air with patriotic tunes. Dogs barked, and babies, startled by all the noise, squalled at their mothers' bosoms. It was minutes before someone realized this was another false alarm. This time, a hay-laden wagon driven by a citizen of nearby Brown Branch was passing through.

The tubas died off, followed by the trombones and cymbals. Eyes returned to the north end of town.

"I'm nervous," Lillian Hubbard said as she tightened little Trish's hair ribbon.

Haleen Lutz fanned herself with a hanky, her matronly features flushed from the heat. Tiny beads of perspiration lay on her forehead. "Well, I'd like to have Mr. Mercer to supper, but I surely do hope he doesn't plan to stay long. We don't need his likes on a regular basis. Got enough riffraff the way it is. Don't you agree, Alvin?" She tugged her husband's sleeve, raised her voice, and spoke directly into his ear. "I said Mercer needs to move on when he's through here. Don't you agree?"

The sheriff checked his watch fob. "Stop

frettin', Haleen. You don't have to yell. It won't take Mercer long to do his job. He's got a reputation to uphold."

Minnie Rayles frowned. "Carl'll make sure he leaves the moment the job is done. I'll have him for pot roast and maybe one of my lemon pies, but I agree with you, Haleen. He cannot be hanging around afterward."

The mayor's features tightened. "Don't start naggin', Minnie. A man don't just clean up a town, eat pot roast and lemon pie, and leave overnight. Ya gotta give Mercer enough time to do what he's gotta do."

"Thou shalt not kill —"

"An eye for an eye, Minnie. I read my Bible too."

"Nonetheless, Carl. Mercer must not be allowed to remain in Barren Flats one moment longer than necessary."

The mayor ground his teeth into his cigar. "Yes, Buttercup."

The excitement was contagious. The town's troubles were over, no doubt about that! Best money they had ever spent.

"He's going to kill the gangs, kill the gangs, kill the gangs," young Mary Hubbard sang, and her sister, Trish, immediately picked up the chant. The two girls held hands and hopped from one foot to the other. Pigtails flew as they twirled in a circle, forcing others to sidestep them. "Kill the gangs, kill the gangs!"

"Trish! Mary! Who's been filling your minds with such thoughts?" Ragan asked. "We must stop the gangs from destroying property and possibly killing one of us." She shaded her eyes, peering down the road.

Judge McMann, Johnny, and the Ramsey family were all gathered to welcome the shootist. Ragan dabbed at the trickle of perspiration on her forehead.

Mary paused, hands on slender hips, eyes narrowed with challenge. "If he's not gonna kill anyone, how come he's called a 'shoots it'?"

Ragan bit back a smile. She glanced at Johnny and blushed when he grinned and murmured, "Why indeed?"

"Shootist, Mary, shootist," Ragan said. "It doesn't mean — oh, look! Is that the stage I see?" Eyes shifted northward again and focused on a coach dragging a cloud of dust as it approached.

A cheer went up as word spread that the legend was, for sure this time, about to arrive.

Ragan pulled Holly aside. "Watch Papa closely this afternoon. With all the excitement, he's likely to wander off."

"Ragan! Yoo-hoo!"

Ragan clamped her eyes shut, and then she reopened them to see Everett coming toward her. She spared him a brief glance before cupping her hand to her eyes and expectantly peering down the road.

Becca poked Johnny, giggling. "Everett loves Ragan."

"Rebecca!" Ragan shot her youngest sister a stern look.

"It's true!"

Ragan glared, but Becca only reiterated, "Well, he does."

"Everett." Ragan smiled as the tall, painfully thin telegraph clerk approached. "You've met Mr. McAllister?"

Everett eyed Johnny, and then he looked back at Ragan. "I've seen him around." He reached out and touched Fulton's shoulder. "Afternoon, sir. It's good to see you out and about."

Reverend Ramsey seemed confused, as if he had just awakened and realized there were people around him. He focused on Johnny, a smile breaking across his features. "Why — who's this fine young man?" He frowned. "Ahh, of course . . . the new schoolmaster. Looks as though we have a good one this time. I've brought the children to meet you. Say hello, children."

Fulton Ramsey's daughters exchanged embarrassed looks before murmuring obedient hellos.

Sliding her arm protectively around her father's shoulders, Ragan said, "Papa, this isn't the new schoolmaster. It's Johnny McAllister. Remember? He's staying with Procky."

"Oh, yes." Fulton smiled pleasantly, extending his hand. "You'll be good for Paradise," he told Johnny. "An education is extremely important for our young people. They can't read the Good Book if they don't have an education."

Everett edged closer to the small circle. "Ragan, you look mighty fetching today."

"Thank you, Everett." Ragan quickly changed the subject. "We'll be meeting Mercer any moment now. Isn't it exciting?"

"I intend to learn to shoot a gun more accurately." His eyes darted to Johnny and then to the stage finally pulling to a halt in front of the mercantile. "Very soon, actually. Just have to find the spare time."

Judge McMann had to shout to be heard over the band. "Better leave the shooting to the experts, son."

Everett ran a finger around the inside of his shirt collar, damp from the building heat. "I can shoot, Judge! I just need more practice, that's all."

Four men piled from the top of the stage. A twitter went through the crowd, and all eyes were glued on the descending passengers. The young men turned out to be area boys, and excitement turned into a disappointed buzz. Not an eye patch in the bunch.

The Thompson sisters alighted from inside the coach, back from their aunt's funeral in San Francisco. For a moment they looked startled at the gathering before they threaded their way through the crowd.

Eyes switched back to the open door. A small, innocuous-looking man stepped off the coach. He couldn't be more than five foot four and a hundred ten pounds, with thinning brown hair. The new arrival paused, squinting over the rims of thick spectacles.

Then a young boy carrying a portmanteau tied with string hopped down. He scanned the crowd, brightening when he spotted his grandparents.

"There's your grandson, Cap," someone called.

Racing toward the older couple, the child embraced Sylvia Kincaid. The three then set off for a nearby wagon, oblivious to the townsfolk waiting for Mercer. Cap's red hat bobbed in the crowd as he lugged the boy's bag.

Eyes shifted back to the front of the coach. Ragan stood on tiptoes, searching the crowd.

Becca pressed closer. "Do you see him?"

"No. I don't think he came." A sick numbness ran through her.

Disappointment spread through the onlookers. The music died away.

"Didn't come? We wired a deposit — he'd better come!"

"Maybe he missed the stage. Maybe he's on the next one."

Tempers flared to match the temperature.

"Of all things! The whole town's out to welcome him, and he doesn't show up. What does that say for his credibility?" Minnie Rayles blustered. "Carl? What's going on here?"

"Don't go gettin' yourself worked up, Minnie. Give the man time."

Johnny focused on the small-statured, bespectacled figure threading his way toward Alvin Lutz and Carl Rayles. Mercer? He'd read stories about the gunslinger, but none ever gave a description that he could recall. He watched the man exchange a few words with the sheriff. Shock registered on Alvin's face. He stepped back, cupping his hand to his ear.

A moment later, "*You're* Mercer?"

Johnny winced at the sheriff's incredulous tone. Because of his deafness he always spoke loudly, and his voice carried well through the crowd.

Heads swiveled. Jaws went slack.

"*That's* Mercer!"

"That can't be the shootist. That man couldn't fight his way out of a wet periodical!"

"It's him, all right. Look at Carl. He looks fit to be tied."

Johnny saw the man's steely stare. It was Mercer all right. The town just didn't care to believe it.

"Oh, for heaven's sake!" Minnie turned away in disgust.

"Now, Minnie," Muriel Davidson was overheard trying to pacify her. "Warren always says it's not a person's size —"

"I don't care what Warren always says. Look at him. He can't fight these gangs. He's no bigger than a termite."

"Send him back, Mayor," Mazilea yelled. Mayor Rayles held up his hand and demanded silence. When the clamor died enough for people to hear, he lifted his voice above the confusion. "Folks, er . . . now, calm down. It seems there's been a mistake

—Warren! Stop playing that blessed tuba!"

Tuba strains died away.

"Is that Mercer?" someone in the crowd shouted.

"Er . . . yes. Now, let's not jump to conclusions . . ."

The crowd pushed forward. Mayor Rayles and Sheriff Lutz were forced to step back or be trampled.

"We want our money back!"

"Oh, my." Ragan pressed her hanky to her forehead. "This is just awful."

Judge McMann stood and tried to peer over the frenzied gathering. "They should at least talk to the man. Why, this is a disgrace."

Johnny parted his way through the crowd, moving toward the gunman. Granted, Mercer didn't look as if he could whip cream, but looks were deceiving.

"Send him back!"

Johnny couldn't believe his ears. In their midst was one of the deadliest guns in the West, and they were complaining because he wasn't as big as they had imagined he would be?

He reached Mercer as the crowd formed a ring around the mayor, calling for his removal. By now Mercer stood to the side, stiffly watching the exhibition.

"Lars Mercer?"

Mercer's eyes narrowed, his hand dropping to his holster concealed beneath a dark blue suit coat. "Who wants to know?"

Johnny extended his hand. "John McAllister."

Mercer ignored the gesture, refusing to shake. "What's going on here?"

Johnny studied the crowd. He wasn't about to apologize for others' bad manners. Then he saw Ragan, and his thoughts tempered. This was her town, and it was a troubled town. "They're having a rough time right now. They don't mean any disrespect."

Mercer leaned over and spat. "Who'd they expect? Wyatt Earp?"

Glancing at the judge, who was moving forward, Johnny said quietly, "Do you know Dirk Bledso?"

Mercer kept an eye on the restless crowd. "Sure, I know the Viper. Why?"

"Have you seen him lately?"

The gunman's eyes returned to Johnny. "What's it to you?"

"I have something that belongs to him." *A bullet with Bledso's name on it.*

Mercer leaned over and spat again. "So?"

Johnny kept his tone casual. "Bledso's a hard one to catch up with. I suppose he and

145

his brothers are still tearing up towns?"

Mercer made a sound like a laugh, but it was easy to see he wasn't amused. "Yeah, those boys are real mean."

"So I've heard."

Wiping his mouth with his coat sleeve, Mercer frowned. "Haven't seen Dirk in a while. Last time I bumped into him was over in Callum County — two, maybe three years ago." The two men turned to look as the noise around the platform swelled again.

"Send him back," the crowd yelled in unison.

Mercer eyed them sourly. "Them people are nuttier than a pet coon."

# CHAPTER EIGHTEEN

Ragan watched the unfolding spectacle, sick at heart.

"Roll me to the platform," Judge McMann said to her. "I'm going to put a stop to this."

Ragan pushed the chair through the noisy crowd, her eyes centered on Johnny and Mercer. What were those two talking about? Her heart sank. Did Johnny and Mercer know each other? Was Johnny thinking about doing something foolish? It would be simple to cause a ruckus and slip off through the crowd. *Don't jump to conclusions.* She was being as unfairly judgmental as the others.

"Mayor Rayles!" Judge McMann shouted above the noise. The crowd parted and allowed the judge access to the platform.

When the mayor spotted McMann, he stepped down, mopping his brow. "Judge." He nodded to Ragan. "We got ourselves in a real fine predicament here."

Judge McMann moved closer. "What's the problem, Carl?"

"Well . . . just look at Mercer. He's not exactly what we had in mind." Carl wiped his nose and then shoved the handkerchief back into his hip pocket. Sweat popped out on his forehead.

Heads swiveled to stare at the shootist.

Mercer stiffened, nailing the entire assemblage with a hard look, his hand perched defiantly on his Colt revolver.

Eyes switched back.

"Exactly what about him don't you like, Carl?" the judge asked.

Carl leaned closer. "Look at him, Procky. He's little — skinny as a rail. And reedy — real reedy. We need a man for this job."

Judge McMann's eyes traveled to Mercer. "Seems to me you're being a little unfair, aren't you, Carl? Can't tell a book by its cover."

"I can read that book, Judge." They turned to look at the spindly shootist.

"We're sending him packing and demanding our money back," Minnie declared.

"We can't ask for our money back." Carl mopped his forehead with his coat sleeve. "The man's come all the way out here. We can't ask for our money back just because he's small."

"We'll pay for his fare, but you'll have to get our deposit back, Carl." Minnie snapped open her parasol. "And be quick about it. No use wasting the man's time."

Carl, perspiration trickling down his face, went to break the unpleasant news to Mercer.

Johnny moved back to stand by the judge as the mayor told Mercer that due to an unforeseen circumstance, his services would not be needed.

Judge McMann said softly, "Something tells me we're making a mistake."

Ragan turned, concern lining her face. "What do you think, Mr. McAllister? Could Mercer do the job?"

Removing his hat, Johnny ran a hand through his hair. What he thought didn't matter. By now, there wasn't enough money in the state to make Mercer stay. "Looks and size don't make a man."

"That's true," the judge murmured.

Everett added his two cents. "That's entirely right, Judge. A man's size don't matter — it's his abilities that count."

The crowd dispersed as Mercer got back on the stage. A moment later, it pulled slowly from the platform.

"Well, so much for a shootist!" Roberta

straightened her hat.

"It's only a minor setback. We've made a sound decision," Minnie said. "To think that a pint-sized man like that believing he could clean up a town."

Snapping open their parasols, the two women went to begin the picnic.

# CHAPTER NINETEEN

The following Monday afternoon, Ragan poured lemonade for the ladies' quilting group in Judge McMann's living room. The subjects of Lars and the raids had been thoroughly discussed, and conversation had turned to the upcoming Founders' Day celebration, held the first weekend in September.

"Why, Frank can't wait for the pie tasting," Kensil Southern exclaimed. "He's talked of nothing else since he was a judge last year. His favorite is blueberry, but Minnie's pecan holds a close second with him."

The mayor's wife blushed. "Oh, Kensil, it's a very average pecan. I use just a dribble of sorghum, you know. That's what gives it that bit of an edge."

"I don't see how your Frank stays so skinny, eating all that pie!"

"He never has been one to put on weight.

Just lucky, I guess."

"Mazilea, are you entering your green tomato chow-chow this year? That's always a winner."

"Yes. Shorty's eaten most of it already, but I have some put back, so I'll have an entry. Bringing some pickled watermelon rind and okra too."

"Oh, you make the best pickled okra around. My mouth waters just thinking about it."

"Alvin's gathering hay and targets for the shooting match. Justine, are your boys shooting this year?"

The blacksmith's wife nodded. "Couldn't keep them away."

"Poor Everett. He'll be in there trying again, though he can't hit the broad side of a barn."

"Yes, dear boy. He really is a dismal shot." Roberta Seeden glanced at Ragan and then back to her sewing.

"Well," Minnie bit off a thread. "One thing's going to change this year."

The ladies turned their attention to the mayor's wife. "There'll be no liquor at the celebration. I've made that very clear to Carl."

"How're you going to prevent it, Minnie? You know some of those men and their spirits. My mister doesn't partake, but it will take more than you to stop the trouble-makers." Though Haleen's hands were now too arthritic to sew, she always came to the meeting.

"I put my foot down, that's how. I've been checking the cellar every evening after Carl's in bed. Nary a drop of spirits down there. And Florence is watching Hubie to be sure none are sneaked from the saloon."

Florence's needle paused. "Well, they are two of the biggest offenders. The past few years, Hubie's stashed away rum for Carl to pick up on his way home in the evenings. Now when Carl comes by, I keep a close eye on those two."

The ladies exchanged sympathies, except for Minnie.

Lillian Hubbard frowned. "Alcohol should never have been introduced to the celebration. If it weren't for that Harold Layman and his shiftless ways, our men wouldn't think about consuming."

Minnie sniffed. "My Carl, for one, will not consume this year."

"Minnie, you always say that, and at every celebration Carl imbibes. The men always find a way," Kensil Southern said.

Haleen nodded in agreement. "Men will be men."

"They won't this year, I tell you. I've made my intentions clear. There's not a single drop in the cellar — nor will there be between now and Founders' Day."

Sighing at the familiar argument, Ragan set aside her sewing and got up to bring more lemonade for her guests. She glanced out the kitchen window and saw Johnny scrubbing screens. Powerful arm muscles flexed as he worked.

With each passing day, she knew, knew in her heart, that he had been falsely accused. Johnny McAllister wasn't a bank robber. He might be guilty of poor judgment, but she knew a criminal when she saw one. And he wasn't one.

# CHAPTER TWENTY

Early the following morning Ragan announced she was out of coffee, so after breakfast Johnny walked her to the mercantile. When they parted at the door, he smiled. "Don't spend all day in there talking."

"Since when did you get to be so bossy?"

Winking, he tugged one of the ribbons on her bonnet and walked away grinning. He could feel her eyes following him as he stepped off the porch.

Minnie Rayles emerged from the general store and looked both ways for Carl. The mayor was across the street at the surveyor's office, but it was obvious Minnie didn't know where her husband had gone.

Johnny sauntered toward her and took the two large bags from her arms. "I'll get those for you, Mrs. Rayles."

Minnie had to take two steps with her plump little legs to his one, and she bustled to keep up. "Thank you, Johnny. You're a sweet man." She reached up and pinched his cheek, and he winced.

He set the groceries on the buckboard seat, his cheek stinging. Tipping his hat, he smiled. "Have a nice day, ma'am."

Minnie tittered. "Oh, I shall. Ta-ta!"

How that woman could be so much like Grandma's sister, Aunt Tess, he'd never know. He felt like a nine-year-old around the mayor's wife. Aunt Tess had pinched his cheek like that when he'd done something to please her.

Leaning against the bank railing, he took inventory of the town. People went about their business as if they hadn't made complete fools of themselves with Mercer. Music already spilled from the open doorway of the Oasis Saloon.

He wondered if there was any real chance Bledso's gang would ever come through Barren Flats. Every other lowlife seemed to.

Removing his hat, Johnny wiped sweat off the headband. It wasn't nine o'clock yet, and it was hot enough to cook an egg on the boardwalk. His eyes swept Main Street as time dragged. Well, if there was anything he had, it was time.

His hand crept down his thigh to feel the space left by his missing pistol. What if he

156

got his chance at Bledso before his gun was returned? The thought plagued him. Judge McMann might let him use an ax to chop wood, but his trust didn't carry over to a gun.

"There is one more requirement you must fulfill before this court is satisfied that the correct sentence has been handed down." Judge Leonard leaned forward in his chair. "John McAllister, I want your word, as a man, that you will serve the sentence and will return before this bench at its completion."

"You have my word, sir."

The judge nodded gravely. "I'm an old man. Some folks don't like my sentences — sometimes I wonder myself if they're sound. Tomorrow morning at daybreak, you'll be transported to Paradise, California, where you will begin your punishment. I'll expect to see you back in this courtroom at the successful completion of your term."

Johnny nodded. He would be back — unless he ran into Dirk Bledso. In that case the judge's efforts on his behalf would be in vain. If, and when, he met up with Bledso, he would kill him. He'd never get Grandpa's gun back, and that bothered him. But the way Bledso had butchered his family in cold blood disturbed him more. Besides, if he killed a man he'd hang. He'd have no need of a gun to hand down to his son.

Was killing Bledso worth it? Sometimes he looked at the people here in Barren Flats and envied their home lives. Their children. When he was twelve he hadn't thought about a wife and kids; only revenge. He hadn't known then that carrying a grudge could wear a man down.

Bitterness gnawed at him, an acridity he couldn't shake. Folks had wanted Mercer to clean up their town. He laughed. Couldn't be done. Justice couldn't be carried out without a lot of violence, and folks here didn't have the stomach for it. Bledso had ended life as he knew it, in one senseless act. He'd destroyed almost everyone who ever cared about him. Grandpa had loved him, but now he was gone too. He focused on Ragan, who was talking to Roberta Seeden in the mercantile. If things were different, he might court a woman like that. Or at least he'd try. But he couldn't have a decent woman and kill Bledso. Ragan was a strong believer, and at times he envied her faith. She might not be the Scripture-quoting kind, but she lived her faith. He'd seen it in the way she took care of the judge and her family. She worked long hours to

158

keep them all fed, clothed, and healthy. Killing wouldn't be in her vocabulary. So he'd go on searching for Bledso. Sleeping in a lonely bed at night. Awaiting a hangman's noose.

His restless gaze traced the streets, pausing at the telegraph office. The clerk — Everett . . . what was his last name? Pidgin? — leaned on the counter, chin propped in his hand, gawking at Ragan through the mercantile window.

Poor besotted fool.

Ragan's laughter floated through the open doorway. A man would be hard pressed not to desire a woman like her. Soft, sweet, smelling of rosewater, exuding domesticity.

An elusive thought teased him. Pidgin had mentioned wanting to learn to shoot a gun. He, on the other hand, needed access to a gun but was forbidden to handle a firearm.

Pushing away from the post, Johnny sauntered across the street to the telegraph window. Everett was so engrossed in watching Ragan that he didn't hear Johnny's footsteps.

"Hot today."

The clerk's head snapped around and suspicious eyes centered on him.

Everett's face was too long, his eyes narrow set. He had a lantern jaw, a five o'clock shadow, thick lips, long sideburns, and he was thirty pounds too light for his six-foot-four frame.

The clerk watched as Johnny approached. "Can I help you?"

Johnny casually adjusted the brim of his hat. "Just waiting for Ragan to finish up at the mercantile. Thought it might be cooler over here."

Everett busied himself straightening papers. His open resentment was amusing — no, actually, it was pathetic. Pidgin carried a torch the size of Texas for a woman he could never have. Obviously Everett considered his presence at the McMann house threatening, though he couldn't imagine why.

Ragan was out of his league. Women like her had always been out of his league. She wanted home and family; he wanted Dirk Bledso to pay for his sins. The two didn't mesh, and it would be foolish to ever think otherwise. That would be a fatal error on his part, and his goal was to make as few errors as possible. The last one had cost him at least one year, maybe two, of his life.

Lifting the dipper out of the water pail, Johnny took a long drink. He glanced at Pidgin, who was now busy scribbling on a yellow pad. It was possible they could accommodate one another. He couldn't be caught with a gun in his possession, but he did need to know where he could get his hands on one if Bledso showed up. Taking a final swig, he tossed the remainder of the water onto the ground.

"Founders' Day a big celebration around here?"

Everett didn't look up. "Somewhat."

Johnny leaned against the counter, scanning the building clouds. A nice shower would settle the dust. "A lot of good food and drink, I guess."

Getting up from his stool, Everett sorted another stack of papers. "You're serving a sentence, aren't you?" He avoided Johnny's eyes. "You're a criminal."

Johnny took a deep breath. Pidgin knew his status, but he'd play along. "Yeah. I'm a criminal."

Everett had decided to press the issue. "What'd you do? Kill someone?"

"I'm accused of robbing a bank."

Everett reshuffled the same stack of papers. He'd be lucky if there was anything left to deliver if he didn't stop moving them around. "Did you do it?"

"A judge said I did."

The men fell silent. Everett finally stashed the papers neatly on a shelf and returned to the window. Johnny glanced toward the mercantile, aware of Everett's curious sideways looks.

"We don't need no more trouble in town. We got enough."

"I don't plan on causing trouble."

"Don't matter. The celebration and picnic this year? It won't be worth attending."

Johnny didn't doubt that a bit. He'd never been one for socializing.

"No whiskey this year."

Johnny's brows lifted curiously. "You a drinking man?"

"Nah. Just on Founders' Day." He straightened, looking proud. Johnny had a hunch he could be easily led.

"Never cared for whiskey myself. A man needs to keep a clear head." At least not all of Grandpa's teachings had left him.

"Whiskey," Everett repeated, frowning. "Minnie Rayles won't let the men have *whiskey*. It's mostly stuff they make. Home brew, a little gin . . . but we can't have anything this year." His eyes met Johnny's. "That's a crying shame, ain't it? It's the one time of year we're allowed a bit of the brew, and now Minnie goes and spoils it."

Johnny shrugged. "Bad habit, one you'd best avoid."

Warming a little, Everett leaned closer.

162

"Well, there's not a thing we can do about it. Minnie is just plain mean-spirited. I don't know how Carl stands it. I wouldn't want to marry a bossy woman like Minnie."

"Not many would."

Silence stretched between them. Everett cleared his throat. "Actually, I don't care all that much for strong drink, but the other men think it's important. Personally, what I look forward to is the shooting contest."

"They have a shooting contest at the celebration?"

Everett nodded. "Big one, every year. The winner this year takes home a brand-new Greener double-barrel shotgun."

"A Greener, huh? Nice gun. Guess you plan on winning?"

"Me? No. I can't hit the broad side of a barn. Hubie Banks will win it. He wins every year."

*Play it easy,* Johnny reminded himself. *Nice and easy.*

Removing his hat again, he studied it. "What makes you say that? You could practice and get better, couldn't you?"

Shaking his head, Everett appeared to consider, and then he discarded the thought. He glanced at Johnny. "You probably know how to shoot a gun — shoot one real well."

"I do okay. What kind of a gun do you have?"

"A pistol." Everett's eyes drifted back to Ragan. "A real man needs to shoot good. Take care of his family, put food on the table."

This was going to be like taking candy from a baby. The subject seemed to be a sore spot with the clerk. Shifting, Johnny said quietly, "I wouldn't necessarily say that. I know women who despise violence."

"Women like their men to be men. And a real man knows how to shoot a gun accurately."

"Most anyone can learn to be a good shot. If a man wanted to learn, I could teach him to shoot a rattlesnake's eyes out at fifteen feet."

Everett's jaw dropped, and then his eyes narrowed. "You're not allowed to have a gun."

"I could teach a man to shoot without touching the gun."

"You could?"

Johnny could almost see the cogs turn in Everett's head. He wanted it, but would he go for it?

"No." Everett shook his head. "I may look like a fool, but I've got more brains than that. You're a criminal. You're not even supposed to be around a gun. I could get in trouble."

Johnny smiled. "I merely mention my services, should you need them."

"I don't need them, thank you. Judge Mc-Mann would be real upset if I was to do anything to interfere with his program." He glanced toward the mercantile. "So would Ragan."

"I understand," Johnny said.

Everett picked up another stack of papers. Sweat stood out on his upper lip and his hands shook, causing several of the documents to fall to the floor. He leaned down to pick them up. "I'd . . . I'd like to take you up on your offer . . . but it just wouldn't be right."

Johnny calmly set the hook. "Don't know of a man who wouldn't give his eyeteeth to own a Greener." He chuckled. "Imagine the look on Hubie Banks's face if you were to outshoot him this year."

"Yeah . . ." Everett paused to imagine it. "I'd love to see that, all right. And the look on Ragan's face when I won."

"Well, looks like Ragan and Mrs. Seeden have finally finished their shopping." Johnny casually pushed away from the counter. "Are you sure they said a Greener?"

Everett looked downright sick. "I'm positive. I had the deciding vote."

"How much do you suppose a gun like that's worth?"

"Ten — fifteen dollars."

Giving an appreciative whistle, Johnny adjusted the brim of his hat. "Nice shotgun. If you change your mind about my help, you know where to find me. I'm sure we could work something out." He stepped down off the porch.

"Er . . . Mr. McAllister?"

Johnny turned. "Yes?"

"Can you really shoot a rattlesnake through the eye?"

"Every time."

He could feel Everett's stare as he crossed the street and took the packages out of Ragan's hands.

She smiled up at him, her pleasant talk with Roberta still evident on her face. "Did I see you visiting with Everett?"

"Just killing time while you shopped." They fell into step, walking down Main Street. They were almost at the crossroads before Johnny offered his thoughts.

"Why does a woman like you stay in a town like Barren Flats?"

Ragan laughed. "What a question."

"I mean it. I know you take care of the

judge and your father, but don't you want more?"

"More?" She appeared to at least consider the idea. "No, not more. Maybe different. Why would I want more?"

He shrugged. He'd want more — or would he? He'd spent years looking for his family's killers. He'd told himself revenge was the driving factor, but maybe what he wanted was a family again. Ties. Roots. Belonging to someone.

"You're smart. You have a lot to offer."

Her smile was almost impish. "To whom? A husband? Everyone thinks I'll always be an old maid, but someday I want to marry. Right now, I stay in Barren Flats because my family is here. And Procky is here. He and his wife were second grandparents to me when I was growing up."

They turned toward Judge McMann's street.

"I have responsibilities here," Ragan said.

"You can't sacrifice yourself forever."

"Family isn't a sacrifice — but then, you wouldn't know about that." She glanced at him, a lighthearted challenge in her eyes. "Since you came from a pea pod."

Wouldn't know about family? She had no idea. He knew what it was like to wake to the smell of ham sizzling in a skillet. Ice on his bedroom windowpane Christmas morning. The sound of Ma humming as she slid a lemon cake into the oven. He knew all right. And it hurt.

"So you'll just stay here and be a nursemaid all your life?"

She let the subject of his origins pass. "Not all my life, no. I'll stay as long as Papa and Procky are alive. Most certainly until Becca's grown. Procky wants me to go to school later."

"You haven't gone to school?"

"I want to go to college. He'd like me to study law someday. Says I'm a natural, but I don't know if it's what I really want to do. Besides, I have plenty of time to think about it."

"Can a woman get into law school?"

"It would be a struggle," she admitted. "Just last year the Wisconsin Supreme Court denied Lavinia Goodell's application to the bar. Apparently, they believed women are too delicate and emotional for the profession."

Her chin lifted. "I may have to go to the Midwest if I pursue a law degree. The University of Iowa and Washington University in St. Louis opened doors to women almost twenty years ago. But whatever I decide to do, I want to make a difference in people's lives." She slowed, turning to face him. A hot breeze ruffled her blond hair, tossing it around her animated features. "Are you surprised that I want to further my education?"

"Nothing about you surprises me." He'd been here long enough to realize she was strong, independent, bossy, and prettier than any woman should be.

She brushed a lock of hair off her cheek. "I want to make a difference, like Procky does. I've watched wayward boys and grown men change into responsible, outstanding citizens because he gave them the opportunity to develop to their potential. Most in our program have failed, I admit that, but a few have been given a new chance in life, and you can't put a price on that. When I lie back on my pillow at night, I want to know I've helped someone headed in the wrong direction to change — to turn his life around."

She touched his arm. "What about you? What do you want to do once you leave here?"

His plans? He had only one: stay alive long enough to kill Dirk Bledso.

"Johnny?"

"I haven't thought about it."

"You're twenty-eight years old. You can't

drift all your life."

"I don't plan to." They reached the judge's front porch, and Ragan reached for her parcels. Their hands brushed in the brief exchange. At the contact, her eyes held his.

"Let's talk about it soon," she said softly. "And someday I'd like you to tell me about your family too."

For a split second, he thought about telling her everything. He'd empty his soul, tell her what his life had been like the past sixteen years, and tell her that he knew all about family and responsibility and loving someone. He knew she would understand his pain.

"Don't hold your breath," he said. What was there to tell? They were all dead.

Her look was indecipherable. Curiosity? Concern?

"Ragan?" The judge's voice came from the back of the house as they opened the screen door.

"We're home, Procky. I have the coffee."

# CHAPTER
# TWENTY-ONE

That night Johnny stood at the east window overlooking the judge's moonlit rose garden. Crickets chirped and an occasional whip-poor-will called to its mate. A barely perceptible breeze stirred the lace curtains. Johnny turned when he heard a soft scratching. The moon shed enough light to see a furry black paw work its way under the edge of his door and then stretch more fully under the crack in search of anything to ensnare on the other side.

Moving away from the window, he lightly touched the tip of his bare toe to the back of the curled paw. It instantly began a frantic clawing sweep, trying to trap the object. He grinned and watched as the leg stretched as far as possible, grabbing, and then retreating to the opposite side. Another tentative try scooping air, and then a plaintive plea for admittance.

"All right, all right. Hold on."

He opened the door a crack and Kitty burst into the room, scolding him for the neglect she had endured.

"You're late, cat."

She arched against his leg, and then jumped to the sill when he stepped back to the window. He let his hand fall on her head and she pressed into his chest.

"Look out there, Kitty. It's too pretty a night to be cooped up inside. You should be out socializing, making small talk with the other cats in the neighborhood."

She meowed.

A sound caught his ear, and he moved to the north window. The cat changed sills, and rearranged herself in front of him. The muted sound progressed slowly until, illuminated by the moonlight, a small, donkey-drawn cart came into view. Two men walked beside the conveyance, occasionally taking hold of the harness to keep it moving. It passed in front of the house, and the creaking wheels could still be heard as it disappeared into the shadows.

Johnny crossed back to the bed, wondering where he'd seen a cart like that before and thinking of the people he'd seen with donkeys. Plummer had a team of mules. There could be a donkey or two on the Banks's land. The Hubbard girls had a pet jenny, but it was smaller than the one pulling the barrow. He mentally went through the town's dwindling stock population.

He could account for six donkeys, but who were these men?

Lying on the bed and stroking Kitty's head, he wondered who was taking a cartload of what, where, after midnight.

The cat stretched along his thigh and purred when his hand settled on her back. Strange, how comforting it was to know another living being wanted his companionship. It had been years since he'd had a pet. Sixteen years if the number mattered. He took a deep breath. Sixteen years. He'd had a dog, Red. Best hunting dog in the county. Bledso had shot her too.

He had no idea how long he'd slept when the sound of the returning cart awakened him.

Kitty hit the floor and jumped back onto the windowsill as Johnny got up and watched until the mysterious wagon came back into view and bumped back toward Main Street. The donkey moved faster now, and both men rode in the obviously lighter cart.

As the puzzling sight disappeared into the shadows, Kitty jumped from the ledge and ran to the door, trying to paw it open.

Johnny stepped over and opened it for her. "Don't go waking up the judge. It's the middle of night, you know." He watched her silently flick down the stairs.

He lay back down and settled his head on the pillow, uneasy. Who were the men with the donkey?

And what had they taken out of town in a cart at this time of night?

# CHAPTER
## TWENTY-TWO

"I understand Dirk Bledso's here in Salt Lake City."

Glasses clinked down on the bar, and silence settled over the room. Eyes centered on Johnny in the barroom doorway. He smiled at the bartender. "Tell Mr. Bledso he has a visitor."

A cowboy waved a mug in the air and then hurled it against the wall. "Tell him yourself!"

Johnny's hand moved to Everett's gun. He'd waited sixteen long years for this moment. The taste of victory was sweet.

Chairs overturned and customers faded into the shadows. There he was, just as Johnny remembered. Dirk Bledso, bigger than life. Drawing his last breaths. Johnny looked his enemy in the eye. Mama's face floated in front of him, terrified, pleading. "Don't kill my babies . . ."

Papa stepped up, yelling for Bledso to leave them be. Johnny watched the impact as bullets riddled his parents' bodies and they crumpled to the ground. Slowly, methodically, he raised Everett's gun and sighted his prey. The shot hit the Viper straight between the eyes. His evil grin hung midair long after his body lay on the floor. A cheer went up from the townspeople.

The crowd pushed close to the platform, but a hood over Johnny's head prevented him from recognizing faces. Voices rose and fell. He felt the noose drop around his neck. Someone needed to return Everett's Greener.

He'd broken his word, his solemn pledge. Grandpa wouldn't be happy about that.

He sucked hot air between his teeth, and the rope pressed, squeezing, squeezing.

"Prepare to meet your Maker, boy."

Ragan. If things were different he'd have been different. Been the sort of man a woman like her could look up to . . . maybe even love. He'd wasted his life on hate. Who had been the victor: Bledso, a man who cared nothing about life or values, or him, a man who'd thrown away his life in pursuit of bitterness?

The floor dropped from beneath his feet, and he fought the weight on his throat, struggling for breath . . .

Johnny's eyes jerked open. Moonlight flooded the room. Sweat pooled on his body, and his heart hammered. He lay for a moment, staring into bright green eyes.

Then he sat up, struggling to untangle himself from the damp sheet and Kitty. The cat hissed, startled by the sudden movement. A flurry of cotton and feline ensued. Kitty emerged from the sheet and stretched, lazily arching her body, and then she rubbed her face along Johnny's arm.

He stared at the pet and then gently pushed her aside. With a protesting mew, she jumped down and stalked to the window. Perching on the sill, she stared back at him with her sleepy jade eyes.

"This place is getting to me," he grumbled. His breathing was ragged, and the image of Dirk Bledso seared his brain. Sisal still bit into his neck.

Hanging wasn't something he often allowed into his thoughts.

Kitty jumped from her perch and rejoined him on the bed. Purring, she nuzzled his neck, forcing him to pay attention to her.

Settling back on the pillow, he let her stay. For once, her company was more welcome than the darkness. He absently scratched behind her ears. "You know, cat, when I do kill Bledso, there won't be a man alive who'll blame me. He's a blight on the face of the earth, a scourge to humanity."

*"I know you're hurtin', boy. Real bad, but killing's not the answer. It'll only bind you to further pain."*

Grandpa's words. Grandpa who'd hurt as badly as him, but he'd read the Bible by lantern light and stoically follow the Word. "Weren't easy," he'd say when Johnny accused him of not caring. "Hard — real hard to live the Word, but it would be harder to stand before the Lord and say you'd killed one of his children in cold blood. The Lord judges, not man."

Kitty rubbed her whiskers against Johnny's chin and purred.

Stupid cat. Stupid him for lying in bed talking to a cat. Regardless of his grandfather's words, Bledso deserved to die. The last time he'd disappeared like this, word was that he was dead, his body lying somewhere in the Sierra Nevadas, bones bleached white by the sun.

Then the murdering started again.

Dirk and his brothers stole for the thrill of it. They murdered for the pure joy of killing. How else could a man take the lives of children — two blue-eyed little girls with golden curls . . .

Kitty mewed, nestling against his cheek.

He brushed her affection aside. "You kill, cat. Crickets, moths, mice. Don't look at

178

me like you're passing judgment. 'An eye for an eye' — that's what the Good Book says."

The cat inched closer, head up and eyes focused on him. A purr answered his accusation.

Johnny lay back, staring at the ceiling.

There was no telling where the lowlifes were. But wherever they were, he would find them.

Someday he would find them.

He smiled, picturing the moment he'd meet Bledso face-to-face. He wasn't proud of taking advantage of Everett, but there were times when honor was just cause. Everett would get his gun back. He'd see to that.

Kitty mewed softly.

Glancing down at her, he ruffled her fur. "You're spoiled, cat, you know that?"

# CHAPTER
# TWENTY-THREE

When Ragan came through the back door the next morning to begin breakfast, there were three cups of coffee waiting on the table. Johnny and the judge already had their hands wrapped around two of them.

She smiled, feeling a rush of gratitude. Any sign of progress with Johnny brought hope.

"You're getting pretty good at making a decent cup of coffee. They'll be hiring you at the Oasis one of these days," she teased.

The faint hint of a smile showed at the corners of McAllister's mouth and her pulse raced.

"Don't bet money on it," he told her.

"I don't wager, sir. Can't quite imagine you in a skirt, anyway."

Judge McMann chuckled, reaching for the cream pitcher. "You two are in a feisty mood this morning."

Bending over Johnny's shoulder, Ragan

replenished the cream pitcher. The faint hint of shaving soap left her feeling a bit heady. She turned slightly, her face shamelessly inches from his. "Good morning."

"You're in a good mood this morning," he murmured.

"As a matter of fact, I am. It's a glorious day." She touched his shoulder briefly and moved on. Sliding into her chair, she opened her napkin.

"More coffee, anyone?" the judge asked.

The judge chatted amiably but Ragan's mind was on the man opposite her. She couldn't wait for the meal to be over and for Johnny to accompany her to the mercantile. Lately, the moments they spent together were the highlight of her days.

Shortly after breakfast she approached the work shed, happily anticipating the outing.

"I'm out of white thread. I need to purchase some this morning."

He quietly laid aside the window frame he was rebuilding. "I'll wash up."

"We won't be gone long."

He nodded, moving to the water tank to wash.

She wished he would say something instead of just looking at her with those dark, brooding eyes. How she longed to know his inner thoughts — his inner purgatory. As he fell into step with her on the way to the store, she racked her brain thinking of topics to discuss. Finally, she couldn't stand the strain a moment longer.

"About this morning," she blurted. "I didn't mean to behave so boldly." Actually, she did, but her conscience nagged her. She was in a position of authority; she should never have trifled with him. Touching his shoulder was bold and completely inappropriate. Had the judge noticed? Heat tinged her cheeks.

"You don't need to explain, Miss Ramsey. You wouldn't deliberately encourage a prisoner's favor, would you?"

She was so taken aback by his swift response, she was speechless. Apparently he'd been thinking about this morning's incident too. "I just don't want you to think . . ."

"Think what?" His eyes skimmed her lightly.

"That . . . I'm a . . . wicked woman."

"Wicked?" He threw back his head and laughed. Sobering, he met her gaze. "Look. If you'll let up on me, I'll ease up on you. Agreed?"

His words were firm but encouraging.

She accepted his offer with grace.

# Chapter
# Twenty-Four

While Ragan shopped, Johnny leaned against the livery building and watched the town activity. A few women stood about, discussing such topics as which fabrics to use for new dresses and whether milk or cream made fluffier mashed potatoes.

He couldn't be certain, but he was beginning to wonder if the newest raids were the work of the red-bearded bank robber, Puet, and his gang. He hated to think he'd brought more grief to the town or Ragan.

He nodded to the Thompson sisters as they crossed the street.

Old-timers stopped by, asking him questions. Did he think it would rain? Had Ragan made him one of her strawberry pies yet? How did he like Barren Flats?

Nowadays, he was beginning to notice when old Mr. Parson's lumbago was acting up, or if Mrs. Keeling was having a particularly hard day adjusting to her husband's passing. He didn't like noticing. It made the people more like family . . . and they weren't his family. They were strangers, and he meant to keep them that way.

He straightened when he spotted Everett strutting up the walk. Good. It would save him the trouble of going to the telegraph office. Had Everett taken the bait?

When the young clerk was upon him, he paused, shifting a sheaf of papers to his opposite arm. "Mr. McAllister."

"Everett."

"Hot today."

"Sure is."

Everett cast a wary glance over his shoulder. Clearing his throat, he lowered his voice. "I've been wanting to talk to you."

"Oh?" Johnny forced a casual smile.

The clerk edged closer, keeping an eye on the mercantile doorway. "I've been thinking about your offer." Everett's voice lowered even further, and he spoke without moving his lips, which made it difficult to understand him. "You said you could teach me how to shoot. I figured maybe if you didn't touch the gun, you could tutor me. I'm willing to pay for your services."

Johnny shrugged. "I suppose I could help. What do you have in mind?" What was this sudden nagging guilt? He had a job to do, and sentiment toward Ragan wasn't going to stop him. The quicker he left this town, and its idiotic ways, the better, for both him and Ragan. They were starting to get a little too comfortable around each other.

Everett glanced toward the sheriff's office. "I know you'd be doing something you shouldn't, but if you give me your word that you won't try and take the gun —"

*Give my word that I won't?* Johnny shook his head at the man's innocence. "All right. I'll give you my word. I'll teach you to shoot, but we'll have to be careful. It's not going to be easy to keep this quiet."

Everett grinned. "Leave that to me. Not a soul will know what's going on. I'll arrange everything."

"Fine. When do you want to start?"

"The sooner the better. Founders' Day is six weeks away. I want to be ready."

Six weeks to teach Everett Pidgin to shoot out rattlesnakes' eyes.

"I intend to win that Greener." Everett's eyes shifted to the mercantile. "A woman would be mighty proud of a man who proved to be the best shot in town. Why, if I could shoot out a rattlesnake's eye —"

"You won't. Not every time."

"But if I could do it even once, that would be enough for me." Everett was so earnest,

Johnny had to look away. Grandpa wouldn't be proud of this.

Ragan's laughter floated across the street as she emerged from the mercantile with Kensil Southern. The two women paused on the top step, chatting.

Everett's mouth went slack. "She's so beautiful, she makes the flowers blush."

Johnny's gaze followed Everett's. He didn't have Everett's poetry, but yes, Ragan Ramsey was a real beauty. "I hadn't noticed."

Everett's head snapped back. "You hadn't noticed?"

Johnny adjusted his hat on his head. "Women will get you in trouble, Everett. Better buy yourself a good horse and forget about Ragan." He stepped off the planked porch and started across the street.

"Mr. McAllister?"

Johnny turned. "Yes?"

"I overheard you the other day at the stage station. You said a man's size didn't matter. Did you mean that?"

At times, Johnny felt sorry for the young man's uncertainties. He didn't like to prey on them, but Everett was his lifeline.

"A man makes his own way in the world. Size doesn't have a thing to do with it."

The clerk's eyes returned to Ragan.

"That's how I have it figured."

The sounds of quickly approaching hoof-beats caught the men's attention.

"I'll talk to you later," Everett called, already running down the boardwalk as two banditos rode into town, firing into the air as the town citizens scattered for cover.

# CHAPTER
# TWENTY-FIVE

Monday morning Reverend Pillton posted a notice that services would be held on the following Sunday, provided the repair work on the church was completed.

Immediately after breakfast, Johnny was sent to the work shed to gather brushes and rags while Ragan got her sewing materials together. When she came out the door, he hefted a ladder to his shoulder, and they set out together.

She gave Johnny his instructions. "The church needs a good cleaning and sprucing up. Sawdust is everywhere, and the eaves need a fresh coat of paint."

"Seems like a lot of trouble to me. The gangs aren't going away."

"I'll be at Minnie's if you need me for anything."

"I won't need you."

Shooting him a dour look, Ragan turned north to join her sewing group, and he continued down the lane, grinning. She sure was pretty when she was riled.

Arriving at the church, Johnny found it empty. So much for town participation. He set up the ladder outside, opened a bucket of paint, and climbed to the highest point. He painted for more than twenty minutes before he heard a hiss from a nearby bush. He glanced down, trying to locate the source.

"Psssssssst. Hey!"

Stepping down a couple of rungs, Johnny leaned to peer over the top of the bush.

"Over here," the voice stated.

"Everett? What are you doing behind the bush?"

"I'm hiding."

"Why?"

"I've got the gun."

Johnny glanced at Minnie Rayles's house. "Stay down. The women can see you."

"Where are they?"

"At the mayor's house."

The clerk duckwalked from behind the bush, a package tucked neatly under his arm. Pausing at the bottom of the ladder, his eye scoured the area for intruders.

Johnny quickly joined him on the ground. Picking the ladder and the bucket up, he moved to the opposite side of the building, out of the women's view.

Everett duckwalked behind him, toting the wrapped pistol. When they reached safety, Johnny said, "Okay, let's see what you have."

The clerk hurriedly unwrapped the gun.

Johnny glanced around to be sure they weren't observed. "Everett, that's a big-bore forty-five hog leg. What are you doing with a pistol like that?"

"It was my Uncle Mort's. Aunt Pearl gave it to me when he passed on last year. What do you think of it?"

Johnny studied the weapon: a blue, eight-inch six-shooter. The pistol could bore a hole the size of a little finger going in, a silver dollar coming out. "It's not exactly a gentleman's weapon."

"I know!" Everett beamed. "It's a man's gun."

Johnny itched to hold the firearm, but he kept his distance. "Do you have ammunition?"

"All we'll ever need. It's behind the counter at the telegraph office, bottom shelf, way back in the left-hand corner. I keep it there in case I ever have trouble at work."

"It's not loaded now, is it?"

Everett took a small paper-enshrouded package out of his pocket and thrust it at

190

Johnny. "The bullets are in here."

Johnny stepped back, refusing the package. "You carry them. And break open the chamber." He wasn't taking Everett's word on the gun's firing capacity.

Everett obediently opened the chamber and Johnny nodded.

"We can shoot it right now." Everett duckwalked to the corner of the building and peered around the corner. After a moment he waddled back. "No one will pay any attention to a little gunfire over in the woods. Hubie Banks practices every morning."

Johnny glanced at the stand of scrub oak over the ridge from the church. The area was small, but bushy and dense.

"I don't know, Everett. The women will hear us."

"So? They'll just think it's Hubie shootin' or another raid about to take place." Everett shifted from one foot to the other. "Come on, just five minutes. I'm itchin' to try this thing out." He patted the hog leg confidently. "This is my ticket to the Greener."

Well, one shot wasn't that hard to account for. One shot would hold Everett for a few days — a small price to pay in order to know where the clerk kept the gun. The hog leg would never make the telegraph clerk the object of Ragan's affection, but Johnny didn't have the heart to explain that. Everett would know it soon enough.

"All right, one shot."

"One shot," Everett promised. He waddled alongside Johnny as they moved away from the church building.

"Stand up and walk straight, Everett."

"Oh, sorry."

Moments later, the two men disappeared into the trees.

# CHAPTER
# TWENTY-SIX

Ragan's head jerked up from her sewing as the floor shook in Minnie's parlor. "What was *that?*"

"Oh, goodness. Another raid." Kensil calmly lay her sewing aside.

A few women dropped to the floor and scooted under the table. Others crawled on their hands and knees to safety. A few moments later the ladies resumed stitching while they waited in hiding for the onslaught. When a second shot failed to materialize, their needles paused, ears cocked to the deafening silence.

"I don't hear anything."

Minnie frowned. "Could be Hubie practicing again. That man is obsessed with winning that silly shotgun on Founders' Day."

"Don't say anything about my Hubie, Minnie. You're just jealous that he wins the shooting contest every year and Carl doesn't."

"That's a terrible thing to say, Florence, and I resent it."

"Well, if you —"

"Ladies," Ragan interrupted, "can we please have a little harmony?" The women quibbled over the silliest things.

"Should never have let them get a Greener in the first place. They'll all make fools of themselves." Minnie stabbed her needle through a patch and yanked the thread tight.

"Shush . . . listen . . . I don't hear any more shots."

"That's strange. If it's gangs, they should be here by now."

"Stay down. You never know."

"I'm not staying down any longer. My arthritis is killing me."

"Arthritis isn't as painful as a bullet, Roberta."

"You aren't old enough to know about arthritis yet, Justine. You and Rudolph are just kids. I don't think there's going to be any more shooting. I'm getting up."

One by one, the ladies climbed from their hiding places. They helped Haleen Lutz out of the back of the closet and sat down in their chairs again and continued to sew.

"These constant interruptions are a nuisance, and I, for one, think it's a crying shame we can't even attend Sunday meeting services without the fear of getting our heads blown off," Minnie said. "I still don't know if the mister and I will come Sunday mornings, though the church has been repaired."

No one had ever actually gotten his or her head blown off, but Ragan agreed that the problem was still there.

Her thoughts centered on her exasperating prisoner. He was far more experienced about these matters than any man in town. Even though it wasn't his responsibility, the raids directly affected him; he could be hurt in one of the rampages. She wondered if he'd ever considered that when he was telling himself it "wasn't his problem." Getting up from her chair, she lifted the curtain to look out of the parlor window.

"Is your prisoner behaving himself?"

Frowning, Ragan searched the grounds surrounding the church. Johnny was nowhere to be seen. She released a pent-up breath when she saw him round the corner with Everett moments later. The men carried paint and ladders.

"Actually, he's been ideal, Haleen. With the exception of refusing to lower his barriers, we couldn't ask for a more model subject."

"I imagine he's rather put out, having to

serve this unusual sentence," Minnie said.

"He should consider himself lucky. He could be sitting in jail, or worse."

The mayor cautiously emerged from his study. "Are you ladies all right?"

"Fine, dear." Minnie smiled and joined her husband as he moved to the front door and looked out.

"Strange. One jarring blast, but nobody's coming. Must have gotten scared off."

"And what would they be scared of?" Minnie asked with a toss of her head. "There's nothing in this town for them to be scared of."

Carl looked both ways once more and then shut the door. "Something must've stopped them."

Estelle Southerland picked through the pile of colorful swatches and selected a purple one. "Maybe they've decided to leave us alone," the seamstress suggested.

Minnie sputtered. "I'm telling you, we need the Brown Branch boys to help us."

Carl paused on his way to the kitchen and turned to stare at his wife. "Who are the Brown Branch boys?"

"A group of young men who keep the thugs out of Brown Branch, that's who."

"How hard is that? Brown Branch is thirty miles from the border."

"Never you mind, Carl Rayles." Minnie gave her husband a warning look. "It would be money well spent, I say."

Carl glanced at Ragan on his way out. "We'd better hope those boys, whoever they are, weigh three hundred pounds each and eat glass. Otherwise, she'll order them back on their horses and send them packing."

Ragan bent her head to her work, covering a smile.

Minnie didn't appear to be affected by Carl's lack of vision. She sat back down in her chair. "My, I don't know how you and the judge do it. Writing that book, taking in those desperadoes."

"Johnny isn't a desperado." The denial was out before Ragan knew it. She hadn't decided what he was, but she sensed that below that embittered exterior was a decent man.

One who was badly in need of love, whether he knew it or not.

"Why, Ragan Ramsey." Mazilea's needle paused. "You sound as if you're actually attracted to this fellow."

"Me?" Ragan's face flamed and she jumped when she jabbed her finger with the needle. "Don't be silly, Mazilea. I would never be attracted to one of the judge's subjects. What a thing to say." She jumped as she accidentally jabbed her finger again.

A series of quizzical looks passed among the ladies.

Noting the exchange, Ragan laid her needlework aside, feeling quite flushed. "Plain silly, Mazilea, and you know it. Anyone else care for lemonade?"

The sun hung low in the west as Ragan and Johnny started home. Ragan had never seen the church looking better. A couple of more days, and the painting would be done.

"You did a wonderful job on the building. I'm surprised more didn't show up to work today."

She glanced at Johnny curiously. He kept tilting his head as if trying to clear his ears. Usually when she talked, he at least looked at her. Tonight he periodically thumped his head, staring straight ahead as if he were deaf.

"Carl said to tell you he'd be available in the morning to paint the inside, if you're willing to help again."

Johnny turned to look at her. "Milk?"

"Help."

He shook his head. "I haven't in years, but I suppose I can."

She shook her head to clear her own ears. "I noticed Everett stopped by. Did he paint?"

When he didn't respond, she tried again. "I had a lovely day. Minnie made a delicious lunch. She had fresh poke from the garden and pork roast."

He glanced at her quizzically.

"Poke. And pork roast."

"Toast?"

"Roast."

"Poke toast?"

"Poke toast? I've never heard of such a thing. She served poke and pork roast! What's wrong with your ears?"

He frowned. "Why would she cry about toast? Did she burn it?"

Ragan stopped and faced him, pointing to her ears. "Is something wrong with your ears?"

His face closed. "No."

They walked on in silence, their boots kicking up bits of dust. Grasshoppers jumped back and forth on the road. The sun sank lower, bathing the sky in shades of pink and red.

"Did you hear that loud gunshot earlier this afternoon? We all dove for cover, but apparently the outlaw rode right through town and never stopped."

He continued walking as if he hadn't heard what she said, let alone a loud gunshot.

"Johnny?"

When he didn't answer, she repeated louder, "Hey!"

His head snapped around. "What?"

This was exasperating! Carrying on a conversation with him was like talking to a fence post. Staring straight ahead, she walked faster. "Minnie thinks we should hire the boys from Brown Branch to get rid of the gangs. She says there are no raids in Brown Branch. The people won't allow it."

"It's going to take more than a branch to scare them off."

She paused, staring at him. Were they having the same conversation? "Minnie says the *town* doesn't have any raids because they have fearless young men in Brown Branch who deal with the problem."

He stopped, his hands coming to his hips in exasperation. "Sideshow freaks? How does being earless qualify a man to clean up a town?"

"I didn't say *earless* young men — for heaven's sake, what is wrong with your hearing?"

"Nothing." He passed her and walked on ahead.

Fine, just ignore her! Stooping over, she picked up a dirt clod and hurled it at him. It splattered at his feet.

Stiffening, he slowly turned around to meet her sheepish gaze.

"Acting like a child, Ragan?"

The sound of her given name startled her. He always called her Miss Ramsey. She hung her head, ashamed of herself. Usually not much could rile her, but he sure could. She straightened her hat brim.

His features sobered. "You really want my opinion on this whole mess?"

Meeting his gaze evenly, she said, "Yes."

"The town is trying to get someone else to solve its problems."

She started to protest, and then she pursed her lips as he continued.

"The people here need to take the situation in hand, stop acting like frightened children, and take care of the trouble themselves."

"How are we supposed to do that? The gangs shoot our stock and take anything that isn't nailed down. They —"

He leveled his finger at her. "If this town doesn't have the gumption to stand up for itself, no one else will." Turning, he walked on.

She watched his retreating back, seething. He had no right to criticize. The town had tried to stop the gangs, and their efforts resulted in nothing but more trouble. While he was offering his sterling opinion, why didn't he explain exactly how to stand up? What more could they do than what they'd already done?

She blinked as he bent over and picked up a dirt clod, turned, took aim, and lobbed it back at her. She hopped backward as dirt splattered near the hem of her skirt.

"It's getting dark, Miss Ramsey! The judge's supper is two, that's *two,* hours overdue."

"Stew?" she mimicked. "I *hate* stew."

He acted as if he didn't hear and walked on.

Swiping the dirt off her dress, she trailed him toward the judge's house. Tonight she was going to write a whole chapter on arrogant men who refused to cooperate. Deaf arrogant men who refused to cooperate.

"And there is something wrong with your hearing!" she shouted at his disappearing back. You'd think the gunshot that afternoon had gone off in his ear.

# CHAPTER
## TWENTY-SEVEN

Ragan was snapping beans when Johnny came in the back door Saturday afternoon. She smiled, one of those womanly acknowledgments that affected him deep in his gut. No wonder Everett was in love with her. When she turned those innocent eyes on any man who was a man, it was all he could do to keep his mind on business.

"Finished at the church so soon?"

It seemed to be an effort for her to speak. Was she feeling poorly today? Walking to the washstand, he poured water into the ceramic bowl, watching her from the corner of his eye.

"The handrail is fixed. I repaired the bottom step while I was at it."

"Roberta will thank you. She's complained about that loose step for months. Her arthritis makes it a real chore for her to climb up or down." She sighed. "And Sheriff and Haleen have stayed home because they're afraid of falling."

"Well, their worries are over. The step's solid as a new stump." He reached for a bar of soap to lather up. The pleasant scent of lye and sun-dried towels reminded him of his mother.

"Supper will be a little late." Ragan sighed again. "I thought it best to finish the beans before we ate."

Nodding, he was about to leave her to her work, when he noticed her red eyes and nose. It was obvious that she had been crying. She fumbled for her handkerchief, touching it lightly to her eyes.

*Leave now, McAllister, before you wade into something that doesn't concern you.* He made it to the doorway before her voice stopped him.

"Mr. McAllister?" Her tone had that helpless inflection that usually — no, always — meant trouble.

"Yes?"

"Would you mind helping me finish these beans?"

He'd mind. Snapping beans was right beneath peeling potatoes, which was right behind mending on the list of his least favorite chores. And he sure didn't want to get involved in whatever had her sniffing and red-eyed.

She briefly touched the corner of her eyes with the hanky again. "The canning took longer than I expected, and the judge will be up from his nap any moment now." She lifted her eyes and gave him a wan smile. "You know how Procky is when his meal is late." She met his uncertain frown. "Do you mind?"

Pulling out a chair, he sat down at the table. A sizable pile of beans immediately appeared in front of him.

"Is there a proper way to do this?" Anything like the complicated instructions he'd received on button sewing?

"Pinch the ends off, remove the strings, and snap the bean in two — unless, of course, it's a long bean. Then snap it in three pieces."

He picked up a bean and looked at it. He turned it end over end. Was this a long one or a short one? "How long is a long one?"

"About this long." She spread her thumb and forefinger to the proper size.

He hadn't known there was a proper way to snap beans.

They worked a few minutes in silence. An occasional furtive glance in her direction assured him she was weeping, all right. He didn't know why, and he didn't want to know why, because he couldn't do a thing about whatever had her upset. He was becoming too attuned to her moods as it was. Before long, they'd be rocking on the front porch together. The reason he was stuck in this godforsaken town in the first place was because he'd stuck his nose in somebody else's business.

But when her sniffling grew more pronounced, he sighed in resignation, crossed his arms, and asked gruffly, "What are you crying about?"

She glanced up, seemingly surprised that he noticed. "I'm sorry. It's . . . it's been a trying day."

He reached for another bean, snapped it, and pitched it into the pan. Trying, was it? She didn't know the meaning of the word. She ought to try teaching Everett to shoot. One shot and his ears were still ringing. "Is the judge ill?"

"No, not Procky. It's my father."

Definitely a subject to avoid. Fathers meant family, and family meant feelings he didn't want to be reminded of.

He sighed again. "What about your father?" He scooped up a pile of strings and discarded them, mentally groaning when she buried her face in her hands and burst into tears.

*Never ask a weeping lady why she's crying.*

She sobbed into her hanky, her slender shoulders heaving with grief. His first instinct was to abandon the beans and allow her privacy. It sure wasn't his place to comfort her, even if for some insane reason he wanted to.

But her soft, pitiful mewlings, so like Kitty's when she wanted something, tore at his gut.

Getting up from his chair, he wet the end of a towel and carried it back to the table. Awkwardly removing her handkerchief, he pressed the damp cloth into her hands.

"Dry your tears," he said softly. "Whatever it is, it can't be that bad."

She held the cool cloth to her eyes.

Squatting beside her chair, he met her teary gaze. "Look. I'm not very good with these things, but if you want to talk, I'm a decent listener."

Wiping her tears, she said, "Mama passed away on this date. Papa and I take flowers to her grave every year." She sniffed. "This morning, when I mentioned going, Papa didn't even know who I was talking about."

She dabbed at the moisture filling her eyes. "I don't know why it still bothers me so. Papa's been getting worse for months now. It isn't as if I just woke up today and realized he would never be back." Her chin quivered. "He's here, but he's not the old Papa . . . my strong, proud Papa."

His eyes softened, and he took her into his arms, where she sobbed softly against his shoulder.

"Would you stop that? It makes me want to kiss you, and I'm in no mood to have my face slapped."

She hiccupped, laughing and crying at the same time. Then she smiled at him. "Are you asking permission?"

Was he? Oh, he wanted to kiss her, wanted to almost as bad as he wanted to find Bledso, but he wouldn't.

"I think we'd better solve your problem first."

He brushed a lock of her hair into place. She looked prettier than any woman ought to look with a red nose and teary eyes. "So," he asked softly, "what makes today particularly difficult?"

"It just seems another part of Papa is gone. I have to admit to myself that both Mama and Papa are gone now."

Removing the towel from her hand, he got up and wet it again. She accepted the cool cloth with a sigh.

"Is your mother's grave around here?"

"No, Papa wanted her buried next to her parents. The family plot is in Searcy County.

Jacob's there too. It's almost a two-hour ride from here."

Two hours? Well, it could be worse. She could need to go to San Francisco. She glanced at him.

He averted his eyes and sat down and concentrated on the beans. He separated strings from the pods. Measured the two halves of the bean. Dropped one in the pot. Then the other. He looked back at her.

The silence lengthened.

Finally, he drew a deep breath. "A two-hour ride isn't that far. It's still early, and the days are long."

She bent her head. "No, not that far. But Procky doesn't like me to go alone — not with so much trouble going on."

"You shouldn't go alone."

"I know."

Only the occasional snap of a bean and a discreet sniffle broke the silence.

"I'd take you, but I don't have a gun." It was a sore spot with him. A gun was a man's only protection.

"Having a gun isn't a problem. There's an old mining road that hardly anyone uses anymore. Papa and I travel it so we won't meet up with the gangs."

The prospect of traveling without a gun worried him. A man could run into all kinds of trouble along the way. Wild animals, robbers, no telling what he might encounter. He didn't like being without protection.

He could ask Everett to come along, but somehow he didn't think Ragan would want that. It didn't appeal to him much either. Throwing a bean in the pot, he made an offer he was sure he would regret. "If you want to go, I'll take you."

Hope sprang to her eyes. "Would you do that? Really?"

It wouldn't be his first choice, but her tears touched something inside him, something he thought he'd buried a good many years ago. The way she looked at him, all soft and needy, stirred his protective instincts, even though he fought it. The grateful look she gave him troubled him even more.

The last thing he or Ragan needed was to involve themselves in each other's lives. He would be dead or behind bars once he found Bledso. She had her whole life ahead of her, and he doubted that her faith would ever allow her to fall in love with a criminal. She was strong in her beliefs. She didn't preach, but she lived her trust. He envied her.

"I'll take you," he heard himself saying. "I'll hitch a wagon."

The smile that lit her face more than assuaged his doubts. A four-hour ride wasn't much — not considering the gratitude shining in her eyes.

# CHAPTER TWENTY-EIGHT

Judith Ramsey's grave lay in a small grove of scrub oak behind Frank and Lucy Daniel's homestead. Her son, Jacob, was on the right. Johnny stopped the wagon and helped Ragan down.

"Thank you. I won't be long."

"Take your time."

He stepped to the shade and waited as she laid flowers on her grandparents' graves, and then she moved to her mother's mound to clear the weeds that had overtaken the simple wooden cross. Songbirds flittered in and out of the bushes. In the distance, a creek trickled peacefully along the edge of the property. The setting was so restful it was easy to see why Fulton wanted his wife and son laid to rest here.

He studied Ragan's expression as she tidied the site with loving devotion, and he thought of his own mother's grave, abandoned now. No one was left to bring her flowers or clear away weeds. Grandpa was gone, and he hadn't been home in years. If he ever made it back, he promised himself he would cover his parents' graves with flowers. And the little girls' too. He'd buy all the flowers they deserved.

"I'm guessing you and your mother were close?"

Ragan got to her feet and brushed the grass off her skirt. "I suppose we were. I was her firstborn, so I had to help out more than the other girls did." She wiped her forehead with her sleeve. The air was close, as if it might storm, but there wasn't a cloud in the sky. "I didn't mind, but sometimes I feel like I never had a childhood."

And not much of a life now. Johnny had heard the whispers around town, the well-meaning but careless remarks the women directed at her. Old maid? He found himself tensing when he heard the insinuations. Ragan outshone every woman in Barren Flats, and she should be applauded because she chose to accept responsibility for her father and younger siblings. Instead, the town hens reveled in discussing poor Ragan and her impossible situation.

"What about you? Are you close to your mother?" She returned to pulling weeds around the other graves.

Squatting on his haunches, he watched her work. "I don't have any family."

She yanked a particularly stubborn yucca root. "Everyone has family at one time or another. You didn't just appear on earth one day a full-grown man, did you?"

"Could be."

She turned to look at him. He tried to stop the slow grin that threatened to reveal itself.

"You most certainly did not appear from nowhere, so you have a mother." Sitting back on her heels, she faced him.

"Had a mother."

She waited.

"She's dead."

Ragan's smile faded. "I'm sorry. She must have been very young."

Nodding, he stood up. "Too young to die."

"John." It was the first time she'd ever called him by his given name.

"Yes?"

Her insistent gaze met his. "Did you rob that bank?"

Their gazes held. "Do you think I did?"

"I think you didn't. I might be a fool, but I don't believe you committed the crime."

He could tell her the truth, but then that would make him more vulnerable to her. "Well, I heard folks say you're a fine judge of people."

He turned away while she resumed her work, tugging another clump of weeds and tossing them aside. "Where's your father?"

"You ask too many questions."

"You don't talk enough." Getting to her feet, she dusted her hands. "There, now. That looks better, wouldn't you say?"

"A grave's a grave." He'd never seen one to brag about yet. He checked the sun. He didn't want to rush her, but it wouldn't be smart to travel after dark. "Only a couple of hours of daylight left."

"I'm through. Just let me say goodbye to Mama and Jacob."

He stepped aside as she turned back to the graves. Though she spoke softly, he caught snatches of her one-sided conversation.

"Papa's not doing so good . . . put up green beans this morning . . . Jo's growing like ragweed . . . miss you both more than I can . . ."

When she returned to the wagon a few minutes later, he helped her aboard. Their clothing brushed, and he moved away. As the wagon rolled from the gravesides, Ragan kept her eyes fixed on the road.

"Thank you for bringing me," she said quietly.

He kept his eyes trained on the trail as well. "You're welcome."

It had been a pleasant outing, Johnny decided. No harm in a man enjoying a pretty woman's company, as long as he didn't forget his purpose.

He kept to the back roads, as they had on the way there. Although he was accustomed to keeping his opinions to himself, Ragan's tendency for chatter drew him into a spirited discussion. The debate involved dogs and skunks. What was worse? A wet dog or a passing skunk?

"Dog," Ragan said. "The absolute worst."

"Skunk. Apparently you've never taken a direct hit from one."

"Absolutely not. Have you?"

"Once. One caught me while I was taking a bath. My clothes were high up on the bank, and the varmint decided to sit down and watch me. "The da—" He caught his language. "That old meany kept me pinned to the water for three hours."

Ragan giggled.

He had become creative in his choice of expletives; he hoped she'd noticed. He felt like a fool talking like a sissy, but then he'd noticed he could get his point across just as easily without vile language. When had he picked up the habit? Over the years, on the trail, around men who lived as though there wouldn't be a Day of Judgment. Living with Grandpa had convinced him there was a mighty God. Over the years he'd just let the knowledge slide by, bent on his own judgments.

"By then the sun had gone down, and I was chilled to the bone. I decided to take my chances and climb out of the river. When I did, the skunk turned away from me, pointed his tail to the sky, and got me. And my clothes. And my horse."

He glanced over when she burst into laughter. "You think that's funny? It took me three weeks to get the smell out of my bedroll. The horse smelled so bad we —"

They looked up as four masked riders darted out of the bushes and galloped headlong toward them.

"I thought no one knew about this road."

"Papa and I never met anyone along here before."

Brandishing a gun, the leader motioned for Johnny to pull over.

Ragan pressed against his side, fear evident in her strained features.

"Let me do the talking," he warned as the bandits approached.

She nodded, huddling closer.

Without a weapon, there wasn't going to

be a fight. He let the wagon roll to a gradual halt. He had no way to defend her or himself.

The men closed in, pistols drawn. "Put your hands where we can see them!" the leader ordered.

Ragan's arms obediently shot over her head. Johnny lifted his more slowly. "We're not carrying any money."

Climbing off his horse, one of the men approached. Time stopped as Johnny came face-to-face with a red bushy beard partially concealed beneath a dirty bandanna — the outlaw from the bank robbery. Recognition turned to perverse humor in the dark eyes that stared back at him.

It would have been easy for Puet to find out where Judge Leonard had sent him. The outlaw was probably convinced that Johnny either had the bank money bag or that he knew where it was, and he'd tracked him to Barren Flats to get it.

"Well, well, well." Puet leaned across Ragan and rested the barrel of his pistol against Johnny's temple. The gunman's stench was worse than his taste in company. "Who do we have here? McAllister, isn't it?"

"We aren't carrying any money," Johnny repeated, lowering his hands.

"No?" The gun dug into his temple. "Why, I'd swear you look like a man of means." He slid his mask off.

Johnny's face remained expressionless. Ragan whimpered, and he quenched the urge to reach for her hand. He doubted the man would pull the trigger, not with the money bag missing, but he wasn't a fool.

"I don't have your money," he repeated.

"No?" The man's fetid breath was hot and potent. His lizard-like gaze darted to Ragan. She inched closer, molding against Johnny's side.

"Johnny?" she murmured.

"Easy," he said. The gun was still pointed at his brain; he couldn't afford any unexpected moves. "They aren't going to hurt you." Her hand slipped into his. He held it, tightening his grip. She trembled beneath his touch.

The man's eyes slid insolently over her. "Afraid for your man, honey?" he mocked.

She glared at him, and he casually switched the barrel of the gun to her temple.

She clamped her eyes shut. "Our Father, who art in heaven . . ."

"Shut up!"

She closed her mouth.

Johnny calmly pivoted the barrel back to his own temple and met the leader's eyes.

"The lady's nervous with a gun in her face. If you want to shoot someone, shoot me."

The gunman lowered the pistol, a smile lighting his eyes. "Now, why would I want to shoot you?"

Johnny stared back at him.

The gang was restless. One man glanced over his shoulder, and another rode back and forth beside the wagon. "Come on, Puet. Stop foolin' around. He ain't got the money. Let's take the woman and get out of here."

*Keep your head, McAllister.* Ragan's only chance was for him to convince the men they were welcome to her.

"Good idea." The leader's reptilian eyes shifted to Ragan. He ran his tongue over his dry lips. "We'll take the woman." He tapped Johnny's shoulder with the barrel of the gun. "Any objections, McAllister?"

"Take her. She means nothing to me. I was just delivering her to Judge McMann's house."

Ragan's gasp cut through the charged silence. She sat up straight, jerking her hand out of his.

The smile was still evident in the leader's eyes. "Take her?"

"Take her. I'll keep the money." If the bluff failed, both he and Ragan were dead, because there was no way he would let them have her — not without a fight. Sweat trickled down Johnny's collar and ran between his shoulder blades.

The man's eyes narrowed and then turned deadly. "Where's the money, McAllister?"

Johnny met his stare. "Take the woman, Puet, and we'll call it even."

"Johnny." Ragan's eyes went from one man to the other. "Do you know this . . . this vile animal?" Disappointment choked her voice.

The gun clicked, and Ragan whimpered. "Please don't shoot him. Take me."

"Take her." Johnny smiled.

"You're bluffin', McAllister."

Johnny shrugged. "Try me."

Puet reached over and jerked Ragan to him. Grinning, he pulled her close, grinding his foul mouth into hers. She fought, struggling to break his hold.

A vein throbbed in Johnny's neck.

When the gunman shoved her back, she fell against the wagon seat. She met Johnny's eyes and then looked away. Her look of betrayal cut him.

The rest of the men moved closer, bunching their horses to vie for space. "Take her, Puet. We don't need the money." They slid from their horses and approached the wagon, their eyes focused on Ragan.

Puet eyed Johnny. "Whatta ya say, McAllister? Can my men enjoy your lady's company? She's a fine lookin' filly."

Johnny held tight; he had no choice but to play his hand out. "Go ahead, gentleman. Like I said, she means nothing to me."

Color crept up Puet's neck. "You're bluffing, McAllister."

"You heard the verdict. I saw you in the crowd that day. I'm her prisoner. Why would I care what happens to her? You'll have a woman, and I have the cash." Johnny leaned back. "Fair trade." If there was a God, Johnny hoped he was watching. Ragan was innocent. He'd put her in this spot and he knew no other way to get her out.

The gang exchanged skeptical looks. Puet rammed the gun against Johnny's throat. "Tell us what you did with the bank money, McAllister!"

Lunging, Johnny knocked the bandit off balance. With lightning swiftness, he reached for the whip. Swinging it above his head, he brought it down on the four horses standing to the left. The animals bolted, breaking for the underbrush. The wagon shot ahead, pitching the highwaymen to the ground. They scrambled to gain their footing as the buckboard shot off through the thicket.

"There are some old mining shafts about a mile up the road!"

"Which way?"

"To the left! There's one particular one with a hole big enough for the rig, but it won't go all the way through the shaft!"

The wagon clattered along uneven ground, bouncing them like nuggets in a sluice pan. Their teeth rattled, and Ragan held on to his arm with a deathlike grip.

"How far?"

"Not far!"

It seemed a hundred miles before she pointed ahead and shouted, "There!" The opening was nearly obscured by undergrowth. He would have whipped past it if she hadn't pointed it out.

The entrance looked small — too small for the wagon to clear. Glancing over his shoulder, he estimated how long it would take for the men to round up their horses and come after them. Five, ten minutes?

The shaft opening was coming up. "Is it large enough to clear the wagon?"

"I'm pretty sure it is!"

Large enough or not, they were going through. Ragan screamed and covered her eyes as the horse galloped headlong toward the cavern. Thick vegetation grew along the sides of the overgrown mining road, obscuring the shaft.

"Come on, girl," Johnny urged. He prayed the mare wouldn't refuse to go in.

Johnny shut his eyes as the wagon sheared the undergrowth and burst through the opening. The scream of metal meeting the stone walls was deafening as the wagon slowly ground to a halt.

Johnny turned to stare at the wheels. Were they ruined?

They both sat in silence for a few moments, breathing hard. Dampness encompassed them, and they could hear water dripping from somewhere inside the shaft.

"Are you hurt?"

"I need to use the necessary," Ragan whispered, pale as a ghost.

Climbing over the seat, Johnny inched his way to the rear of the wagon. The bed was just inside the shaft, and the wheels were sheared to the spokes.

Hoofbeats pounded down the road, and Johnny quickly climbed back to shove Ragan to the floor of the seat and crouch over her.

The riders galloped by, and then the vibrations of their horses' hooves receded into the distance.

Ragan's voice was muffled beneath him. "Are they gone?"

"Yes." Helping her onto the seat, he leaned back, taking a deep breath. "If this isn't a mess."

She threw her arms around him. Her mouth consumed his, pressing him back in the seat with such force he struggled to breathe. When she lifted her head a few moments later, he murmured, "You pick the oddest times to turn woman on me."

She grinned, leaning her forehead against his. "I'm just so very grateful to you."

"Grateful?" He hadn't expected her gratitude. He thought she'd fly into him like a banshee. "For what?"

Looping her arms around his neck, she met his eyes. "For protecting me. Thank you."

"You're welcome."

Sitting up, she drew a shaky breath and then she hauled off and smacked him in the middle of his chest.

"What was that for?"

"How *dare* you give those vile men permission to take me!" She whacked him again.

Pinning her hands in front of her, he struggled to control her. "It was a bluff — one that saved your life, lady!"

She stared defiantly back at him. "What would you have done if they had accepted your offer?"

He released her hands. "They didn't." He didn't want to consider the prospect.

Rubbing her wrists, she refused to look at him, so he turned in the seat to take further stock of the damage. The wagon was sitting on the frame, the back wheels wedged securely in the opening.

He climbed over the front of the buckboard and released the harness. No sooner had the last tether loosened than the mare bolted, the reins slipping out of Johnny's hands before he could react.

"Now the horse is gone." He turned to look at Ragan.

"This shaft opens up just around the corner. Not much gold was ever found in this area, and the mine shafts are all very shallow." She climbed over the front of the wagon, and they walked out the back of the shaft.

"Do you see the horse out here?" she asked.

"No. I'm sure she's headed for her stall in town. We're going to have to get back on our own."

Darkness was closing in, and they had a good hour's walk ahead of them. If they didn't show up soon, the judge would have a posse out after them.

"I thought you said the opening was wide enough."

"I said I was *pretty* sure it was." She primly straightened her collar.

"Well." He assessed her inappropriate hour-walk-to-town footwear. "I'm *pretty* sure you're going to have a blister the size of a washbowl, Miss Ramsey. We have a long walk ahead of us."

She seemed unaffected. "You'll have blisters just as big as I, Mr. McAllister."

She speeded up to walk ahead of him, turning to call over her shoulder, "And don't come whining to me for relief!"

"Miss Ramsey?"

She refused to turn around. "What?" Her skirt tail flounced in the dust.

"Those 'vile men' are still out there."

Her footsteps slowed and then stopped. Without turning around she said tightly, "Hurry up. Procky will be worried sick about us."

Lifting his hat, he brushed his hand through his hair. The judge could send someone back for the wagon. He fell into step with her, and they walked on.

"For what it's worth, I take responsibility for what just happened. I shouldn't have brought you without a gun."

He was surprised when she said, "It's not

227

your fault. It's nothing short of a miracle that the horse and wagon cleared that opening." She paused, and he slowed to face her. "I'm also sorry I lost my temper. I know you saved me from certain . . . shame."

"What do you take me for? I wouldn't have let them hurt you." He didn't know how he would have stopped it, but they would have had to kill him first to get to her.

Her face softened. "Really?"

"I'll protect you the best any man can without a gun."

She took a step toward him, her eyes softening. "I wasn't certain."

"Look, Ragan." He put his hands on her arms, holding her politely. "You're a good-looking woman and I'm a red-blooded man. I'm not immune to you, and I would not stand by and see you compromised."

"Thank you for informing me. I will remember that the next time you offer me to a gang of thugs."

He gave her a pained look. He couldn't get involved with her, tempting as the idea might be, but she didn't make it easy. With every passing hour it was harder to ignore her.

"Can't we just be friends?"

His tone gentled. If things were different

— "I'm not in any position to be a friend or anything else to you. I'm a prisoner, Ragan. I'm here to serve a sentence."

"Fine. You have my permission to kiss me."

"Kiss you!" She could come up with the nuttiest notions at the nuttiest times.

He groaned when she lifted her mouth to his. "This is exactly what I'm talking about," he murmured. "We cannot be friends or personally involved."

"I didn't ask for lifetime commitment. I asked for a gentleman's kiss."

"I am not a gentleman."

"Stop talking and kiss me."

He took her mouth passionately and surrendered to the certainty that she was different, and he didn't know what he was going to do about it.

But at the moment, he plain didn't care.

# CHAPTER
## TWENTY-NINE

Ragan jumped as Judge McMann slammed his fist on the desk, rattling Maddy's china cup and saucer. In all the years she'd known the judge, she'd never seen him this upset. "I'll not have it! I'll *not* have it! Whatever it takes, we're getting rid of these gangs. You and Johnny could have been killed!"

It was late by the time Ragan had calmed the judge enough to insist that he go to bed. He had assembled a posse and Alvin Lutz was fit to be tied. They had had to roust him out of bed. Procky had thought the worst when she and Johnny hadn't shown up when expected. They hadn't returned until well after dark.

After helping Ragan assure the judge they were both unharmed, Johnny saw Ragan safely home before lying down in his own bed and trying to put the incident behind him. He thought about the good night kiss she had given him instead.

■ ■ ■ ■

Early the next morning a knock sounded at the door, and Ragan hurried to answer it. When word had spread that a gang had attacked Ragan and Johnny, the whole town went into an uproar.

"Oh, good morning, Everett."

"Morning, Ragan." The telegraph clerk tipped his hat, his face lined with concern. "Are you all right?"

"Fine, thank you, Everett. It was nothing, really."

"Nothing! You could have been killed." He handed her a wire. "Mayor Rayles said to see that you got this quick as possible. It's from the Hostetler boys over in Brown Branch."

The judge rolled to the doorway. "And not a minute too soon."

Ragan took the wire, scanning the message. "Isn't there some kind of law that keeps you from reading other people's wires, Everett?"

Everett colored. "How can I not read it? I have to write it down as it comes in. Job hazard, you know."

"What's it say?" the judge prodded. "Can they come right away?"

"Mmm," she mused. "Yes, they can come, but you may change your mind when you read this."

"Never you mind. Minnie's already called a town meeting for this afternoon. We'll pay those Hostetlers whatever they ask."

"Well, Mercer was cheap. The Hostetler boys want a *hundred* dollars to do the job."

The judge blanched. "A hundred dollars! The Roman army would be cheaper!"

Everett nodded. "That's what I say."

"Must think mighty highly of their services." The clerk trailed Ragan and the judge into the kitchen.

"Land sakes! Do they think we're made of money?" Judge McMann fumed. "They might as well use a mask and gun."

Sighing, Ragan put the telegram down. "Should we give in to this kind of blackmail? These ideas seem silly and juvenile. The Bible says 'thou shalt not kill,' but the Old Testament is filled with retribution. We can't let gangs destroy what we've worked for all our lives. Perhaps it's time for violent measures."

"I know it's pure foolishness to ask someone like those dumb Hostetler boys to do anything, but we're desperate, and the town doesn't want killings unless it's absolutely necessary. We'll have to pay those boys what they want and pray they can rid the town of trouble."

"I hear those boys aren't known for their brains," Johnny mused.

"No." Ragan pursed her lips. "They're not. Actually, it's rumored they haven't got the sense God gave a goose, but they do keep their town free of gangs."

"Minnie says not to be late for the meeting this afternoon." Everett swallowed, his Adam's apple bobbing. "Five o'clock. Everyone's required to be there."

"Required?" the judge blustered. "Who made Minnie queen?"

"She says we have to do this democratically. After the Mercer thing, folks are pretty antsy. The town has to vote on calling the Brown Branch boys and then figure out how we're gonna come up with the money to pay them."

"Dadburn it. Supper'll be late again."

"Judge," Johnny said, "let your nays be nays and your yeas be yeas."

The judge nailed a fly with a swatter. "Everett, you tell Minnie to make it brief. Why even vote? What choice do we have? Gangs riding around, attacking young couples. It's a disgrace." Still grumbling, he rolled out of the room.

# CHAPTER THIRTY

The thermometer hanging on the Oasis porch registered one hundred and one at five o'clock that afternoon. Anyone with a lick of sense knew you didn't call a meeting at this hour of the day, and more than one person informed Minnie of the fact. Townsfolk wiped sweat, and ordered lemonades from Mildred Crocker, who was as cross as a bear for having to work late.

"Everyone sit down and hush up!" The stout-framed woman stood in the middle of the room, hands on hips, hair hanging in her flushed face. "I'm serving up drinks as fast as a body can. I didn't invent this heat."

"I don't know what's worse, Millie, your sour attitude or your sour lemonade. Is there a sugar shortage?"

"No, there's a brain shortage, Jesse. I thought you of all folks would know that."

Ragan pushed Judge McMann's chair through the crowd. Johnny was already seated toward the front with her family. Jo had planted herself next to McAllister. What was she going to do with that girl?

She caught Johnny's eye and frowned her disapproval. A moment later he got up and moved to the back of the room. Jo turned in her seat and shot Ragan a glare.

The room was abuzz with today's topic. Roberta Seeden's high-pitched voice carried above the noise. "Well, yes, I am concerned when I think that the rest of my life is going to be spent crouching under a table or hiding in a closet. That's not easy for some of us, you know. A hundred dollars is highway robbery, but I'm willing to pay just about anything at this point."

"Maybe you are, Roberta, but there's others in the room who can't pay it. You and Tim got a little money put back, but what about the rest of us? We ain't got that kind of cash."

"It's all I can do to keep the wolf off my doorstep," one man complained.

"You ain't gonna *have* a doorstep if the raids keep up," a woman reminded him.

Calling for order, Judge McMann whacked his cane on the bar. Millie flinched and dropped a full tray of lemonade on the floor.

"Effie, help Millie clean that up. Everyone

else, sit down and let's get this meeting underway. It's twenty minutes past my suppertime as it is."

The din quieted with the exception of Effie Willoughby, who crawled on her bony hands and knees, picking up broken shards of glass.

"Get on with it, Judge," a farmer yelled. "You ain't the only one hungry, and besides that, I got cows waitin' to be milked."

Judge McMann gave him a repressive look. "All right, now. As you all know, Everett sent the wire over to Brown Branch inviting the Hostetler brothers and the Jurley boy to come in and do something about the raids." His eyes moved to Minnie. "They're available, for a price."

"We know the price, Judge." Carl Rayles's mouth was set, and a deep flush rose from his collar. "Might as well stick a gun to our heads, but they got us over a barrel. We'll have to come up with the money somehow. It's a sad day when we can't even visit loved ones' graves without being harassed."

Clifford Kincaid got to his feet. The small-statured man adjusted the red cap on his head. "I say we offer 'em ten dollars apiece. That's a fair price for anyone."

"That's more than fair, Cap," the judge said, "but they want a hundred dollars."

The room hummed with indignation.

"A hundred dollars? How many are there?" a woman asked.

"Four in all. Three Hostetlers, and the Jurley boy."

"A hundred dollars is outrageous. Can't we offer them twenty-five?"

"We can, but they won't accept it." Florence Banks stood up from where she was helping Effie wipe up the sticky floor. "I've heard about these boys. They're not real bright, but they're stubborn as mules when it comes to money."

"If they're not real bright, why would we hire them?" asked a woman sitting near the back, fanning herself with a piece of paper.

"Bright or not, we'll have to pay whatever they ask," Minnie declared. "We can't go on like this."

"I agree with Minnie! A hundred dollars ain't much when you consider it's our lives you're talkin' about."

"Let's get on with it!"

Clifford used his cap as a fan. "Do something, even if it's wrong. Won't be the first time."

A hat was started around. Amid complaints and disgusted grunts, folks dug in their pockets. When it reached the back of the room, a man carried it to the front and counted the donations. "Three dollars and eighty-seven cents."

An uneasy silence gripped the room.

Austin Plummer said, "I put in a dollar! That means the rest of you yokels only contributed two dollars and eighty-seven cents!"

Eyes lowered. Feet shuffled in the back of the room, some in the crowd looking contrite.

"Okay," Judge McMann said. "We're going to have to assess each family a flat fee."

When a few protested, the judge rapped on the bar with his cane. "People! Do we want help or not?"

Holly stood, clearing her throat. "Judge, I understand your need to assess a fee, but Tom and I need every cent we have." She blushed, glancing at her fiancé. "We hoped to marry late fall or early next winter, and we're both saving every bit we can get our hands on."

Other protests echoed her words. The judge's cane rapped again for silence.

A lone voice spoke up. "What's wrong with doing the job yourselves?"

Heads swiveled to locate the speaker.

Johnny McAllister met a sea of curious eyes. "Why not do the job yourselves?" he repeated.

Ragan felt a stab of relief. She held her breath, praying he would suggest a viable way for the citizens to defend the town.

"I say we assess a dollar a household," Minnie butted in. "McAllister is a . . . an outsider. He should not have a say in our business."

Ragan shot her a glare. Why couldn't Minnie keep her opinions to herself just once?

"That's only sixty-seven dollars," someone offered.

"What if there're two families in one household? Would that be one dollar or two dollars?"

"Two dollars! That wouldn't be fair."

"Paying one price for a family isn't right, either. There're only two people in our house, but others in this room have six or seven. They should have to pay more than a dollar!"

"Are you out of your mind? More than a dollar?" Jim Allen turned red-faced. "Why, Polly Ann and I can barely keep food on the table for the eight of us. Where are we going to get that much money to give to the dumb Hostetler boys?"

"What's wrong with doing the job your-selves?"

Heads switched back to Johnny.

"Stay out of this, McAllister," a man called.

"Shopkeepers should put in two dollars each," another man suggested. "They ought to pick up the slack for those of us who can't afford to chip in."

"Now, see here!" Frankie Southern objected. "Kensil and I can't afford two dollars just because we own the mercantile!"

A timid hand raised in the back row. "How about fifty cents an adult and twenty-five cents a child?"

"What are you calling an adult? I'm not paying fifty cents for my fifteen-year-old."

"Friends! Please!" Judge McMann rapped for order again. "You want the help, but you're not willing to pay for it. I'm putting five dollars on the table, and then I'm going home. I suggest you do the same and think about this. I'm not sold on the Hostetlers, but since I can't come up with a better idea, I'm willing to give it a shot." He slapped down the bills and then motioned to Ragan and Johnny. "It's past our suppertime."

The Brown Branch boys were hired for the job. Within the week they rode into town, looking like the cavalry to the beleaguered citizens of Barren Flats. The oldest boy, Billy, was a big, tall blond whose hair stood straight up at the crown. He was almost scary looking, but the town couldn't be picky.

The second brother, Buck, bore a striking resemblance to Billy. He was dirty, hadn't been near a razor in months, and a tad shorter and rounder around the middle than his older brother, but a Hostetler, no doubt.

A missing front tooth in no way hindered his friendly smile.

Cisco, the third Hostetler, didn't resemble either a choirboy or his brothers. Ragan studied his swarthy looks and decided the town had another chicken killer on their hands. And a high-priced one, at that. He wore his raven black hair slicked back and tied with a leather thong. His dark, brooding eyes constantly searched the crowd that had turned out to watch the boys' arrival.

Rantz Jurley, a strange character with Spanish heritage, hung back and waved at everyone as the crew rode in.

"Maizie Jurley's boy," Minnie Rayles whispered. "Dropped on his head at birth. Pure old mean. Maizie's moved him from one town to another to keep him out of trouble. He's lived with every cousin and relative she could convince to take him for a spell. No one's been able to straighten him out."

"Do you know any of these men?" Ragan whispered to Johnny.

"Sure. They're all close friends."

She gave him a prickly look.

When the judge saw the motley group, Ragan heard him mutter under his breath before he turned and rolled his chair back into the mercantile.

# CHAPTER
# THIRTY-ONE

The Hostetlers set up camp in back of the post office. They pitched a tent and hobbled a couple of shaggy pack mules, which brayed day and night. The noise was deafening.

Ragan passed a bowl of gravy to Johnny the second morning, bleary-eyed from lack of sleep. "Well, what do you think?"

He broke open a biscuit and ladled gravy over it. "I think it's going to be a hot one today."

Judge McMann rolled his eyes.

"What do you think about the Brown Branch boys?" she persisted. "And none of this 'it's not my problem' nonsense. It *is* your problem, whether you like it or not."

Johnny chewed a bite of biscuit and gravy, and then he calmly drained his coffee cup and pushed back from the table.

Ragan waited. This time he was going to answer, or she was going to throttle an opinion out of him.

"I think they could use a haircut and a bath."

She calmly picked up the bowl of gravy and dumped the contents in his lap.

Johnny shoved back from the table. Kitty seized the moment and began licking gravy off the floor. He shot Ragan a look that would have scared most women.

Casually reaching for the bowl of scrambled eggs, Ragan studied it. "Surely you have some teensy, tiny comment?" Her expression hardened. "Don't you?"

The judge hurriedly took a sip of coffee, and then he backed his chair to safety.

"Ragan —"

Her eyes snapped fire. "Don't you?" She hefted the bowl threateningly.

Johnny mopped gravy off the front of his clothes. "The town doesn't want to hear what I think. They made that clear at the meeting."

"The town might not, but I do," the judge said, returning to the table, interest lighting his eyes. "I would value your opinion, John."

Kitty jumped onto the judge's lap, sniffing his hand for a treat. Dipping his fingers in the remains of the gravy, he allowed the cat to lick them clean.

Carrying a stack of dishes to the sink,

Johnny deposited them in the dishpan. "I don't understand why they want to hire someone to do their job."

The judge leaned back, studying him. "You're saying you think we haven't tried to defend ourselves?"

Johnny's eyes met Ragan's. "I know how you've been terrorized, your father burned out, and the town shot to pieces." He looked at the judge. "I know about Ragan's brother, and I know about being scared and helpless, but you can't expect others to protect you. You want my opinion? I think you're a community of gutless cowards who won't stand up for what's rightly yours."

He turned on his heel and left the room.

For a moment, neither Ragan nor the judge could find their tongues.

Finally Ragan picked up the empty gravy bowl and wiped the table clean.

"Well," the judge observed. "As I said, we have to consider all communication as positive."

# CHAPTER
# THIRTY-TWO

That afternoon Johnny stayed behind while
Ragan and Judge McMann visited Main
Street to see the Hostetlers' progress. A
gang hadn't come through since their arrival, and things were uncommonly quiet.

"Are you sure you won't come?" Ragan
asked as she pushed the judge's chair past
Johnny and through the open gate.

"No. I promised Mrs. Curbow I'd fix a
loose shutter for her this afternoon." Johnny
closed the gate behind them and latched it.

Work around the judge's house had slowed
to the point that Ragan had started to loan
Johnny out to the town's widows. Between
painting and gardening, he was busy most
of the time.

"Mind if Kitty goes with me?"

The judge and Ragan turned to look over
their shoulders. He met their stunned gazes
easily.

"No, go right ahead. She'll enjoy tagging

along," the judge said.

When they reached Main Street, Ragan braked the chair, eyeing the activity. The three Hostetlers and Rantz ran back and forth from one side of the street to the other, stringing rope across the north entrance.

"What on earth are they doing?" Squinting, the judge leaned forward in his chair, shading his eyes against the sun's glare.

"Looks like they're tying rope to posts at the telegraph office and then tying the other end to the mercantile across the street. Maybe they're going to hang a sign." Ragan couldn't imagine why they'd do that.

Billy snapped orders while Cisco tied the rope on one side and Rantz tied it on the other. Buck measured out another length and started toward the south end of town, dragging the hemp behind him. He grinned, tipping his hat as he passed the judge. The tip of his tongue protruded through the gap from his missing front tooth.

Billy barely glanced up when Ragan rolled the judge's chair within hearing distance.

"What are you doing, son?"

The boy looped the rope around a post and tightened it. "Strangin' rope."

"I can see that. What's the plan?"

"Gonna strang rope 'cross the road for

when the gangs ride through again."

The judge glanced at the rope and then at Billy. "And what's supposed to happen?"

"The gangs'll ride in, and the rope'll catch 'em right here." He gave a hard chop to his sternum.

Rantz snickered as he came over. "Knock 'em right off their horses."

"Knock them off their horses?" The judge studied the rope. "That's your plan?"

Buck approached, sweat rolling down his baby-faced features. "Knock 'em offen their horses, and then the sheriff's deputies can arrest 'em and throw 'em in jail."

Ragan was glad that Johnny wasn't witnessing this. "Is that wise? The impact could hang a person, couldn't it?"

"Naw, jest knock 'em offen their horse, ma'am." Billy pointed to several coils of rope lying on the ground. "We got us four ropes." He grinned. "We'll catch 'em all, don't you worry none."

Her heart sank.

"Billy, let me see if I understand you." The judge appeared to study the plan. "The gangs will ride into town. You're banking on them being blind; that they won't be able to see the rope strung across the road. When they stupidly ride into the rope, they'll be knocked off their horses, and all the deputies have to do is sashay out there and tie them up. The gangs will just keep riding into the rope until there are no more to ride in, or the four ropes give out. Is that your plan?"

Buck nodded. "Yessir." He flashed a toothless grin.

"Ragan?"

"Yes, Judge?"

"Take me home. I have a splitting headache."

"Yes, Judge." She turned the chair and started off.

"String a rope! I've heard it all now."

"Yes, sir." She bit back a grin. "Can we agree not to mention this to Johnny?"

"Have mercy. Maybe the boys will change their minds before they can put the plan into action."

They passed Rantz, who was trekking across the street, dragging a trail of rope behind him.

"Then again, I guess that's too much to hope for."

A commotion had erupted at the saloon. Ragan moved the judge's chair to the shade of the building, and they watched as a crowd of men hustled in and out of the bar, carrying chairs.

"Morning, Shorty, Hubie."

"Morning, Judge, Ragan."

"What's going on?"

Hubie hoisted another chair onto a buckboard. "Hostetler told us to make space for the prisoners."

"You honestly believe there are going to be some?"

Shorty frowned. "Well, shore. Billy says the jail ain't gonna hold all the gangs."

"Ragan?"

"Yes, Judge?"

"My headache's getting worse by the minute."

# Chapter
# Thirty-Three

Saturday morning dawned dry with a hot breeze. Ragan wiped her forehead with her apron hem before setting eggs and ham on the table. "Is it ever going to rain again?"

She poured coffee, watching Johnny salt his gravy. "It's been three days and no raids."

The judge grunted, reaching for the sugar bowl. "Through no virtue of the Brown Branch bunch."

Unfolding his napkin, Johnny laid it in his lap. "I understand those ropes are causing quite a problem." He met Ragan's eyes, and she could swear he was laughing at her. Well, who wouldn't laugh? The Hostetlers' idea was downright embarrassing. To think the town had spent money on this fiasco.

"Most idiotic situation I've ever had the misfortune to witness," the judge grumbled. "Everyone's complaining because they have to park their buggies outside of town.

Harold Bradshaw was mad enough to eat nails yesterday. He had to carry fifteen sacks of grain to his wagon because of that rope. Lowell Homer turned his wagon upside down when he tried to cut between the mercantile and Sheriff Lutz's office. Dumped the whole load of hay on the jail steps. Where the cat hair is Alvin Lutz?"

Ragan carried a skillet to the sink. "He's down in his joints, Procky."

"We might as well not have a sheriff."

"Was Lowell hurt?" Ragan asked.

"No, you know Lowell. Hardheaded as a gourd. That team pulled the wagon on its side and strung hay all the way down Main Street. It's a disgrace, I tell you. We'll be the laughingstock of the county."

Johnny reached for the butter, trying to catch Ragan's eye, but she refused to accommodate him. "Ahh, yes. The old rope trick." He casually buttered a biscuit and then bit into it. "Who knows?" Ragan finally looked at him, and he winked at her. "It might work."

"Five days and no raids," Judge McMann said.

The silence of the last few days was unsettling, and Ragan's nerves were on edge. A rope wasn't going to keep the gangs away.

252

The outlaws were only biding their time until they could devise their own plan. In the meantime, everyone in town was inconvenienced.

"Well, it's what we wanted," Ragan said as she turned a shovelful of potatoes in the garden. "You're not unhappy about that, are you, Procky?"

"Of course not. Just wondering if anyone's actually dumb enough to ride into those ropes."

"Actually, one person has. Holly mentioned last night that one of Ted Rowser's boys from Tom's Canyon rode into town yesterday and hit the rope. Knocked him clean off his horse. Almost hung himself, Holly said. He has a fierce rope burn across his neck."

She wasn't at all surprised at Johnny's snicker. Naturally he found the situation amusing, but poor Keith Rowser had failed to see the humor.

"Keith was real upset. When he finally got up, he threw a punch at Billy. Sheriff Lutz had to separate them and threatened to haul them off to jail." She knocked a clod of dirt off her hoe, pinning Johnny with a critical look. He was still snickering. "It's not funny. Keith could have been seriously hurt."

Johnny's features immediately sobered. "I

don't doubt that. If a rope's taut enough, it'll take a man's head off." He pitched a potato into the pan.

Judge McMann shook his head. "How long is this nonsense going to last? Townsfolk inconvenienced, Lowell tearing up his wagon and losing all that hay, the stage not getting through, and now we've nearly decapitated one of our neighbors' sons." He sighed heavily. "I don't think we can afford the Hostetler boys."

At the sound of gunshots, the judge straightened in his chair. "Listen."

Hoofbeats and rounds of fire sounded near the south edge of town.

"They're coming!" Ragan threw the hoe aside, and reached for Kitty. She thrust the cat toward the judge. "Quick! Into the house."

"Wait!" The judge held up his hand. "Listen."

The noise of horses and guns gradually receded.

"They're leaving."

They stood silently, straining to make out the retreating hoofbeats.

"Doesn't seem as if they captured the riders," Ragan said.

The three exchanged looks.

"There wasn't enough time," the judge

replied. "Let's go have a look."

The Hubbards and Kincaids joined them as they hurried toward the post office. An air of expectancy hung over Barren Flats.

"We made the girls stay home," Lillian explained breathlessly. "We don't want them witnessing all this violence."

People streamed into town to see the first evidence of their hard-earned money at work. Florence and Hubie Banks stood in front of the saloon, discussing what had just happened.

"What's going on, Hubie?" the judge called as they got closer. "We heard the riders coming, and then it sounded as if they turned around."

"There were eight to ten of 'em, Judge. They rode up and saw the rope. That must have caught 'em by surprise, because they turned around and hightailed it out of town. Jim Allen followed them, and he rode back a minute ago and said they were still out there, huddled together on that ridge out near Coyote Road."

Johnny turned to look over his shoulder. "They're just sitting there on their horses?"

"Yeah, that's what Jim said. Wonder what they're up to now?"

Billy and Buck strode down Main Street, smiling. "No need to get upset, folks. We skeered 'em off." Billy gave the judge a smug look. "Our plan worked. The minute they spotted that thar rope, they decided not to try their luck."

Buck chortled. "Skeered 'em to death."

Thundering hoofbeats interrupted them.

Riders appeared, guns blazing. Reining in at the rope, they slashed it with their knives. Then their horses trampled the tattered remains as they galloped into town.

The townsfolk scattered, and the marauders charged toward the saloon. Ragan pushed Judge McMann through the open doorway. The front window shattered and shots ricocheted off the Oasis sign. Glassware exploded and bottles flew from the shelves. Florence groaned as a bullet hit the gold-framed mirror hanging behind the bar. The frame split and crashed to the floor. A single triangle of glass dangled from the right-hand corner.

The hoodlums rode up and down Main Street, whooping and firing. Then they sliced the rope guarding the north end of town and galloped off.

An eerie silence settled over the stunned population.

Hubie slowly crawled to his feet, setting a chair upright. "Anybody hurt?"

Ragan felt Johnny's hand on her arm.

"Thank you," she murmured as he helped her up.

He moved to assist the judge back into his chair.

"I'm okay, son. Thank you. I'm so thankful Maddy isn't here to see this. It would break her heart."

As they descended the Oasis steps, Buck ran past carrying what was left of the ropes. Flashing his toothless grin, he called out, "Jest a small setback. We'll git 'em. Don't you worry none."

"Idiots," the judge grumbled as the crowd dispersed. "We've bought ourselves a hundred dollars worth of idiots." He motioned for Johnny to take him home, and the three were silent as they left Main Street.

# CHAPTER
## THIRTY-FOUR

"You know . . ." Everett closed his left eye and squeezed off another round. The bullet missed the target. "I never believed that rope trick would work in the first place."

"Really." No one in his right mind would think the rope plan would work. The idea was laughable, though the town's situation wasn't at all funny.

It was only a matter of time until a tragedy was sure to happen. A toddler was almost trampled yesterday. Johnny hated to think of another family suffering as the Ramseys had.

"You're jerking your arm, Everett. Hold it steady."

"Sorry."

Squinting first one eye and then the other, Everett took aim and fired again. That bullet also missed its mark, and wood chips flew from the base of a nearby scrub oak. At this rate, the clerk wouldn't be ready for the Founders' Day shooting contest in six months, much less six weeks.

"If that don't beat all!"

Johnny bent to pick up the spent shells. "Rome wasn't built in a day."

"It went up faster than I'm learning to shoot."

The two men scanned the practice area. They'd been at it for more than an hour now, and Everett had leveled everything in sight with the exception of his intended target.

"Well, Founders' Day is still a ways off."

Everett eyed the barrel of his pistol sourly. "I'm never going to make it." He glanced Johnny's way. "How come you're allowed to move about on your own so much lately?"

Johnny felt a prick of conscience. The judge had sent him to repair the church bell tower this morning, but he had slipped off with Everett for a few minutes of target practice instead. The judge's trust was misplaced, and he didn't feel good about it.

"Ragan's canning beans today. Judge Mc-Mann told me to come alone."

Everett whistled. "You must be gaining Proctor's trust."

"Looks that way." He could walk away from Barren Flats and never be seen again. Hadn't the judge thought about that? The old man had a heart of gold. Unfortunately, he left himself wide open for defeat.

It was a shame he would be the one to derail the judge's program if he found Bledso. It wasn't right, seeing how McMann had been so good to him. He treated him more like a son than a prisoner. But then, whoever said life was fair? It wasn't for Judge McMann, with his stove-up limbs, or for Ragan's brother, and certainly not for his family, lying cold in their graves.

Everett settled himself on a log. "You know, Judge McMann and Ragan work hard to prove lawbreakers sometimes deserve a second chance." He slid Johnny a hopeful look. "You wouldn't do anything to mess that up, would you, John?"

"Why would I do anything to mess it up? I'm living in paradise."

He had good food, a roof over his head, a clean bed to sleep in, and a woman who cared more about him than anyone had in a long time. Her affection came too easily lately. She was the last thing he thought about at night, and the first thing he looked for in the morning. His resolve was slipping. He couldn't have both Ragan and Bledso, and it was getting harder to remember that.

Everett polished the pistol handle with the

cuff of his shirt. "No . . . don't suppose you would. You haven't tried anything funny with the gun or anything like that."

Nor would he try anything funny with the gun or anything like that. Not until he needed it. Still, the admiration in Everett's voice bothered him. He'd be yet another to be disappointed in him, another who would walk away and say, well, what did we expect from a man like Johnny McAllister?

Lightening the mood, Johnny smiled. "I had the distinct impression you didn't like me when you met me, Everett."

"Well, I didn't. Not at first."

"Because of Ragan?"

Everett's face flamed, and Johnny felt a little sorry for the lovesick kid. He'd been tempted to impress her a time or two himself.

"She's some woman, isn't she? Pretty as spring grass. Someday I'm going to marry her. She isn't interested in me right now, but she will be, someday."

The artless declaration disturbed Johnny. Not just because of the stab of envy; it also bothered him because Everett was so gullible, and he was sure to be disappointed when his dream failed to materialize. Ragan had made her intentions clear. Everett was just too blind in love to accept them.

"Well, I'm sorry I was so rude to you when you came to town, John. I thought Ragan would fall like a rock for you, but she didn't." Everett brightened. "She doesn't appear to care any more for you than she does for me."

If the cheerful observation was meant to comfort him, it missed its mark. But then, Everett was a pitiful shot. And Everett had never held Ragan in his arms . . .

Johnny glanced at the sun. It was close to noon, and he still had repairs to do at the church.

He nodded for Everett to precede him out of the grove of trees.

A few moments later Johnny followed. The two men exited the woods at different points, Johnny turning toward the church lane, and Everett heading to town.

# CHAPTER
# THIRTY-FIVE

Ragan was churning butter the next morning when young Clayton Miller showed up on the porch looking hungry.

"Mornin', Miz Ramsey."

"Come in, Clayton. What brings you out and about so early?" She motioned the boy to the table and placed a plate in front of him. Filling Clayton was like filling a hollow stump.

But Clayton had more than biscuits on his mind this morning. He was breathless with excitement. "Got me a job! The Hostetlers hired me and Junior to —"

"Junior and me," Ragan automatically corrected, pouring a large glass of milk.

"Hostetlers hired Junior and me to tell everybody in the area to bring what cattle they have left to Main Street, quick as they can."

"Cattle?" Judge McMann wiped his mouth and then pushed back from the table.

"You know, cows."

"I know what cattle are, son. Why do the Hostetlers want everybody to bring their cattle to the middle of town?"

"Buck said they're gonna pack the town plumb full of cattle so the gangs can't ride through." His message delivered, Clayton helped himself to two slices of bread and spooned a heap of apple butter in the middle. Folding each slice in half, he set upon the food with the gusto of a growing fourteen-year-old.

Ragan glanced at Johnny. He gave no indication that his opinion of the Hostetler's newest plan was any higher than the last one. He kept his head down and avoided her eyes. Sighing, she realized that though he warmed at times he didn't intend to thaw. The thought made her heart ache, and she realized she had grown far fonder of this man than prudence and common sense warranted. Perhaps he was a criminal at heart. Perhaps she'd let her attraction to what seemed vulnerability override all that she had been taught. Papa's mind wasn't good enough to notice his daughter's plight. How she wished she could go to him, pour out her heart, and ask for wisdom. Of course, his first concern would be for Johnny's soul, and Ragan didn't know if the man's soul belonged to God or Satan, but the Johnny she caught occasional glances of suggested he knew about God. He knew passages from the Good Book, so somewhere in the life he refused to talk about someone — perhaps his mother — had instilled a sense of accountability in him.

Clayton finished the last of his treat and washed it down with a long swallow of milk.

The judge chuckled. "Have some more, son. There's plenty."

The boy pushed back from the table and stood up. "No, thank you, sir. Junior and I are going to borrow Mr. Banks's cart and mule and spread the news." He puffed out his chest, and he would have looked very important if it weren't for the apple butter ringing his upper lip. "I'm to tell folks to bring those cows pronto, 'cause we don't want no more —"

"Any more," Ragan said, handing the boy a clean napkin.

"Any more raids," the boy finished as he swiped his mouth clean. His freckled face beamed. "Thanks for the bread and apple butter."

Ragan stuck a thick slice of ham between two pieces of bread, wrapped the sandwich in a clean towel, and handed it to Clayton as she walked him to the door. "All that work is bound to make a body hungry."

"Yes, ma'am. It sure does. Thank you kindly." He tucked the food into the bib of his overalls and jumped down the steps, turning to wave as he headed off. Ragan returned to the kitchen to clear the table.

The judge shook his head. "How do those numskulls think our own wagons and horses are going to get through Main Street if they pack it with cattle? Not to mention the stage and the neighbors' wagons."

Johnny reached for the butter. "Wonder which one of them is considered the brains behind this operation?"

The judge's mind was still on the cows. "Who's going to keep all those animals from wandering off?" He drew on his pipe. "And the mess. Wonder if those numskulls have thought about the mess a herd of cattle that size can make?"

Johnny passed the bowl of gravy. "Do they think?"

"When they were handing out brains, those boys must have heard 'trains' and said they didn't have anywhere to keep one." The judge grunted, laying his pipe aside. "This is turning out to be a big headache."

Judge McMann was up early the next morning. When Ragan came to work, he was already sitting at the kitchen table, eating a bowl of oatmeal.

After stoking the fire, Ragan slid the stove lid back into place. "I thought you didn't like oatmeal."

"I don't, but I'm in a hurry this morning. Didn't sleep a wink last night. I want to get a look at this riduculous plan those Brown Branch boys have thought up."

Ragan didn't have to get a look; it already sounded like a cattle drive out there. Cattle bawling, flies swarming. The stench was awful.

"Why don't you come with me?"

Ragan glanced toward the parlor. "I need to fix Johnny's breakfast."

Judge McMann pushed his empty bowl aside. "Who do you think made this oatmeal? You know I can't cook. John ate with me, and then he went out to the shed for a minute. We're ready to go when you are."

"But the housework —"

"Just leave the housework. It'll be here when you get back."

Johnny returned, and the three had walked less than a block when they met Julia Curbow standing at her gate. Her bright red hair was done up in curls this morning. "Morning, Judge, Ragan. Isn't it exciting?" She smiled at Johnny, and Ragan could swear that even this woman had set her cap for him.

Johnny graciously returned her smile. "You look mighty fetching this morning, Mrs. Curbow. That right foot bothering you today?"

"Why, thank you, darlin'. No, my foot's much better." She beamed. "Once these raids are taken care of, I'm going to make myself a new dress." She eyed Johnny coyly. "A lady can never have too many pretty dresses, don't you agree, Mr. McAllister?"

Johnny shrugged pleasantly and called back as they continued toward town, "That's what the pretty ladies say."

Cattle milled back and forth in front of the saloon. Lowell Homer was trying to move them on down the street. Removing his hat, he scratched his head and said, "Can't quite figure how having all these cattle in the street is gonna help solve our problem."

The judge shook his head and gestured toward the north. "Is that Plummer coming?"

Lowell shaded his eyes with his hat. "Looks like Austin's brought what's left of his herd."

The livestock bore down on the town. Occasionally several would break into a gallop, stirring up whorls of dust.

Ragan flattened against a hitching post as one ornery longhorn pushed down the walk, brushing her with its fat sides. The animal bounded up the title office steps. Lowell struck the beast on the rump with a prod, but the steer kept going.

When the dust cleared, Ragan ducked into the general store as a shouting match erupted behind her.

"It's a real mess out there, Mazilea," she said. "Tempers are flaring."

"Tell me about it."

"Problems?"

"Those cattle! They're stirring up terrible dirt. We'll be the laughingstock of the county when word of this spreads." She swiped the counter with a rag, and then she moved to the front window where she rubbed a clear spot on the glass. "Just look at this." She shook the blackened rag at Ragan. "And cows don't buy groceries."

Ragan peered out. Cattle clogged the boardwalks, where red-faced shop owners tried to beat them back with brooms. "Wonder how long the Hostetlers plan to keep this up?" Dust boiled as more and more livestock crowded onto Main Street.

"Oh, brother!" Mazilea took a step toward

the door.

Ragan whirled in time to see a water barrel in front of the store tip over. The barrel spun off the porch, careening off the steps and into the crush of cattle. The lid rolled one way and the barrel the other.

"I'm not risking my life for a barrel," Mazilea declared, watching a big Hereford trample it. "I'm closing the store and going home. No one's going to brave a stampede to buy groceries. I'll have to close permanently if this keeps up."

"Now, Mazilea, people still need flour, tea, and sugar, no matter what they have to do to get it." Ragan handed over her list. "I need a tin of baking soda too."

The storekeeper bustled around the room getting Ragan's order together, complaining all the while. Ragan didn't blame her; the cow stench was enough to put anyone in a bad mood.

"I saw Julia on our way over." Ragan prowled the narrow aisles, glancing over the merchandise.

"Oh? How is Julia? She was in last week, complaining about feeling poorly." Mazilea stuck her head around the corner of one aisle. "You know, she's smitten with your prisoner. Thinks he's the best-looking man she's ever seen. Most excitin' too. He's all

270

she talks about. Jonathan this, Jonathan that."

Ragan frowned. "Yes, she's very taken with him. Why does she think his name's Jonathan?" He did talk to the elderly neighbor from time to time. She felt a prick of envy. Did Julia know something Ragan and Procky didn't?

"She thinks it is. Don't ask me why, but you know how Julia is. Once she gets something in her head, wild horses can't change her mind." Mazilea measured out sugar into a bag. "But then, she doesn't have to contend with him like you do. She claims the boy's been framed, that he didn't rob that bank, and you know Julia. She might be meddlesome, but she's a fine judge of character."

"I agree with her." Heat colored Ragan's cheeks when she realized how easily she leapt to Johnny's defense.

"Julia says he likes cats."

"Oh, I wouldn't exactly say that. How would Julia know, anyway?"

"Says he stops and scratches her tabby under the chin when he passes by."

Well, maybe he did love animals. In spite of all their sessions with the judge, he'd revealed nothing about his life except for the brief information at the cemetery that day. And Kitty was awfully fond of him lately. The women turned as Shorty burst through the door and dumped five loaves of bread on the counter. "Get busy and make up a couple dozen ham sandwiches. I'm going back for the pies."

Mazilea stared at the bread. "Hold it right there, Shorty. I just baked those pies last night; they're for us to enjoy for the whole week. So is this bread. Take it right back where you got it."

Her husband stopped to catch his breath. "You can bake more bread tonight. The Brown Branch boys can't handle all the cattle. They've had to ask the town to help. Think about it, Mazie. These folks are gonna be hungry. I've been telling everyone to come by here for food." He jerked open the door and disappeared before there could be any argument. "We're going to have more business than we can handle."

The door opened again, and half a dozen hungry men came in. Mazilea flew into action, and Ragan quickly excused herself, gathered her groceries, and left.

Outside, the din of the animals was deafening. Ragan tried to read Judge McMann's lips when he spotted her. She was able to make out ". . . are going to camp in town . . . haul water and feed . . ." and "lucky to sleep tonight."

Hopefully she'd filled in the blanks correctly, and she was not the one expected to camp in town, haul the water, and feed the cattle. Lifting the hem of her skirt, she waded across the street.

Everett appeared out of nowhere. "Allow me." He laid out an expanse of heavy butcher paper for her to step on.

"Thank you, Everett. I'm afraid my skirt is already beyond saving. This is some mess, isn't it?" She picked her way to Judge McMann's side, and Johnny took her elbow as she stepped to the wooden walk in front of the title office.

Everett waited until they were on their way home before he made his way back across the street.

# CHAPTER
## THIRTY-SIX

That night, Ragan lay in bed and listened to her father's restless movements. She could hear the cattle in town even from this distance, and the incessant bawling frazzled her nerves.

Every time she squeezed her eyes shut and tried to block out the racket, an image of the vile red-bearded man and his gang arose in her mind.

Who were those horrible men who had seemed to know Johnny? She didn't want to admit that it mattered. He would serve his sentence, and be gone before she could wave goodbye, but it did matter. Drat it all. It mattered a great deal.

There was a quiet movement somewhere in the house, and her eyes flew open. She sat up, trying to distinguish that sound from those made by the noisy cattle. A door creaked, and she was instantly on her feet. "Papa. Papa!" She flew through the rooms, outside, and down the porch steps to catch up with Fulton Ramsey, who was already at the gate. He fumbled with the catch. "Papa, it's nighttime. Where are you going?"

"They're coming."

"Who's coming?"

"Listen. Can't you hear them? They're going to hurt my family. I have to protect my girls. Hurry, help me find your sisters."

She turned his frail form back toward the house. "Your daughters are asleep, Papa. You come back to bed too."

His bare feet were wet and muddy by the time she got him inside. "Let's get you washed and then back into bed."

Holly stood in the doorway in a sleepy stupor. "Is something wrong?"

"No. It's all right."

Becca and Jo appeared. Ragan sent them all back to bed, and then she led Fulton to the kitchen table and sat him down.

"You know this is never going to end, don't you?" There was no hesitation in his voice now. His eyes were clear and keen, his tone lucid. "No one is going to take care of this town. You might as well accept that."

"We're doing all we know to do, Papa." She rinsed the mud off his feet and gently toweled them dry.

"Others can't make decisions for you."

He stood up, his chin firm. Ragan followed him to his room, and when he sat on his bed, he looked at her with eyes so sad her heart wrenched. Then he was gone again. "You must listen to me. Noah listened when God told him what to do, and he —"

"I know, Papa, I know." She helped him lie back on the pillow and then pulled the quilt over his gaunt frame.

"And he took two of each . . ."

How she longed for the old papa, the one she'd briefly glimpsed moments earlier. She needed his advice, not about the town but about her heart. The feelings Johnny McAllister stirred alive in her. A man deemed criminal. There could be no future between McAllister and her. She felt hot tears roll down her cheek.

Later she softly closed the door, the sound of bellowing cattle drowning out her father's repetitive words about the animals Noah had taken into the ark. Tears spilled down her cheeks, and she whispered softly, "I know, Papa. I know."

# CHAPTER
## THIRTY-SEVEN

Cattle packed the streets of Barren Flats for five endless days. It seemed the animals were everywhere. There was talk of little else, and the subject was close to being exhausted in the McMann home.

"If I never hear another steer bawl, it will be too soon," the judge declared after dinner Saturday. "Ragan, I don't even want you to cook a roast anytime soon."

She put a thick slice of apple pie on Johnny's plate. Their eyes met and she looked away. This fascination with him had to stop. There could be no future together; he cared nothing about her or her town. "We have to be encouraged that the raids have stopped."

"Humph. Gunshots are preferable to this constant racket and the flies."

"I don't want gunshots or cattle." Ragan dropped the knife into the sink and then took the end of her apron and wiped her forehead. "I'd prefer a good, old-fashioned thunderstorm."

A streak of lightning flashed, followed by a deafening clap of thunder that shook the kitchen floor.

Laugh crinkles formed around Johnny's eyes. "Be careful what you wish for."

The judge chuckled. "Sounds like you have a connection with a powerful force."

She did have such a connection. God could do all things. Apparently he chose not to answer her pleas for the time being. If her every prayer were to be answered, she would ask that Johnny McAllister was an upstanding, solid citizen. That he wasn't a prisoner. And that she could act on these perfectly irrational feelings she was having about him . . .

Another loud *crack* followed, and Ragan went to look out the window at the building storm. The air was as still as glassy water.

A low rumble began and quickly grew into a roar.

Turning away, she whispered, "Tornado."

Johnny took hold of the judge's chair. Lightning illuminated the kitchen as they headed for the doorway. Closer and closer, the roar increased. The house shook with pounding vibration.

Ragan grasped the door frame as the porch quivered beneath her feet.

Johnny paused, grabbing the porch rail and listening as rain drummed down on the roof. He shouted. "It isn't a tornado!" His eyes swept the sky, and then he looked in the direction of town. "It's cattle!"

"Cattle?" Ragan frowned, trying to shield the judge from the rain with her apron.

"Stampede!" He pointed toward a dark mass moving from Main Street.

Ragan's eyes widened at the sight. "The cattle. They're coming straight toward the house!"

Riders rode the perimeter of the giant herd, trying to gain on the lead animals. Rain pelted the outbuildings and ran in rivulets on the parched ground. Blurred images thundered past, trampling shrubs and flower beds. The din of pounding hoofs competed with the sound of the driving rain; it was impossible to distinguish one from the other. When the chaos moved past and on down the road, Ragan turned to stare in shock at Johnny.

His words barely penetrated. "On to the next plan."

The skies cleared from the brief shower, and the sun came out. Lifting the kitchen window, Ragan wrinkled her nose at the strong odor.

"The air smells of sulfur," the judge

remarked, sitting at the open front door.

"Sulfur? Smells like —" Johnny glanced at Ragan. "Like the Hostetlers have a manure problem."

Hot, damp air enveloped the house. The stench spread throughout the rooms, saturating furniture and drapes.

Ragan pressed a hanky to her nose. She could just throttle those Hostetlers! How would she ever get rid of the odor?

"We might just as well go look at the stampede damage." Judge McMann fanned the air in front of him as he rolled out the door and down the walk. "Phew-ee."

Phew-ee, indeed. This was ten times worse than the raids! Ragan hurried to catch up with the two men.

The three held handkerchiefs to their noses. Ragan felt something bite her left ankle. She lifted her leg and kicked at a fly at the same time Johnny slapped his neck. The judge shook his foot to ward off two large, green, buzzing insects.

The stench was more pronounced now. The downpour had turned the rutted street into liquefied manure. It was impossible to walk anywhere except the wooden walkway without shoes slipping and hems and cuffs sucking up the muck. Huge flies buzzed, landed, and then bit. Mosquitoes attacked in angry swarms. Ragan's nose wrinkled, and she pinched her nostrils tight.

"I've seen all I need to see." The judge wheeled his chair around.

Everett hurried toward Ragan with a clean roll of butcher paper.

"Oh, Everett, thank you, but it's no use. There's no way to salvage this dress now." If that boy would just find someone to care for besides her!

The judge patted the clerk's arm. "You'd better get back inside before these bugs eat you alive, son . . . or you're overcome by the fumes."

Everett obeyed, for once seeming anxious to leave.

People stood in doorways. A few balanced on hitching posts, and some high-stepped their way across the street.

On the other side, an angry mob surrounded Rantz and the Hostetlers.

"How do you expect us to conduct business in this stinkin' mess?" Shorty Lynch demanded.

Trish Hubbard buried her nose in her mother's skirt. "I'm going to spit up, Mama. Honest."

Lillian guided her youngest to the side of the general store and held the little girl as she doubled over.

"Now, folks." Buck Hostetler waved his arms above his head. "Folks, let me have your attention, now. There's no harm done here. Don't get excited."

"No harm? Our town stinks like a privy, the road runs with cow manure, and the flies are eating us alive! What do you mean no harm?" Rudolph Miller's massive form towered above Buck. He crossed his beefy arms over his chest and stared. "What are you gonna do about *this* mess?"

"Well." Buck glanced at Billy. "Give us a minute to think about it." He took off running when Rudolph came after him.

Florence Banks slapped a fly off Hubie's back, and then she pinned Billy with a withering look. "You'd better do something, and do it quick, young man."

Billy swatted a fly. "Now, folks —"

"Clean up this mess!" the crowd roared.

Billy lifted a manure-stained hand for quiet and started to pace importantly in front of the crowd. "The way I see it, this is your town, and we gotta have more cooperation outta you." He motioned for Buck to come back and stand by his side.

"Taking care of our town is what we paid *you* fer."

"And what we want you to do," Buck continued, ignoring the jeers, "is for each family to come up with a barrel of lime and a rake." He paused, making a dramatic, wide-armed sweep of the area. "Line those barrels up and down the street — the whole street, both sides — and dump the lime in piles from north to south. Then everybody rake the lime until it covers the whole street. That will take care of the smell and the flies."

The crowd fell silent.

Buck, who apparently sensed confusion, went on. "The sooner you get back here with the rakes and lime, the sooner we'll get rid of the stink. Once we get rid of the stink, then me and my crew can get on with another plan."

"We've had enough of your plans, Buck," someone called.

"Go back to Brown Branch!" Timothy Seeden yelled. "Thanks to you, we live in Manure Hollow."

Buck's hands shot to his hips resentfully. "I *said* we're going to clean this up. You'll get your money's worth."

Jesse Rehop approached Judge McMann and his party. "I think I've had about all I want for my money. How about you, Judge?"

"Disgraceful," the judge snorted. He nailed a fly on his knee and brushed the squashed remains aside. "We can't have Sunday services this week. No one could stand it."

Carl Rayles moved to the front of the crowd. "People! Listen! Buck's suggestion isn't a bad one. The lime will quell the odor, and when the manure is covered, the flies will quieten down. I say we bring in the lime and take care of this disgusting problem as quickly as possible."

The town finally agreed they had little choice. The flies were eating them alive.

The barnyard stench imprisoned Barren Flats as the citizens set to work. The first barrel of lime arrived, and the men raked it from boardwalk to boardwalk. Flies scaled walls and clung to screens and windows.

An occasional "Those stupid Hostetlers" marked the strained silence.

By late afternoon, some progress was noted. The flies still buzzed, but the lime made it possible to walk without the aid of a handkerchief blocking the nostrils, even though it caked trouser cuffs, skirt hems, and boots.

The judge, Ragan, and Johnny stood at the edge of town, watching the cleanup.

Everywhere they looked, a thick layer of white dust crusted the ground. "Looks like a summer blizzard," Ragan murmured.

"Doesn't smell like snow." Johnny's observation made her smile.

Mazilea was in front of the general store, sweeping the porch in a mad frenzy. Leaving Johnny and the judge to their own devices, Ragan approached the harried shopkeeper.

"Can I help, Mazilea?"

Mazilea shot her a hopeless look. "President Grant couldn't help with this one! Just *look* at this. That . . . that stuff is everywhere. On my floors, in my curtains, clogging the air. I can't sweep it out, dust it off, or mop it up." To prove her point, she picked up a broom and attacked the white substance marring the porch. Her efforts merely rearranged the white powder. "Someone ought to tar and feather those Hostetlers."

"What are you doing now, Buck?" The judge stood up in his wheelchair, a vein throbbing in his neck. Buck and Billy were digging a hole in the middle of the road.

"Easy, Judge," Johnny said.

Buck glanced up and swiped his shirt sleeve across his sweaty forehead. He flashed a toothless grin. "We're diggin' a ditch clean 'cross here, so when the raiders come, they'll fall into it. Then we'll all run out and capture them."

Johnny laid a hand on the judge's shoul-

285

der. By now, Proctor's face was red, and the blood vessels pounded in his forehead.

"A ditch doesn't stink," Johnny reminded him in a low undertone.

The judge looked at him, aghast. "You can't mean you think any of this nonsense will work!"

"No, it won't work. But you're already out a hundred dollars. What do you have to lose?"

"Buck," the judge began again, "that is about the dumbest idea I've ever witnessed. And I've witnessed some dumb things lately. How will the stage or our own wagons get through?"

The boy paused, scratching his head. Billy looked blank as he considered the question.

"Have you given any thought to the damage this ditch will cause to animals? If a horse hits that hole, it'll break its legs. If you think cow manure stinks, wait until you have a ditch full of rotting horse carcasses."

"Well," Billy viewed Judge McMann as if he were the simpleminded one. "The horses will jump *over* the ditch. Jest the riders will fall into it. I think. Least ways, that's the way I have it ciphered." He looked at Buck, and they both nodded.

"Yep. That's how I got it ciphered too," Buck agreed.

The judge looked at Johnny, who shrugged. "Maybe the gangs are also idiots." He looked around at the townsfolk. They didn't deserve this. These were good people.

Mazilea and Shorty were trying hard to eke out a living in this forgotten little town. Their trade was affected by the marauders. Jim and Polly Ann, down the street from the judge, were trying to raise their boys to be upright citizens, and as far as he could tell they were doing a good job of it.

The Homers, the Plummers, Widow Keeling, Julia Curbow — all were suffering. Maybe it was time to step in.

"Now see here, Judge." Billy was clearly getting put out. "We got us a job to do, and we intend to give Barren Flats its money's worth. You're jest gonna have to step back and let us do what we was paid to do."

Closing his eyes, the judge took a deep breath. "Billy, with all due respect, I believe it is time for you to go home."

A few bystanders stepped forward, ready to back up the edict.

"Yeah, Billy. It's time for you to go on back to Brown Branch," Mayor Rayles said loudly, and others joined in.

Austin Plummer nodded. "Go home, Billy. And take your adolescent ideas back to Brown Branch."

All eyes switched to the road as the sound of approaching hoofbeats interrupted the conversation. Billy, waist deep in the ditch, turned to see what was causing the ruckus. Horses bore down on the town in a swirl of dust.

"The stage! It's the stage!" someone yelled. Wide-eyed, Billy scrambled out of the channel and took off running down the middle of Main Street, his boots kicking up manure and lime behind him. Johnny reached for the judge's chair and moved it to safety as the stage approached. The crowd scattered, ducking for cover.

Buck threw his shovel aside, dirt flying as he tried to climb out of the ditch. He turned toward the stage, wildly gesturing at the vehicle bearing down upon him.

Stumbling, he went down on one knee, still frantically signaling the driver. But the team didn't slow. When the driver finally spotted Buck, he sprang to his feet, throwing on the foot brake as he frantically hauled back on the reins.

The coach whipped past Buck, knocking him backward into the ditch as the horses bounded over the trench. The animals whinnied and the old stage threatened to break apart as it slammed to the ground, rocking wildly side to side until it ground to a halt in front of the mercantile.

A passenger's head popped up in the window, hat askew, his eyes bulging with fright.

As the dust settled, Johnny calmly rolled the judge's chair to the gaping hole, and the two men peered over the rim.

Buck slowly pulled himself up out of the ditch, his dirty, sweat-streaked features clearly shaken. He looked at the judge and then broke into a lame grin. "Didn't I tell you? Those horses jumped that ditch clean as a whistle."

# CHAPTER
## THIRTY-EIGHT

Lantern light spilled from the livery doorway. Mellow rays fell across the white-
covered ground, softening the thick coating
of lime. Johnny rubbed warm oil into a
saddle, listening to the activity outside.

The Hostetlers had cleared out, and Barren Flats was settling down for the evening.
Haleen's annoyed voice drifted to him, fussing at Alvin for tracking lime on her clean
floors. If the smell of potatoes and onions
frying in someone's skillet hadn't reminded
him it was past suppertime, his stomach
would have. Home life. Family. Funny how
he'd forgotten how good it could be.

The Brown Branch boys' fiasco had left
an impact on Barren Flats but life went on.
The familiar was taken for granted — unless you didn't have a home to go to or a
mate to fuss at. Your own table to sit down
to at night.

Johnny glanced up when he heard a

sound. Jo stood in the doorway, framed by lantern light. The warm rays caught the red in her hair, and he was struck again by her resemblance to Ragan. Like her older sister, Jo was going to be a beautiful woman.

He turned back to his work. "Shouldn't you be home for supper?"

She crossed the hay-strewn floor, pausing in front of a buckskin's stall. "I'm on my way there now. I saw the light and hoped it might be you." She reached out to pat the mare's nose. The animal whinnied her appreciation, nuzzling the offered hand for a treat. "Aren't you eating supper with the judge and Ragan?"

Johnny massaged oil into the finely tooled leather. "Ragan will keep a plate warm for me. I wanted to finish up here before I went back." The smell of hay and saddle leather mingled with the scent of fresh lime.

"You work for Rudy now?"

"No. Just lending him a hand." There were only so many widows' sheds that needed painting, and he welcomed the chance to keep occupied.

Giving the mare a final pat, she moseyed over to sit close by. "Got a minute?"

He had more minutes than she could count, but he didn't think Ragan would want him spending them with her little sister. "Better run along home, Jo. Your family will be worried about you."

"I won't stay long." Settling her skirts, her gaze skimmed the stable. "I've got a problem, and I need a man's advice."

Johnny continued to polish the leather. "Can't be much of a problem at your age."

"I'm fourteen, and it's a boy problem." She turned doleful eyes on him, and sighed. "Benny Dewayne Wilson."

He flashed a grin. "Benny Dewayne, huh? What's Benny done other than set you to thinking about things a girl your age shouldn't be thinking?"

"Benny doesn't even know I exist." She sighed again, crossing her hands in her lap. Her hangdog expression tugged at his heartstrings. Ragan had the same look when she had to do the mending.

Dipping his fingers into the oil, he gazed at her. "How do you know he doesn't?"

"I just know. He never looks at me, and if he does by mistake, he makes a horrible face, or does something mean like yanking my hair."

"Sounds to me like he's noticed you."

She exhaled noisily. "Not the way he notices Emma Tracy. He eats lunch with Emma. I hear them laughing sometimes."

"Laughing doesn't mean anything." He

thought about how he laughed with Ragan. She could put him in a good mood real easy. "Just because a man spends time with a woman doesn't necessarily mean he's got his eye on her."

Jo brightened somewhat. "Emma is quite homely. I don't mean to be spiteful, honest. She's my very best friend, and I truly love her. She's funny and thoughtful and doesn't have a mean bone in her body, but I suspect you'd have to tie a pork chop bone around her neck to get a dog to play with her if you went solely on looks."

Johnny listened to her worries, smiling on the inside. Lara and Elly would have had these problems by now. And a hundred more.

He was aware of Jo's eyes dissecting him as they talked. How was he going to discourage her interest without hurting her feelings? Jo brought out his brotherly instincts, and he felt partial to her, protective.

When she continued to gaze at him, he asked, "Do I have lime on my face?"

"No." She smiled. "You're very handsome, you know." Her eyes went all dreamy. "Almost as handsome as Benny." A heavy sigh escaped her.

Aha. So that's the way the wind blew. Johnny chuckled and pushed the stopper back in the oil bottle. "Well, I have a confession to make, Miss Jo. I thought you might be getting a crush on me. Guess I was making a mountain out of a molehill, what with Benny Dewayne and all, huh?"

She started giggling, the snickers ballooning until she was in the grip of a full-blown laughing fit. Holding her sides, she laughed until his stern look finally halted her.

Did she find the idea that amusing? "What?"

Pointing at him, she laughed until tears coursed down her cheeks. "You thought . . . you thought I was smitten with *you?*"

"Well . . ." He colored, setting the bottle of oil back on the shelf. Ragan was the one harping on him to discourage Jo's attention. It clearly wasn't needed.

Jo doubled over, and her youthful shoulders shook with mirth. "I think you're a wonderful man, but I'm not smitten with you! You're so . . ."

"Old," he guessed.

Grinning, she said, "I want you for Ragan, not for me." Her pretty features sobered. "I want Benny Dewayne."

He felt three times a fool. He'd been sweating bullets over her, taking all kinds of heat from Ragan, and she was wanting him for her sister!

Women were all alike. A man didn't stand a chance around them.

"I have only one concern regarding you," Jo confessed.

"And what's that? That I'll have store-bought teeth before I marry your sister?"

"No." She turned pensive. "Are you a man of God, Mr. McAllister?"

Johnny reached for a bolt. "Isn't a man's belief private?"

"Well, it shouldn't be."

"No?"

"No, and I only ask because I know that as much as Ragan cares for you — and she truly believes you are innocent of the crime you've been convicted of — she would never marry a man and be spiritually unequally yoked."

"She wouldn't, huh?"

"No." She turned grave eyes on Johnny. "You do believe in God, don't you?"

Smiling, Johnny eased her fears. "I believe in God. I just happen to be a little upset with him at the moment."

Releasing a pent-up sigh, Jo wilted. "That's perfectly acceptable. I get mad at him myself at times, but I always know if anyone steps away, it's me, not him."

# CHAPTER
# THIRTY-NINE

Ragan rounded the corner, high-stepping through the lime as she made her way to the stable. Supper was on the table, but both Johnny and the judge had wandered off. She'd had to come clear to the other end of town in search of the men. You'd think they'd have enough sense to stay close when told supper was five minutes away.

Her footsteps slowed as she neared the livery. Jo's laughter drifted from inside. What was she doing here at this time of day? She should have been home an hour ago. Stepping closer to the doorway, Ragan listened to her sister's and Johnny's low voices.

"You should let your sister pick her own men," Johnny said.

"She won't do that. She's so busy taking care of the judge and Papa that she forgets all about herself."

"Still, it's not your place to hustle men for her."

Ragan couldn't stand it any longer. She risked a peek around the door corner.

Jo touched his arm. "Don't be upset. I like you a lot. And you're just perfect for Ragan."

Jo trailed Johnny to the back of the livery, where he hung a bridle on the far wall.

"She's never going to find a man she loves in Barren Flats. Have you heard how the town whispers about her being an old maid, and how she'll always have to put her life on hold so she can take care of Papa and the judge? But I see how she looks at you, all starry-eyed and love struck."

"You want Ragan marrying a bank robber?"

"Did you do it?"

Stepping around her, he moved to the back stall.

"Did you rob that bank, Mr. McAllister?"

He stood in the silence, listening to the gelding shuffle in its cubicle. An ache settled around his heart, a pain so hurtful he wanted to tear it out and get rid of the constant reminder. Jo made him want family, want a life of his own where his every thought wasn't consumed with hatred.

"Did you, Mr. McAllister?"

Johnny closed his eyes. "No."

A soft breath left her. "I knew it! You're exactly the kind of man I want for my sister." A delicate hand came up to touch his shoulder. "And though you won't admit it, even to yourself, I believe you'd like to be that man. I've also seen the way you look at Ragan. All soft and needy-like."

Shaking his head, he said softly, "Your sister deserves more than I can give her, Jo."

"My sister deserves love, Mr. McAllister, and I'm bettin' you could love her better than any other man could even think about."

How simple her trust was. How much he wanted to deserve it.

"You remind me of my sisters, Jo."

"I take that to be real special. Where do they live?"

Johnny sat down on a bale of hay, removing his hat. "My sisters are dead. They were murdered, along with my ma and pa."

Jo's face registered shock. "How dreadful for you." She reached for his hand. "That must be powerful hard to accept. Do you know who killed them?"

"I know. Dirk Bledso and his gang."

Jo shook her head, wordlessly sharing his pain. "They must be awful, vile men. Do you have any other family?"

"None." He stared into space. Bledso's ugly face swam before him. "Bledso took them all but my grandpa. He's gone now too."

"You must be very angry at God about that."

Getting up, Johnny adjusted his hat on his head. "Yes, I am. I'm going to kill Bledso."

"And his gang?"

"If necessary."

Jo's eyes widened. "Mr. McAllister!"

"Sorry. That's what I intend to do."

Her pretty features knitted with concern. "But . . . then you would be hanged."

Johnny tossed a forkful of hay into a stall. "That's why you can't be getting your hopes up about me and your sister."

"The Good Book says 'thou shalt not kill.' "

He turned to look at her, his features tight. "I don't claim to be perfect. I'm just telling you not to get any ideas about Ragan and me. Even if I'm cleared of the bank robbery, I still have a score to settle. I'll never be free to marry your sister. And even if I were, she deserves better than me."

# CHAPTER
## FORTY

Sagging against the side of the livery, Ragan pressed her knuckles against her mouth. Tears smarted in her eyes.

The poster she'd seen of the murdering cutthroats floated to her mind, and she recalled how innocently she answered Johnny's questions that day about Bledso and his gang, assuming he was simply making idle conversation.

But he had been dead serious.

She didn't for a minute believe he had robbed that bank, but was he capable of something more horrendous? Was he capable of killing a man in cold blood?

If he were out to kill Dirk Bledso, then the judge's work was in vain. Her work was in vain. Should she tell Procky what she'd just overheard, or should she plead with Johnny to reconsider before he destroyed not only the program, but more importantly, his life?

Turning away, she walked back to the house, struggling to regain her composure. If she told the judge, he would surely be forced to confront Johnny about the matter. But what if Johnny were only trying to scare Jo? Yes, scare her! That was very possible.

*If Johnny kills Dirk Bledso, he's as good as dead.*

Biting her lower lip, she sidestepped Minnie Rayles.

"Oh, hello, dear. I was —"

"Not now, Minnie. I'm sorry. I have something cooking on the stove." Hurrying up the judge's porch steps, she entered the house, slamming the screen door behind her.

" 'Dearly beloved, avenge not yourselves, but rather give place unto wrath: for it is written, Vengeance is mine' . . ."

The words lodged in Ragan's throat.

"Go on," the judge said, rocking in his chair. The evening air had cooled pleasantly; the scent of wild grapevine was sweet in the air.

She glanced up to see if Johnny was paying attention. She had deliberately selected this section of Scripture tonight. If he was attentive, he gave no indication. Her heart ached with the terrible knowledge of his secret.

" 'I will repay, saith the Lord,' " she read a little louder.

Judge McMann insisted on daily Bible readings. Some days he'd take the Bible from its stand right after breakfast, and other times the devotions were observed in the late afternoon following his nap.

On soft summer evenings such as this one, he often asked if Ragan would mind staying to "sit a spell" before she left for home. Tonight Ragan's chair was turned in order to catch the light from the inside lamp on the entryway table.

Johnny rested his back against a porch column and idly moved the stem of a dried weed in front of Kitty, who was sitting at his feet. The cat's head moved from side to side, her paw occasionally stabbing the pretend prey.

Smiling, he surrendered the weed to the cat and picked up a slingshot he was whittling for one of Jim Allen's boys. He held it to catch the light, tracing his fingers over the wood to check for smoothness.

Christian Allen had cajoled Johnny into showing him how to down flies with a rock and a slingshot, then he had entreated him, "Make one for me, Mr. McAllister. Pleeeease."

When the other five boys surrounded

Johnny with pleas for him to provide them with a weapon too, he'd been outnumbered. He was fashioning the second one tonight.

He held up the sturdy forked stick and sighted Ragan in the Y, moving it forward and back. Laugh lines appeared around his eyes, and he winked at her.

"Procky's asleep, and you're not listening," she said crossly. She snapped the Bible closed.

The judge flinched but didn't awaken.

Johnny laid the slingshot aside. "I am listening. Heard every word."

"You are not!" Eyeing him sourly, she opened the Bible and read. " 'I will repay, saith the Lord —' "

He finished by memory: " 'Therefore if thine enemy hunger, feed him; if he thirst, give him drink: for in so doing thou shalt heap coals of fire on his head,' " he supplied.

If Johnny could quote the Good Book by heart, why didn't he apply its teachings to his life? It had been on the tip of her tongue to tell Procky about Bledso all evening, yet she'd held back. Why? Was she afraid Johnny would leave Barren Flats if the judge confronted him?

Chirping crickets and the sound of tree frogs blended with the judge's even breathing. She forced her mind back to the Scriptures. When she thought of Johnny pursuing revenge, the tightness in her chest nearly squeezed the life from her.

The moon seemed to settle over the housetop, bathing the old porch in its amber light. The judge snorted and then settled deeper into his chair.

She sat up straighter. "What's that noise?"

"The judge snoring."

"Not that." She turned to locate the barely perceptible squeak. "That sound, like a wagon's coming." She got out of her chair and walked to the end of the porch.

Johnny joined her and peered down the darkened road. "It's a cart."

"Whose cart?"

"I don't know. It comes by once or twice a week."

Ragan strained to make out the cart's moonlit silhouette. "It looks like Carl Rayles's rig. What would the mayor be doing out at this time of night — and who's that with him? Minnie?"

"It's not Minnie. It's another man."

She turned to face him. "How do you know so much about that cart?"

"I told you. It passes by here two, three times a week. It's usually close to midnight, but lately it's been coming by earlier. It turns just past the house and heads out toward Coyote Road."

She turned back to have another look. "I never noticed it before."

The squeak gradually receded into the distance.

"That's strange. Where do you suppose it goes?" She wasn't convinced it was Carl, but it did resemble the cart he used to haul wood for town events.

"Looks like it heads toward the dynamite shack."

"I wouldn't think Minnie would allow Carl out every night."

"Maybe she doesn't know he's out."

She glanced at him, and they both grinned.

"Whatever he's hauling, he's not bringing it back with him. When they return, the wagon bounces. And the men ride back, not walk."

"Odd."

They returned to their seats. Ragan closed the Bible. Johnny tied a rawhide thong onto the slingshot.

Judge McMann's chest rose and fell in steady rhythm, and he exhaled with a light whistle.

"There's lemonade if you want it."

"No, thanks." He studied the piece of

wood. "Why didn't you tell him?"

Ragan rearranged the buttons in her sewing basket. "Pardon?"

"Why didn't you tell the judge what you overheard in the barn earlier?"

Her gaze flew to his. How did he know? Had Jo seen her?

Clearing her throat, she said quietly, "I trust you'll do the right thing." She desperately wanted to believe that.

The judge stirred, and Ragan set her sewing basket aside. A moment later he drifted off again.

She got to her feet. "Let's walk," she said softly.

They stepped off the porch and went down the flagstone path to the gate. Johnny unlatched it, and they walked down the street in silence for a while.

"How did you know?"

"I saw the hem of your blue dress as you left."

"You'll put an end to the judge's program if you follow through with this plan."

"I know that."

"But you're willing to do it? To put the judge's program in jeopardy?"

A muscle in his jaw tightened. "I don't want to hurt the judge, but nothing will change my mind."

"You know what the Bible says about vengeance."

"If you're suggesting I feed the hand that killed my parents and my sisters, forget it, Ragan. I'm not proud of what I'm going to do, but there's no choice for me. From a hiding place in the barn I watched Dirk Bledso destroy everything I loved. I heard my parents plead for their children's lives. I smelled the blood when he slit their throats." He paused, turning to look at her, and his eyes narrowed. "Years, Ragan. For sixteen long years I've hunted him. I won't rest until he's dead."

Emotion choked back her words. Until this moment, she hadn't known she was fully and deeply in love with him. Somehow he'd found his way into her heart, and the thought of losing him to Dirk Bledso was more frightening than anything she'd ever faced.

"If I asked you to give it up, would you?"

He touched her cheek with his knuckle. "Don't ask me. I don't want to hurt you." His gaze softened. "If I could, I would. But there are some things a man has to do. This is one of them."

"But I care for you — care very deeply."

His smile was a sad one. "I never intended for anyone to care what happened to me.

That way, when the time came, I could do what I had to do and no one but the guilty parties would be involved. I'm sorry you're part of it now."

His touch, fleeting as it was, profoundly affected her. Warmth spread from her cheek throughout her body and into her heart, where it somehow gave her courage to speak. Her answer came from her soul. "John, I don't want you to do it."

It was moments before he answered. "It's what I have to do."

She blinked back tears as he turned and walked back to the house. The sight of his lone figure tore at her heart. That was to be Johnny McAllister's life: alone and lonely. Did she blame him for his bitterness? Not at all. Did she understand his pain? In every imaginable way. If Bledso had murdered Papa and her sisters, she would have the same hatred festering in her heart. But she wouldn't let it devastate her. That hatred would destroy Johnny McAllister.

Even worse, now that she'd fallen in love with him, it might well destroy her too.

# CHAPTER
## FORTY-ONE

Founders' Day approached, and Barren Flats shifted into full swing for the yearly celebration. Held the first weekend in September, the holiday provided a time to let down. The raids were still coming on a weekly basis, but as Carl Rayles declared, "No ill-mannered, foul-smelling roughnecks are gonna spoil this year's festivities."

It was August now, and the town had voted to place guards at opposite ends of Main Street for the big day. Men would spell each other, allowing all to enjoy the celebration.

For the past three weeks Johnny and Everett had practiced out by the dynamite shack, near the first of the old mineshafts. Most of the town's men now regularly visited the small stand of timber behind the church to practice for the contest, so it was much too risky to go there to shoot.

The mining road was farther away, and

the spot of scrub timber was small but secluded. No one would be concerned about gunfire coming from out this way, since hunters often foraged the area, scaring up grouse, jackrabbits, and other fresh meat.

And since several of the men had declared their intentions to practice for the upcoming shooting contest, most gunfire was considered commonplace these days.

Everett fired off another round, ducking when the wild shot snapped a limb and sent a hail of dead branches crashing to the ground.

Johnny threw his arms over his head, protecting himself from a shower of dried acorns. He straightened, pinning Everett with a stern look. "You're still jerking your arm."

Everett fired again and grazed a chicken that had escaped its pen and wandered away. Feathers flew and the bird set up an earsplitting squawk, beating its wings through the undergrowth.

"Shoot." Everett slipped another round into the cylinder and shot. Another miss. Heaving a sigh, the clerk turned to face Johnny. "I got something on my mind, and I need to ask it."

"What's that?"

"Well, I figure you and me well . . . we're

friends now. Right?"

Johnny smiled. "Right."

"Good friends. And good friends tell each other the truth. Right?"

Johnny felt this one coming. He hated to tell the guy he couldn't hit a barn door with a banjo. "Right."

Everett sobered. "Did you rob that bank, John?"

The first choice felt better. But Everett was right. They were friends. "No."

Nodding sagely, Everett lifted the gun and aimed. "Your word is good enough for me." He fired again and missed again.

Gathering the spent shells, Johnny eyed the target. Everett might as well forget the Greener. There was no way short of a miracle he would ever win it.

The clerk took studious aim, and Johnny's hand shot out to relocate the barrel. Everett glanced up, frowning. "Thanks." He fired, shearing the top off of another scrub oak. The shrub caught fire, and fizzled out in a puff of smoke.

Johnny shook his head. "I say we quit for the day." Everett had been shooting for more than an hour, and he was wild as a March hare today. "We'll try it again tomorrow. It's getting close to suppertime." He thought about the roast he'd smelled cooking in the oven earlier. Ragan would be mashing potatoes and making gravy. She'd smell like vanilla, and her face would be rosy from the heat. "We'll come back tomorrow."

"Okay. Just one more shot." Everett leveled the pistol and closed one eye.

"Don't aim over there!" Johnny reached to move the clerk's arm away from the direction of the dynamite shack, but it was too late.

The bullet flashed and drilled toward the old building. A second later, a horrific explosion knocked both men flat on their backs. Timber and rock shot straight up in the air.

Shielding their bodies from the falling debris, they watched in horror as the blast collapsed the dynamite shack.

# CHAPTER
# FORTY-TWO

Female shrieks erupted, horses squealed, and men shouted as the ground rumbled beneath them.

"Earthquake!"

"That's no earthquake, that's an explosion! Look at the smoke!"

Men, women, and children ran down Main Street, past the churchyard, over the rise, and out to the old mining road.

"It's the dynamite shack!"

Johnny and Everett, lying amid the rubble of rock and timbers, listened to the pandemonium.

"The shack's gone!" Everett exclaimed.

"Oh, brother. We're in trouble," Johnny murmured.

"What happened?"

"Everett." Johnny shut his eyes and laid his head back in the mud. He opened one eye and then shut it again. Groaning, he touched a wet cut on his forehead. "Didn't

I tell you *not* to shoot over there?"

Hubie Banks and Carl Rayles dashed into the clearing, panting, each wielding a shotgun. When they spotted Johnny and Everett lying prostrate on the ground, they stopped dead in their tracks. Hubie's eyes focused on the hog leg still clutched in Everett's hand, and then his gaze shifted accusingly to Johnny. Other eyes switched to the crumpled dynamite shack and then back to Johnny.

Struggling upright, Johnny cradled his aching head. "What was in that building?"

"Home brew," the men answered in unison.

"And the town's supply of dynamite," added Carl.

"You actually had dynamite in that shack!"

"And home brew for the Founders' Day event. We . . . er . . . didn't want the wives to know about it." Carl leaned down and sifted through the debris. He picked up a jagged piece of glass with the letters "brew" visible on it. Hubie looked as if he would burst into tears.

"Everett! Are you responsible for this?"

Everett roused enough to weakly lift his head, and then he fainted dead away.

# CHAPTER
## FORTY-THREE

"Son?" Judge McMann tried to make his voice heard above the hullabaloo in the packed room.

Hubie and Carl were carrying on like crazy folk. Red-faced and shouting, one or two men accused Johnny of ruining Founders' Day. Minnie and Florence paced back and forth, fit to be tied.

"Is it true?" asked Minnie. "Were Carl and Hubie hiding liquor in that old shack? Did you and Everett blow it up?"

Johnny glanced at Jim Allen and Austin Plummer as they passed by with Everett's supine form on a stretcher. He touched a knot the size of a goose egg on his forehead. "I didn't know what was stored in that shack, ma'am. I know it said dynamite, but I figured maybe a stick or two, if anything."

"Everybody knows there's dynamite in there. When the miners didn't find any gold, they left it and moved on."

"Everybody knew about this dynamite, but you still stored liquor in there?"

"Well, sure. Dynamite's not gonna blow by itself. Safe a place as any for the liquor. Why'd you and Everett go and blow it up?"

He'd like to deny that he had anything to do with the accident, but that would leave Everett to face the town's wrath alone. As furious as he was at Everett, he couldn't let him take all the blame.

"We didn't know liquor or dynamite was stored in the mine, Mrs. Rayles."

"Hubie Banks!" Florence screeched. "How dare you store that devil's brew! Did you think Minnie and I wouldn't find out?" Hubie ducked when she landed a solid blow to his back with her umbrella.

Minnie was in Carl's face now. "The very nerve! I distinctly told you there wasn't to be any liquor at this year's Founders' Day celebration. Did you think I wouldn't notice?"

The solemn expression on Judge McMann's face bothered Johnny more than the town's outrage.

Ragan's expression was grim as she dabbed cotton on Johnny's facial cuts. "Hold still," she admonished softly when he flinched from the sting.

316

He met her eyes, holding her gaze. He'd disappointed the judge and made her unhappy. He didn't know which he regretted more. "We didn't know there was anything in that building," he repeated. "Everett wanted to improve his aim, and I told him how to do it. I was trying to help him win the Greener."

"You're aware of the terms of your sentence." He winced as Ragan dribbled something that stung like fire on his open cuts. "You have a couple of places that should be sewn up. Someone will need to go for Marta when she finishes with Everett."

"How are we supposed to deal with this?" someone shouted.

"Yeah, Judge. He's your prisoner!"

Florence and Minnie lit into Hubie and Carl again, and the noise level rose until Johnny couldn't hear himself think.

Judge McMann picked up a glass and banged it on the bar, trying to restore order. "Settle down! I can't hear myself think!"

Eventually the hubbub quieted enough for the hearing to proceed. Accusing eyes centered on Johnny, now standing beside the judge.

"Excuse me . . . pardon me." Jo threaded her way to the front to stand beside the accused.

"Go sit down," Johnny said under his breath.

She stiffened her stance and remained.

"Jo!" he snapped. She didn't realize what trouble her show of support would cause.

Ragan took a posture on the opposite side. The two women took hold of his hands and held on tight.

"Both of you sit down. This doesn't concern you."

They ignored him as if they didn't hear. The judge rapped for order again. "Folks! The least we can do is hear John's side of the story."

He wished he had one. Wished the town's animosity wasn't directed at him. Wished Ragan and Jo weren't risking their reputations for him.

The judge turned to look at him. "Son?" He wished he could erase that betrayed look off Proctor's face.

"I was teaching Everett to shoot." A hush fell over the crowd. Hubie Banks stared daggers at him.

"Everett was practicing for the contest, the bullet went wild, and the shack exploded."

His stomach tightened when he felt Ragan's grip tighten.

Shaking his head, the judge looked away.

"You both could have been killed."

"We didn't mean to cause any trouble." Everyone present knew the incident had not only shaken the town, it had also put the judge's program in more jeopardy.

Jim Allen slowly got to his feet. "What are you going to do now, Judge? McAllister isn't supposed to handle a gun."

Judge McMann's eyes focused on Ragan's hand resting in Johnny's. She met his visual warning with respectful defiance. He turned back to face Johnny.

"Teaching someone to shoot isn't the same as handling a gun. You don't have to plow and plant a garden to explain how it's done," Johnny argued.

Proctor shot him a stern look. "The matter is out of my hands. The shack's gone. It's up to the residents as to how they want to punish the culprits."

"Everett should be here. He's in on this too," Millie Crocker complained.

"Everett's out cold," someone pointed out. "No tellin' when he'll come around."

Ragan tightened her hold on Johnny's hand and spoke. "It's only nails and boards. Nobody was hurt or fatally injured in the accident."

The crowd fell strangely quiet. Anger was still evident, but it was obvious that tempers

319

had begun to cool. Would they demand that Judge McMann send Johnny back to Judge Leonard? If so, Judge Leonard would order him to be hanged.

"I won't let them send you back," Ragan murmured.

"How can you stop them?"

"I'll think of something. I can't imagine why you would betray the judge for such a silly cause, but I know you well enough to believe you must have a reason."

The judge rubbed his lined forehead. "Austin, will you accompany Mr. McAllister to Rudolph's stable and stay with him until we can determine what to do about this matter?"

The farmer slid out of his seat and made his way to the front. Giving Johnny's hand a final squeeze, Ragan released it, smiling. What he saw in her eyes was almost worth the misery.

Austin took his arm and walked him through the crowd. Julia Curbow reached out to pat his shoulder as he passed, her eyes warm with affection. "You're a good boy, Jonathan. You were only trying to help Everett."

Nodding, he allowed Austin to lead him away. It wouldn't take long to find out if the rest of the town shared Julia's opinion. Common sense told him they wouldn't.

# CHAPTER
# FORTY-FOUR

"Austin?" Ragan stood in the livery doorway, holding Kitty in her arms. The town had been meeting for more than an hour now.

Austin glanced up. "Any decision yet?"

She shook her head. "May I have a moment with Johnny?"

The farmer got up from the pile of hay, reaching for his battered hat. He looked worn out, older than Ragan remembered. Austin used to give her brown sugar treats when she was a child. She'd always sought him out in a crowd, holding tight to the old farmer's callused hands. When he reached the doorway, he turned to look back. "Can I trust you to be alone with him? You won't do anything foolish, will you?"

"I give you my word."

He nodded. "Gonna get a dipper of water. A little parched." He left the barn, and Ragan listened to his footsteps fade into the shadows.

Johnny refused to look up as she approached.

"I brought Kitty."

He raised his head, frowning, and then dropped his gaze back to the floor.

Lowering the cat to his lap, she sighed. "I thought you needed a friend."

"Darn cat. Nothing but a nuisance." He reached for the animal just the same, scratching her behind the ears.

He could deny he loved that cat all he wanted, but Ragan knew differently. He could deny that he cared for her, but she knew differently. She took a seat beside him.

"You shouldn't be here."

"Why not? I have a stake in your future."

He kept his eyes down, his features sober. "What future?"

"Your future. Our future."

He slowly turned to meet her gaze.

"Our future," she repeated softly. "We could have one, you know, if you weren't so bent on destroying it."

"You don't need a man like me. Ragan, be realistic. You need a man you can be proud of, a God-fearing —"

She rested a finger across his lips. "Johnny, maybe you're a more God-fearing man than you imagine yourself to be."

"I'm a man who's not worth all this trouble. Get that through your head."

She reached for his hand.

"Didn't anyone ever tell you a man's supposed to make the first move?"

"I don't hold with *all* rules." She smiled. "And by the way, you haven't kissed me today."

"Come on, Ragan. You can't be seen kissing a convicted bank robber."

She feigned surprise. "Don't tell me you haven't thought about it." She removed her hat.

A grin played at the corners of his mouth. "I thought about it."

"When?"

"This morning, when you were dusting the parlor. Your cheeks were pink, and that piece of hair was in your eyes. And I thought about it when you were treating my head wound."

"What piece of hair?" She unconsciously smoothed back a strand.

"The piece that's always in your eyes."

"So, hush up and kiss me now." She leaned closer, drawing his mouth over to meet hers. He tasted cool and sweet.

"Ragan, I'm bad for you." He set Kitty on the ground and drew her closer, holding her. "Why can't you see that?"

"You'd like nothing better than to convince me that you're bad to the bone, but so far, you haven't even come close. I've seen you with the town widows and Papa."

Settling against his shoulder, she sighed. "You're a gentle man at heart, Johnny. You've made some foolish mistakes, and this thing with Everett is just plain poor judgment, but we're all guilty of poor judgment at one time or another. I think since I'm in —" She caught herself. "Very fond of you, I'm entitled to be curious about why you decided to violate the terms of your sentence." Her gaze met his in the dim barn interior. "Wouldn't you say?"

His eyes focused on her lips, and she knew he was considering kissing her again. Knew it with every fiber in her soul. And there was nothing she wanted more.

"You're fond of me."

"Yes, I am."

"That's crazy —"

She laid a finger across his lips again. "You can't stop me from liking you very much. We may not always see eye to eye on everything —"

"Name me one time we've agreed on anything."

"*And* I'm worried sick about your spiritual state, but I figure God will deal with you on

325

his terms. You have a friend in me, Johnny."
She sighed and went on bravely. "Believe
me, I've tried to deny I feel anything but
compassion for you. But today, when I realized you could very likely be hanged, it
only reinforced my knowledge that my feelings went much deeper than that. I don't
expect you to be in love with me, but I think
it's important that you know there is someone in this world who loves you."

"How did your feelings go from fond to
love so quickly?"

She blushed, but her eyes locked with his.
"You know what I mean. I will be heartbro-
ken if you carry out your threat to kill Dirk
Bledso." She knew her heart was in her eyes
now. "Don't do it, Johnny. Don't let Bledso
take your life too. Anger is eating you alive.
I understand your need to avenge your
family's deaths, but by doing so, you will be
giving Bledso the victory. Is that what you
want?"

"Bledso *slaughtered* my family."

"An eye for an eye?"

"That's right."

"Why not 'Vengeance is mine; I will repay,
saith the Lord'?"

He stood up, running his hands through
his hair. "Stay out of my problems, Ragan."

"I almost wish the town would ask the

judge to send you back."

He stared at her in disbelief.

"It's true. If they send you back, Judge Leonard will sentence you to prison."

"That's what you want? He could order me hanged."

"It's not what I want, but I think Procky could dissuade him from hanging you. If you're in prison, you won't be able to continue this insane search for Bledso."

"Do you know what you're wishing? If I'm sent to jail, I could be there a long time."

"Death is longer. If you kill Bledso, they'll for certain hang you. If you serve your time, you walk away a free man. Free, Johnny. Free to fall in love, free to marry, free to live again."

"Meanwhile, Bledso is also free. Free to go on killing. I can't buy your argument, Ragan." His eyes softened. "I wish I could."

She rose and stepped over to him. Hooking her arms around his neck, she pulled his mouth down to meet hers.

The contact was electric. All reason left her, and all she wanted was his embrace. She was prepared to do whatever she had to, to spend a lifetime in his arms.

They stepped apart when they heard the barn door open, and Austin appeared in the shadows. "Judge wants to see you, McAllister."

"I desperately hope he sends you back." She kissed him once more and then whispered, "Don't do it. Whatever the judge decides, don't continue this search for Bledso."

The citizens of Barren Flats wore solemn faces when Ragan and Johnny entered the Oasis. Judge McMann looked drained, his complexion pale. This couldn't be good. What would she do if something happened to Procky? The day had been taxing beyond belief.

He motioned toward a couple of stools. "Sit down."

Johnny sat down, and Ragan stood beside him. The room fell silent.

"The town has made its decision."

Johnny nodded. Ragan's hand tightened on his shoulder, and he knew he was only kidding himself. Feelings for her were starting to override his attraction for blood. That couldn't be. He had spent sixteen years of his life looking for Bledsoe. What had Ragan Ramsey ignited in him that no other woman had ever set fire to? The thought scared him.

"Everett regained consciousness a few minutes ago. He sent word that he, and that he alone, was responsible for the accident."

Johnny stood and took a step forward. "That's not true, Judge. I took advantage of Everett."

The judge peered over his spectacles at him. "In what way?"

If he told them he wanted access to a gun, that admission would seal his fate. If he didn't, Everett would shoulder the blame. He couldn't do that to a friend.

Ragan spoke up. "Isn't it obvious, Judge? Mr. McAllister is feeling a sense of guilt for his part in the accident. He was befriending Everett and feels they both share equal blame."

Proctor eyed her impatiently. "Mr. McAllister is capable of speaking for himself."

"He's capable, but he won't do it."

Julia Curbow was on her feet in Johnny's defense. "The gun was never in his hand. Everett swore to that."

The town murmured in agreement.

"Speak up, son. Did you handle the gun?" Procky asked.

"No, sir." That at least was the truth.

The judge smiled. "I'm glad to hear that." He looked at Ragan and then at Johnny. "The town has decided to let you stay."

"Yesss!" Jo bounded to her feet, and Holly pulled her back down to her seat. She flashed Johnny a smile.

He couldn't let them believe a lie. "Judge, I —"

"Order! We aren't accepting testimony from the accused." The judge's voice was firm. "The decision to let you stay in no way excuses what you've done, John, but it seems the consensus is we want that dynamite shack more than we want a piece of your hide. You and Everett will rebuild it, at your own expense, and you'll start come daylight tomorrow morning."

"Yes, sir." Johnny exhaled in deep relief. Building the shack back wasn't a problem — leaving Ragan would have been.

# CHAPTER
## FORTY-FIVE

After supper Johnny excused himself and went to the porch. Sitting down in the rocker, he reached for Kitty. The town had gone easy on him. He didn't deserve their clemency, but he was grateful for it. Rebuilding the shack would take every cent he had, but he didn't begrudge the lost funds. It could have been much worse.

The screen opened, and the judge wheeled out. When his honor saw Johnny, he nodded. Proctor had been unusually quiet during supper. Johnny had the feeling that the town might have forgiven him, but it was evident Proctor hadn't.

"Thought I'd get a breath of air. The house is hot tonight."

Johnny got up to give the judge his favorite seat. "It's cooler out here." He helped the judge from the wheelchair, into the rocker, and then he sat down opposite him.

Kitty bounded onto his lap, and he smiled.

The cat purred and rubbed against his shoulder, wanting attention.

"Get down, Kitty."

"She's not bothering me, Judge."

Pulling his pipe from his pocket, the judge packed it with tobacco. Johnny stroked Kitty's head. The two men sat in silence on the porch, enjoying the faint breeze.

Proctor struck a match, and the flame illuminated his weary features. Johnny wished he hadn't been the one responsible for the dark circles under the old man's eyes tonight.

"I'm disappointed in you, son."

"I know, Judge. I didn't mean to endanger your program. I was wrong, and I apologize."

Fanning out the match, Proctor drew on the pipe stem. A pleasant cherry scent perfumed the air. Kitty settled herself on Johnny's lap and stretched out. In a few moments, she was purring softly.

"It isn't so much the program. I knew when I started it that I would have setbacks. It's more about you. I want you to get back on your feet and start living life to its fullest. I've known you long enough to form my own conclusions, and you *know* the Lord, son. You've just blocked him out of the way. You stepped back; he didn't. Take your problems to him. Let him guide your decisions. You're smart enough to know life goes a whole lot smoother when you follow the plan God has for you."

At one time Johnny would have stopped him, but he knew he spoke the truth.

The judge settled back in his chair. "I know you must wonder why I allow myself to be wide open for defeat, but there's something you need to understand. Giving a man more freedom is the only way I can be assured he can be trusted, that he does what he does because he wants to, not because he's made to. I want to feel, beyond a doubt, that the person I'm working with can be rehabilitated. In your case, I had no doubt you were a man of your word, that I could trust you."

Johnny wished the judge's words were filled with condemnation; it would have been easier. He heard failure instead, and he knew he had put it there.

"You can trust me, Judge. I give you my word. There won't be any more problems."

The judge snorted. "Hubie and Carl should've known better than to store liquor in there in the first place."

Johnny leaned back, absently stroking Kitty. "I suppose you can take comfort in the knowledge that Hubie and Carl have a much bigger problem than a dry Founders' Day."

The men chuckled softly at the thought of Minnie and Florence lighting into the mayor and his bumbling accomplice in front of the whole town.

Then Johnny said quietly, "I am sorry, Judge."

Drawing on his pipe, the judge set his rocking chair into motion. The gentle squeak mingled pleasantly with the sounds of tree frogs. "I'm an old man. I've learned to roll with the punches. It's Ragan I'm concerned about." He turned back to face Johnny. "She'd never fall in love with a man who didn't know and respect the Lord. Don't let her down, son. If you do one thing in life right, don't let down the Lord or Ragan."

Johnny didn't have to ask how he knew about Ragan's feelings. The judge had witnessed her openly holding his hand that afternoon. Proctor didn't want her hurt. Neither did he.

The old chair creaked back and forth. "She's like a daughter to me. I love that girl, and wouldn't take kindly to anyone who would cause her a moment's grief." The old man's eyes drifted shut. "Do we understand each other, John?"

"Yes, sir. We understand each other."

"Good." His head bobbed. In a few minutes, soft snores filled the porch. Johnny leaned over and gently removed the pipe from the judge's hand.

Ragan pushed the screen open with her hip, balancing a wicker basket.

Johnny got up to help. "I'll get that for you."

She smiled. "Thought you might walk me home."

"I'd like that."

A full moon lit the path to the Ramsey place. As Ragan walked hand in hand with Johnny, the companionable silence was a far cry from the turmoil of the day's events.

"It's been quite a day, hasn't it?"

"I could have lived without it."

"Johnny." She paused in the middle of the road, moonlight playing across her feminine softness. "I'm glad you're staying."

He couldn't resist teasing her. "Three hours ago you wanted me sent to prison."

"I want you alive."

His hand tightened on hers, and they walked on. "I'll be staying a while."

"For me?"

"Might be. You or Kitty." He drew her closer as they walked.

"What about Bledso?"

He wished he knew. "Maybe someone will mistake him for a polecat and shoot him."

She leaned up for a kiss. "Just so it's not you."

Maybe someone *would* mistake him for a polecat and kill him. Stranger things had happened. It would be nice to think about settling down in a place like Barren Flats with a woman like Ragan Ramsey.

When they set off again, Ragan giggled. "Some thought the blast was an earthquake. What did you think?"

"I didn't have time to think. I was flat on my back, staring up at the sky."

They broke into infectious laughter. Each time one gained control, the other burst out laughing again.

"I thought Florence was going to beat Hubie with that umbrella!"

"She did! I saw her whack him a couple of times on the way back to town."

"She was as mad as that old hen Everett nicked during the practice." He told Ragan about Everett's wild shooting and his attempts to teach him to hit the target. "I was trying to help him win the Greener. But in addition, I wanted to know where I could put my hands on a gun if Bledso ever rode through. I'm not proud of it, and I knew I was putting the judge's program in jeopardy, but I didn't touch the gun, Ragan, and I wouldn't have unless I'd had to."

She sighed softly. "I understand what drove you to that, but it worries me that you would consider putting the judge's program in jeopardy for any reason. God has shown you mercy, Johnny. Judge Leonard could have hanged you that day."

"I've considered that."

It was hard to confess his motives, even to her, but he was proud of the friendship he had established with Everett. And it felt good to no longer be hiding anything from her.

"At least the mystery of the donkey cart is solved," Ragan said.

"I wonder how many late-night trips Carl and Hubie made carrying that home brew out there."

"More than they'd admit, I bet. There was a lot of fuel for that fire." They broke into laughter again.

When they arrived at the Ramseys', the house interior was dark. Ragan stepped up on the porch and peered in the front window. Everyone had retired for the night. "I didn't realize it was so late. I hope the girls weren't worried about me."

Johnny set the basket on the step. "Do you have to go in this soon?"

"Well," she sighed, coming back down the steps. "It's been a long day, and you have to be up earlier than usual in the morning." She met his gaze and burst out laughing again.

It took a second for him to join her. "Not funny," he said reaching for her.

"Shhh." She giggled, laying a finger across his mouth. "We'll wake the family."

He slowly pulled her to him, lowering his mouth to taste each sweet-smelling fingertip that still held the flavor of supper. When she murmured her pleasure, he drew her into his arms. "You're beginning to grow on me, you know that?"

She leaned closer, offering her neck. Pushing her hair aside, he kissed her fragrant skin, resting his mouth against her ear. "You smell good too."

Closing his eyes, he drank in her essence. Moonlight and the faint scent of the judge's tobacco on her dress. She fit him as if she were made for him. Maybe God was trying to make up for a wrong.

"It's Maddy's lemon water. I sneak a dab here and there." Her breathing switched tempos. "Procky said he didn't mind. It makes him think of his wife."

Turning her into him, he kissed her, lightly at first, then drawing her deeper into his

338

embrace. When their lips parted, she rested her head on his shoulder. "What am I going to do about you?"

"I don't know, but for what it's worth, I'm real fond of you too," he murmured.

"You are?"

"I am."

"That's not good enough," she whispered. "Say you're fond enough of me that you'll stay alive for me."

He pulled her to him again, his mouth closing over hers. He wanted to live for her, more than he'd wanted anything for a long time, but something inside refused to let go of his quest for revenge. A lifetime of hatred was difficult to put aside.

Later that night, when he lay back against his pillow, the faint scent of lemon still lingered on his skin.

Kitty turned around on his chest a couple of times and then plopped down. Twitching her tail, she eyed him sleepily.

Could he give up his pursuit to kill Bledso? Once the issue had been so clear cut, but it was murky now.

Maybe his family's vindication wasn't in seeing a worthless, no-good piece of humanity eradicated, but rather from seeing the surviving son productive and happy and going on with his life. It was a new thought, one he'd never imagined before. He closed his eyes, the taste of Ragan still on his lips.

Was it enough for him?

# CHAPTER
# FORTY-SIX

A thunderstorm threatened the Founders' Day celebration during the night. Thunder and lightning shook the ground, but by morning the skies had cleared and a bright sun shone on the town. The grass dried, and outdoor activities began in earnest. Teams strung red, white, and blue bunting across both ends of Main Street, and store owners tacked patriotic streamers to their storefronts.

Men swung heavy scythes, and weeds disappeared like magic. Women set up long tables in the churchyard and arranged chairs. The south end of Barren Flats began to look like a county fair.

Ragan waved to Jesse Rehop as his wagon rumbled past, loaded with benches for the spectators at the shooting contest. As the mule team topped the rise, Jesse turned and yelled over his shoulder. "Hey, Cliff. Come up here!"

Carl Rayles and Shorty Lynch dropped what they were doing and followed Clifford Kincaid up the hill.

Ragan frowned. What were they gawking at? Johnny and Everett were building the new dynamite shack just beyond the rise. She could hear the ring of hammers from where she stood.

"Excuse me, Minnie. I'm going to see what's so interesting over there." She laid a tablecloth aside and walked up the rise to join the men. She could hear their conversation as she approached.

"Now, that's a fine piece of work. Makes the old structure look downright embarrassing."

"Shore does. Didn't know Everett had it in him."

"Don't think it's so much Everett as it is McAllister. I was watching them work the other day. McAllister seems to know what he's doing with a hammer," Carl offered.

The four men eased closer and peered at the construction.

"Built real sturdylike. Take a cyclone to topple this one."

"Or a big blast." Shorty winked at Carl.

"Admiring the new building, gentleman?"

Ragan tried not to let her pride show, but it was nearly impossible. The new construction was more than lumber and nails. Johnny was creating one fine piece of work.

"Yes, sir," Cliff said. "That boy's a real carpenter."

Ragan swelled with bliss, and she had to be careful not to strut as she walked back down the hill to rejoin the women. She glanced back over her shoulder, grinning when she heard Carl yell at Johnny and Everett to stop work and come join the festivities.

"C'mon up here, Everett!" Cliff echoed. "You need to get in a little practice before that shootin' contest this afternoon."

The thought of Everett throwing his hammer aside and vaulting over the sawhorse tickled Ragan.

The past month, the change in Everett was one more thing the town could attribute to Johnny McAllister.

These days, Everett walked with a new confidence. The strenuous physical labor had produced muscles that were invisible a month ago. Long hours in the hot sun had tanned the clerk's skin nut-brown, and the hard work had perked up his appetite. He'd packed a good ten pounds of muscle on his lanky frame, and the extra weight suited him well.

By nine o'clock, Main Street was full.

Neighbors welcomed relatives from surrounding counties, and friends gathered in small groups.

After lunch, Ragan saw that Julia Curbow had Johnny cornered near the watermelon table, introducing him to all her friends.

"Jonathan, this is my best friend, Lydia, from Cedar Gulch."

Then a moment later, "Jonathan, this is my best friend, Lucia, from Brown Branch." The spunky widow dragged Johnny through the crowd, showing him off. "And this is my best friend, Mona Joann, from Tom's Canyon."

When Johnny passed Ragan for the third time, she teased in a loud whisper, "Why Jonathan, you are just the sweetest man. Let me introduce you to my best friend."

Johnny finally escaped Julia's clutches and found a shady spot for himself and the judge. The two men seemed to be deep in conversation when Ragan noticed them later. She considered taking her two favorite men some lemonade, but she decided they had more important things on their minds.

# CHAPTER FORTY-SEVEN

The judge tapped his pipe bowl. "I'm proud of you, son. You made a mistake, but you're paying your debt. One slip isn't going to impede your progress. And you've been good for Everett."

Everett was busy entertaining several of the town's eligible young women. The new dynamite shack had made the telegraph clerk somewhat of a celebrity.

"He's a hard worker."

"That boy was raised in a strange family. His daddy took off soon after Everett was born. An uncle moved in and helped Everett's mother and grandmother put food on the table, but he was an overbearing man and never had much good to say about the boy. Everett's mother never quite took to her son, though she raised him with strong moral convictions, and he always did well in school." The judge sighed. "I suppose that's why Ragan's always been so good to him.

Over the years, Everett has latched onto her like a lifeline."

Johnny smiled. Who could blame him?

"Working with you these past few weeks has turned him into a man."

When Everett spotted the two, he excused himself and walked over to join them. "Afternoon, Judge."

"Afternoon, Everett. Turned out to be a nice day."

"Yes, sir, real nice. Can I get you a cool drink, sir?"

"No, think I'll just go over and help myself to another piece of Mazilea's chocolate cake. My, that woman can cook." He wheeled off, heading for the desserts.

Everett fell into step with Johnny, and they walked to the area where the shooting contest was scheduled to start in little under an hour.

"How's your aim today?"

Everett shrugged. "Not worth a hoot."

Johnny grinned. "Just remember to keep that arm steady."

"I'll try, but however the contest turns out, I'm not doing it for Ragan anymore."

"No?"

"She's in love with you, John."

Johnny shook his head. He was in love with her, but he didn't know if he could saddle her with a man with a record. "Once my sentence is served, I should be moving on."

"You'll break her heart."

The last thing he wanted to do was break her heart, but he loved her enough to walk away. All of her life she'd been a caretaker; he wanted more for her. Her law degree and eventually a man solid with God and in good standing with the community. He was none of those.

"When I leave, Ragan can go on with her plans. She'll go off to school, and someday she'll find a man deserving of her love. I'm not the settling-down kind."

Clearing his throat, Everett dropped his voice and glanced around. "Shoot fire, I'd hate to see you leave myself. I've never had a real friend before . . . hope you don't mind."

"I don't mind, Everett. I was thinking the same about you."

*What are you going to do, McAllister? Put your life on hold forever? Let a woman like Ragan slip through your fingers so you can pursue scum like Bledso? Ignore something like Everett's admiration and loyalty? Friends like him rarely come along. A friend like that would stand beside you through thick and thin.*

Bledso wasn't worth a hair on Ragan's or

Everett's head. Why couldn't he let it go and get on with his life?

"We're good friends now," Everett reminded.

Nodding, Johnny concurred.

"I'm giving her to you, John."

"Who?"

"Ragan." Everett paused and turned to face Johnny. "I've loved her for as long as I can remember, and she likes me — in a brotherly sort of way. But she loves you."

"You don't know that."

"I may not be the biggest or smartest man around, but I know Ragan. And she's in love with you. You're the best man for her."

"Best man?" Johnny paused, digesting the gift. "Between the two of us? I'm not the best man, Everett. I'm the ordained man."

"Huh?"

"I may be the one God has in mind for her, but I cannot imagine why. You're the best man, and the woman God has for you is out there. You'll meet her someday, and then you'll understand just how complex love can be."

"Well." Everett grimaced. "She's taking her own good time getting here."

The hour for the shooting contest arrived. The men, faces drawn with concentration, had taken their three shots at their targets. There'd been some mighty fine exhibition.

Now, all eyes were centered on the last contestant.

Silence gripped the area.

Everett clutched his big blue pistol and steadied his arm. Sweat beaded his lower lip. Staring down the sight, he slowly squeezed the trigger. His arm jerked upward, and the bullet actually landed on his target.

Carl Rayles checked the board for accuracy and then shook his head. "Well, that was close."

Everett craned his neck to see. "It was?"

"Weren't bad. Take your second shot." Mayor Rayles stepped back, his eyes on the large X.

Hubie Banks paced behind the benches, his eyes glued to the target. The brand-new Greener double-barrel shotgun, displayed in a leather-tooled case, rested on a nearby table.

Everett closed one eye, squeezed the butt of the pistol between both fists, and sighted. His eyes closed as the shot rang out.

"Hit it square in the middle this time!"

"Let me see that!" Hubie Banks pushed through the onlookers and snatched the board from the mayor's hands. He studied the bullet holes, then silently handed back the target.

Everett's eyes narrowed. "You're not the judge, Hubie. Go sit down."

The saloon owner stalked off.

Everett returned to his mark and, taking careful aim, fired his last shot.

"Half inch to the left of the X," the mayor called out.

Everett bit his lower lip.

"Still pretty good shootin'. Definitely in the running."

The mayor added Everett's target to the pile, and the men began to put away their guns. "That's it for the contest, gentlemen. I'll announce the winner of the Greener before the fireworks tonight."

Everett flashed Johnny a relieved grin, and Johnny released the pent-up breath he hadn't realized he was holding.

Now he knew what it was like to have a kid.

Toward dark, the festivities started to wind down. Women gathered the leftover food and packed it away, and lanterns were lit. Older children played stickball or captured fireflies in glass canning jars.

Mothers with small babies spread blankets on the ground and settled down to nurse their infants before the annual fireworks display started.

The brand-new shotgun went to Hubie Banks again this year, but Everett came in third. The telegraph clerk shook Banks's hand and warned him that next year would be different. He turned and met Johnny's eyes in the crowd, and with a huge grin he saluted him.

While the prizes were distributed, Johnny wandered through the crowd until he located Jo, sitting with Fulton Ramsey. During the day he'd noticed that Ragan's father seemed more lucid than usual. Tonight his eyes were bright as he watched the activity going on around him, even though it was getting close to his bedtime.

Seating himself on the ground beside Jo, Johnny grinned at her. She smiled back.

"Guess who I just saw at the lemonade stand?"

She lifted her brows. "Who?"

"Benny Dewayne I-can't-live-without-you Wilson."

Her eyes lit with excitement. "Is Emma with him?"

"No, I saw her talking to Austin Plummer's boy." He leaned closer. "Benny looked like he could use a pretty girl's company."

Jumping to her feet, Jo tidied her hair. "Really?"

Chuckling, Johnny said, "Go on. I'll keep your father company."

Jo hurried toward the lemonade stand, still fussing with her hair as she walked.

"Enjoying the events, Mr. Ramsey?"

Fulton turned his head. He smiled vaguely, digging in his vest pocket. A moment later he produced a wooden giraffe and pressed it in Johnny's hand. "God watches over them."

Johnny nodded. "Yes, sir, he sure does."

Then Fulton's face sobered. "But he also expects his people to look after themselves."

Johnny studied the older man. Ragan favored him in some ways. Same blue eyes, same shaped nose. Those eyes focused clearly on Johnny now, not clouded as they usually were. "Because I didn't stand up to the gangs, my son was taken from me. You can't let that happen. Give me your promise that you won't let that happen again."

"Mr. Ramsey —"

Fulton took Johnny by the arm, his eyes burning with conviction. "If I had stood up, the town would have followed me. If we had stopped the raids, Jacob would be alive."

Johnny was relieved when he caught sight of Ragan crossing the lawn, balancing three pieces of watermelon in her hands. Concentrating on the melon, she called out, "Anyone still hungry?"

Her smile faded when she looked up and saw Johnny's somber expression. She glanced at her father and then back at him. "Is something wrong?"

"No. Your father and I were talking."

She frowned. "Talking?"

"Yes. Your father was talking about your brother."

"Oh, Papa." Ragan set the watermelon slices aside and leaned down to adjust the light throw draped across Fulton's legs. "Do you want to go home now? Are you tired?"

Fulton rummaged in his pocket and came up with a wooden fish. He handed the treasure to her. "Two fishes and five loaves of bread were all that were needed to feed the multitude."

"Come, I'll —"

He flashed a smile, his eyes clear again. "No, daughter, I don't want to go home. I'll stay for the fireworks, thank you."

# CHAPTER
# FORTY-EIGHT

"I thought I might find you here." The following Monday morning, Ragan set her bundles on the general store floor and knelt beside Johnny, who was loading nails into a sack. Their eyes met, and she drank in the sight of him. He looked so handsome this morning, his dark hair damp with rain. "Good morning."

He checked to see if Mazilea was at the front of the store before leaning to steal a brief kiss. "I thought you had baking you wanted to do this morning."

She pressed her forehead against his. "Bread's cooling on the counter. It's raining."

He checked Mazilea's whereabouts again, and then stole another kiss. "Did you come all the way over here to remind me that it's raining?"

"Of course not. But that means you can't work on the tower."

354

He dropped the last nail into the sack and stood up. "Not until it lets up. Everett's catching up on some work at the telegraph office, so I decided to come for supplies. Do you need something?"

She rose to face him. "You." Slipping her arm into his, she led him toward the front door. "Come with me."

"Where are we going?"

"You'll see." Breezing by the register, she called, "Mazilea, put two dozen nails on Johnny's account."

The store's owner was busy sacking corn-meal. She tied off a bag and set it on a shelf, waving an acknowledgment as they went out the door.

The couple stepped onto the porch, and Ragan popped open her umbrella. The sky was dark; the steady rain that had fallen since daybreak drummed on the tin roof. The drought was broken.

"What's this about?" Johnny asked, ducking under the canvas awning.

Flashing an impish smile, she inclined her head toward the end of the street. "Follow me!"

They darted down the steps and across the street, sidestepping mud puddles. They were halfway down Main when the sky opened and rain fell in torrents. Racing up the porch steps, Ragan flung open the door, propped the dripping umbrella on its handle, and dashed into the foyer.

Johnny, close on her heels, closed the door behind him. They stood in the hallway, dripping on the polished oak floor.

"I'll clean that up later." Ragan impatiently grabbed his hand and proceeded up the stairway, dragging him behind her.

The noise prompted the judge to wheel his chair to the parlor doorway. "That you, Ragan?"

She stopped midway and turned to lean over the railing. "It's me, Procky. I have something to show Johnny in the attic."

"In the attic?"

"I'll leave the door open!" she called.

Frowning, the judge patted Kitty, who was stretched lengthwise on his lap. "Can't imagine where she gets all her energy," he said to the cat. Shaking his head, he returned to his journals.

Johnny and Ragan exchanged conspiratorial glances, and she continued up the stairs.

Rain pattered off the eaves of the musty-smelling attic. Ragan lit a candle and set it on a nearby trunk. Rubbing her arms, she smiled. "Procky hasn't quite gotten used to the idea that he can't run up and down the stairs anytime he wants to anymore."

Johnny returned her smile. "Should he check on us?"

She shivered, ignoring the innuendo. He was still a bit rough around the edges, but that would change. "It's chilly up here," she murmured, trying to still her chattering teeth.

His gaze scanned the cramped quarters. "Just show me what you want to show me, and I'll be running along. Got a lot a work yet today."

She picked up an old blouse, and started drying off. "We are courting, aren't we? Sort of."

His gaze sobered. "I'm not in any position to be courting."

"That's for me to decide."

He stepped deeper into the attic, his eyes scanning the discarded furniture and crates.

"Do you spend much time up here?"

"Some. It was Maddy's sewing room. She said it was the only peace and quiet she could find, so she came up here most every day and sat in that corner by the window to read or sew or to just think about things. I've sorta picked up her habit. I do quite a lot of thinking up here, myself."

Johnny bent to look out the window. "Not much of a view. All you can see is the porch roof."

357

"I didn't bring you up here for the view." He turned around, and her eyes met his. "I have something for you." Taking him by the hand, she moved toward a table on the other side of the window. The surface was cluttered with sewing notions and stacks of cotton material. Scissors, thread, pins, a tape measure, and patterns attested to its recent use.

Ragan picked up a wrapped bundle and handed it to him. "Go ahead and open it," she said with anticipation.

Johnny unwrapped the package and removed two new shirts. Holding them up, he stared at them.

"Do you like them? I finished them after breakfast this morning."

"They're . . . real nice."

"Just nice?"

He looked at her, confusion evident in his eyes. "Who are they for?"

"For you, silly." She moved around the table, tidying up. "I had all this material just lying around. I made the judge shirts for Christmas, and I thought you'd enjoy having something new too." The two shirts he owned were threadbare, and they'd been washed so many times the colors were faded to nothing.

He appeared to be struggling with accepting the gift. Had she embarrassed him? That wasn't her intention — far from it. She longed to take care of him, the way a wife cares for a husband.

Thunder shook the old house, rattling the windows. Rain sluiced down the glass panes. Johnny held one of the shirts up to his chest for fit. "I can't pay you for your work."

"Pay me?" She paused, overcome with disappointment. "I wouldn't accept money, Johnny. They're a gift."

"I don't remember the last time I had a gift — or a new shirt, for that matter."

"Well, you have two new ones now. I have a good eye. I think they'll fit," she said as he stepped in front of a mirror and held a shirt up to his chest.

Slipping the new shirt on over his old one, he assessed his image.

"What do you think?" she asked. He looked powerfully handsome in the blue-and-black plaid.

"You did a good job."

"Thank you, sir."

Drawing her closer, he bent to kiss her. She looked up at him, her heart hammering. "I love to make things for you."

"You want to know something?"

She nodded, loving him so overwhelmingly she felt that she might explode.

"I like you to make things for me." They were the most heartfelt words she'd ever heard from him. And the most welcome.

Resting her cheek on his shoulder, she savored the moment. There had been too few good ones lately. "You've been so quiet the past few days. Withdrawn, the way you were your first few weeks in Barren Flats. I thought we had moved past that."

"Sorry. I've had things on my mind."

"Still Dirk Bledso?" she guessed softly.

Gently releasing her, he stared into the mirror.

How could she reach through this shell he'd built around himself? How could she make him see that all he wanted was right here, standing beside him, with her heart in her eyes?

"It's funny," he mused.

"What's funny?"

"I'm twenty-eight years old. I have no home, no family, my horse was sold for restitution, and someone other than family has Grandpa's pistol."

She heard what he couldn't say, that he had no purpose other than to kill a man. "Papa would say a man makes his own purpose."

"Your papa's wiser than I am."

Johnny fell silent as he reflected on his

360

mirrored image.

Was she getting through to him? It was hard to tell. His hurts were buried so deep. But she wouldn't stop trying until she did.

He turned from the looking glass and drew her back into his arms. Closing her eyes, she held him tightly, surrounding him with her love. *Please God, let me make a difference in this man's life.*

But for the first time in her life, she wasn't sure her Maker was listening.

# CHAPTER
## FORTY-NINE

The rain slacked off shortly before noon.
The sun popped out, and the air grew
steamy. Ragan mopped her forehead with
her sleeve, but she smiled when she saw the
rainbow over the shed. Johnny was inside,
working on window frames for Widow
Keeling's house. The widow had caught him
on his way back to the dynamite shack. The
man had more work than he had time.

In addition to the dynamite shack, new
church pews were in progress. A special
Transformation Fund had purchased the
lumber, and the church members donated
the other supplies.

Town projects were mounting up too.
Minnie had put in her bid for a speaker's
platform in the open space east of the
churchyard. After donating a nice sum, she
challenged others to do the same to build
back the town. Contributed materials were
accumulating at an amazing rate. Barren

Flats had enough work to keep Johnny busy for years. Gangs were inevitable, but the town would repair and keep rebuilding. They would make Barren Flats a decent place to live, regardless.

"Johnny! Ragan! Judge McMann! Johnny! Ragan! Judge McMann!"

Ragan's heart lurched to her throat, and she reached the front door just as Everett burst through the gate.

"Johnny! Ra—"

"Everett, what's wrong?"

Johnny rounded the corner of the porch, hammer in hand.

The judge's cane pounded the oak floor. "What in the world? What's happened?"

Kitty darted out the door in front of him and disappeared under the rail.

Everett stood at the foot of the porch steps, his sides heaving, gasping for breath. He waved a paper in his outstretched hand. "Just came in . . . for . . . the judge."

Johnny took the paper out of his hand and handed it to Judge McMann.

"It's a telegram," Everett managed between gasps.

"We can see that, son. Who died?"

"No one died. They found the money."

"The money? What money? Just take a minute to get your breath." Judge McMann

363

scanned the wire and then reread it.

"Well, well, well." He turned to Johnny, his weathered face breaking into a smile. "It's from Robert. They've found the bank money pouch. Located it in a pile of brush two miles out of town."

"That's . . . that's what I was trying . . . to tell . . . you." Everett pressed his side, nodding vigorously. "Word just came in."

Julia Curbow came through the gate like a shot, then Millie Crocker, followed by Maggie Anglo. Shorty Lynch and Hubie Banks followed Roberta Seeden.

"Is it true?"

"What does it mean?"

"Did they find the money?" Shorty demanded. "Is Johnny cleared of the charges?"

"Whoa, now." Judge McMann raised his voice and rattled the paper for attention. "Let me read this again so there'll be no mistakes." He bent over the paper and took his time reading the message for the third time.

"Says right here the money's been found and it'll be returned to the rightful owners, the patrons of the First Territorial Bank of California in Canyon City." He looked up. "Sadly, that doesn't mean John's sentence will be excused."

A chorus of disappointed murmurs

rippled through the audience.

"Seems to me that if they found the money, that'd be good enough," Julia said.

Hubie turned to look at Johnny. "Guess that proves you've been telling the truth all along."

Johnny took off his hat. "I had nothing to do with the bank robbery or the money. But like the judge says, finding the money doesn't prove that."

Disappointment colored Everett's features. "I was hoping Judge Leonard would at least reduce your sentence."

"I've been praying so hard." Ragan came down the steps to join Johnny. They locked hands, and Ragan didn't care that Roberta's brows lifted.

"Well, the boy's a fine carpenter, and I believe he's innocent of the charges." With that declaration, Hubie turned and headed out the gate. Shorty followed.

"A hard worker," Roberta added as she turned to leave.

"Deserves a break."

"Got a bad deal."

"Building a shed fit for a king."

Julia waved her fingers at Johnny as she left. "Keep your chin up, Jonathan. You're a good boy."

"Thank you, Julia."

Ragan squeezed Johnny's hand, and he squeezed hers back.

"Plain ain't fair," Everett mumbled.

# CHAPTER
# FIFTY

By mid-October the new dynamite shack was finished and pronounced far sturdier than its predecessor. Gangs still rode through, shooting up the place, but the dynamite shack sat impenetrable. It would take an act of God to destroy it. Barren Flats declared Johnny, in Mayor Rayles's words, "The finest carpenter this side of the Mississippi River."

As far as Ragan was concerned Johnny was the finest everything, and she didn't let a day go by without reminding him of it. Each week drew them closer, and she dreaded the day he'd ride away. She had failed to convince him that Bledso had already stolen sixteen years of his life; he shouldn't allow him to have more. Johnny still searched the faces of every gang that rode through, convinced that one day Bledso would show up.

He caught her in the shed late one rainy

afternoon in a playful mood.

"Johnny —"

Drawing her away from the open door, he kissed her soundly.

"I am going to miss you so much when you leave," she whispered when they came up for breath. *Please, God, let him realize that what we have together is more important than seeking retribution.*

"I'm not going anywhere for a while."

But in her heart Ragan knew it was only a matter of time before Johnny would be tested, perhaps far beyond his newfound strengths.

"In conclusion, I feel the program, while experiencing occasional setbacks, has proven effective. In the future, I recommend that the penal system offer rehabilitation to those first-time adult violators exhibiting the willingness and common sense to change."

Judge McMann closed the folder, and sighed. Outside a humid wind whipped against the kitchen windowpanes. "And that's that."

Ragan drew a stitch through the pillowcase she was embroidering. "Feels good, doesn't it."

"Indeed, it is gratifying to know the book

is completed. And while the program wasn't as successful as I had hoped, it wasn't a total failure."

Ragan glanced at Johnny, who was stacking wood next to the cookstove. "So what do you think?"

"Me?"

"Yes, you, sir. Did we leave out anything?"

"Nothing except you don't know the outcome of my case."

Ragan glanced at the judge. "We feel certain we do."

"This project," the judge declared, lifting the manuscript to study it, "is the most important thing I've accomplished for society, with the exception of marriage and fatherhood, in my lifetime. I wish Maddy were here to share this."

Ragan smiled, taking another stitch. "She doesn't have to be here. She knows, Procky."

Proctor's gaze moved to Johnny, even though he still addressed her. "Don't ever forget what's important in life. Love, family, loyal friends. It's easy to lose sight of the things that matter."

Ragan bit off a thread and tied it. "Couldn't agree more."

"Well." The judge yawned. "It's past my bedtime. I assume you'll be mailing the manuscript first thing in the morning?"

"First thing in the morning. Then I have an errand afterward. Did you know that Mary Linder is getting married next week?"

"Yes, her mother cornered me after church. I hadn't realized Mary was old enough to get married."

"She's seventeen, Procky."

"Couldn't be. She was born just a few weeks ago."

Ragan grinned. "Mary's not feeling well, and in order for Estelle to have her gown finished on time, she's asked me to stand in for Mary's final fitting tomorrow. I'll mail the book and then stop by the seamstress's on the way home."

"Take your time; no hurry." The wheels on the chair squeaked as the judge rolled out of the kitchen calling for Kitty. "Come on, old girl. It's bedtime."

Early the following morning, Ragan watched Everett unlock the telegraph office.

"You're sure up and around early this morning."

"I want to get this mailed right away."

"Stage won't be here until late afternoon."

"I know, but once I mail it, I'll relax."

"Proud of it, huh?"

Ragan grinned. "Very proud."

Writing this book meant more than she'd

ever imagined. The hours of research, then putting words to paper, were all most gratifying.

She hovered over Everett's shoulder while he weighed the heavy manuscript and figured proper postage. With a dramatic swoop, he held it over the mailbag. Then, in a loud, authoritative voice, he announced, "I declare this project officially completed."

By now a group had assembled to watch the historic moment. When the parcel hit the bottom of the mailbag, they broke into a round of applause.

Ragan took a mock bow. "I hereby faithfully promise to remain humble, although I'm sure the book is destined to elevate Judge McMann and me to the ranks of the famous." She bowed again to another round of applause.

Still laughing and accepting congratulations, she left the post office. Bumping into Jo, who was on her way to the mercantile, Ragan said, "Hi, there. What brings you to town so early?"

"Papa wants an apple pie and we're out of cinnamon," the young girl explained as Ragan fell into step with her.

"Then by all means, we are off to buy cinnamon." The two sisters locked arms and giggled as they playfully skipped down the center of Main Street.

Ragan was on top of the world today, carefree. The money had been found, and Judge Leonard was bound to reduce Johnny's sentence if Johnny kept up his present cooperation.

"What are *you* doing in town so early?" Jo asked.

"Oh, I mailed the book this morning."

"Really!" Jo stopped to hug her. "Congratulations!"

"Thank you!"

They fell back in step, and Jo glanced at her, grinning. "Have you seen Johnny today?"

"I see him every day, nosy."

The sound of hammers and saws coming from the church attested to his whereabouts. Johnny had mentioned over breakfast that the new pews would be done in time for the next Sunday's services. Lately, he hadn't missed a Sunday preaching.

Jo sighed. "He's sure good, isn't he?"

"Yes, he's an excellent carpenter. And a good listener, and a wonderful friend." Ragan's cheeks flamed. *The man I adore.*

"You're blushing."

"I am not. It's just warm this morning."

"Huh-uh. You're beet red. All I said was that he's good. That made you blush?"

"No, Jo. Drop it."

"You don't think I'm old enough to understand, do you? Well, I am. I love Benny Dewayne, and I know what love is."

Benny Dewayne! Ragan resisted the urge to tell her sister this was puppy love, not the love of a woman for a man. That would come someday, and Jo would realize the difference. The way she'd discovered the difference when Johnny came into her life.

"It's true. Benny Dewayne is my absolute one true love. There's never been a truer love, except for maybe Holly and Tom, or you and Johnny. But Benny Dewayne and I —"

"Are much much too young to be talking such nonsense," Ragan said, walking ahead and leaving Jo to try to catch up.

"I wish you'd talk to me about you and Johnny. I am old enough."

"Jo, there's nothing to tell. I admit, I care about Johnny —"

*Way too much.*

"And sometimes I think he cares for me —"

*Not nearly as much as I'd like.*

"But there are many reasons we can't be together at this time."

*None strong enough that with God's help we couldn't overcome.*

"I know he loves you," Jo stated.

"You don't know that."

"Yes, I do. I feel it in my bones, Ragan."

Ragan sighed. Arguing with Jo was never productive. "Feel it in your bones — you sound like Grandma Ramsey. I have to stop by Estelle's. Mary Linder is ill, so I'm going to do her final gown fitting. Want to come?"

"I guess so. I hear the gown is lovely."

"It is if Estelle's making it." The two sisters climbed the outer stairs to the seamstress's two-room apartment over the title office and knocked on the door.

"You'd think Mary would want to come for the final fitting, ill or not."

"You know Mary. If she can get someone else to do it for her, she will."

A short while later, Ragan stood in front of the mirror, staring at her image. Mary's bridal gown was exquisite. Yards of tulle and lace, puffed sleeves, and a delicately embellished neckline. Estelle was simply gifted with a needle and thread. Ragan turned, studying the way the dress lay in perfect symmetrical folds. *If God makes it possible for me to marry Johnny . . .*

Her thoughts wavered. God wasn't standing in the way. Johnny refused to release his anger.

*When I marry Johnny,* she amended, *I want a gown exactly like this one.*

"It's beautiful," Jo murmured, fingering the delicate Queen Anne lace. "Estelle, you're marvelous."

"Speaking of wedding lace," the seamstress murmured, eyeing Ragan, "when are you going to tie the knot, young lady?"

"Someday."

"Well, it had better be soon or I'll be too old to make the dress." She swatted Ragan's backside affectionately. "Turn. Step back." She bent, adjusting the hem.

"Is Mary feeling better?" Ragan asked.

"I believe so. She wants me to thank you for the favor. I think she just has wedding jitters, but you know she's a little spoiled. Too pampered, I say. Good thing you gals have the same size waist. Don't know of anyone else who could oblige her."

A sudden ruckus outside drew their attention.

Ragan caught Estelle's eye in the mirror and frowned. "A raid?"

Estelle shrugged and knelt, slipping a pin into the hem. "I hope not. Don't have time to put up with one today."

Jo opened the door and peered down the stairway.

"What's going on?" Ragan preened in

front of the mirror, admiring the gown.

"Nothing that I can see."

The seamstress and Ragan joined Jo on the porch, and then they cautiously descended the stairs.

Jo peered around the corner. "I still don't see a thing."

Estelle shrugged again. "Must have been a false alarm. Be careful with that hem coming back up. Mary will have a fit if it gets soiled."

Ragan lifted the skirt and turned to follow. "Jo, could you help with the train back there, please?" As Jo gathered the trailing hem, the sound of thundering hooves approached and the women turned in alarm. Four riders were coming in hard, their dusty coats whipping in the wind.

"Run!" Ragan grabbed for Jo's hand to pull her back up the stairway as the riders galloped straight at them, firing pistols into the air.

Ragan frantically tried to push Jo ahead of her to safety, but the lead rider swooped down and scooped the young girl into his arms, laughing.

"Jo!" Ragan screamed, grasping for her sister's arm.

"Ragan!"

Horrified, Ragan felt her sister's fingers

slip through her desperate clutch. For an instant she met the evil eyes of the red-bearded horseman.

"Put her down!" She leaped forward and grabbed her sister's skirt. The outlaw threw back his head and laughed harder as Jo thrashed about, fighting him. The horse reared, and he jerked back on the reins, and then he swung Jo up in front of him, wrenching her from Ragan's grip. Kneeing the stallion, he galloped off with Jo's frantic screams filling Main Street.

Estelle fell back against the stair railing, holding her hand to her heart. "Oh, my! Oh, my!"

Ragan bolted after the horseman. "Stop. Stop!" she screamed, watching in terror as the gap between her and her sister widened. "No, no, not Jo! Please, not Jo." She stumbled and fell to the ground. The train of the wedding dress caught between her feet as she tried to regain her footing. "Not Jo. Please dear God, not Jo," she sobbed.

The three accompanying riders shot the bank's front window, shattering the glass, then wheeled their horses and hightailed it out of town.

Ragan got to her feet and ran, oblivious of Mary's beautiful gown. Though she thought her lungs would burst, she ran faster and

# CHAPTER
# FIFTY-ONE

Stumbling up the church steps, Ragan yelled McAllister's name. She could hear her voice, but it was as if it came from somewhere far off.

Johnny dropped his saw and charged toward her, meeting her halfway up the aisle.

"What's happened?"

At first nothing registered in her brain. His mouth moved, but she couldn't make out his words.

He lightly shook her, but she didn't feel his hands on her arms. He shook her again. She knew he was trying to reach her, but she couldn't break free. Powerless to speak, she opened her mouth, suddenly aware she was crying hysterically. His look of stark fear finally brought her to reality.

"Ragan!" His eyes searched hers. "Calm down and tell me what's wrong."

"They have Jo!"

"Who has Jo?"

"That red-bearded outlaw and his men!"

Panic seized his features, and he grabbed her arm, and they were running. Out the door, down the steps, across the churchyard.

He ran faster, pulling her along, shouting to the town's men as they passed each business. "Hubie! Shorty! Carl!"

People spilled from doorways and followed Johnny and Ragan down the street.

Rudolph Miller ran out of the livery to meet them. "What's going on?"

"One of the gangs has Jo!"

Timothy Seeden fell into step. "Why would they take Jo?"

Johnny's features hardened. "They don't want Jo. They want me, Tim. I'm going after her."

Carl Rayles took two steps for every one of Johnny's. "Now hold on, son. We need to talk about this. You can't go after her alone."

"Then form a posse."

"A posse!" The men exchanged dubious looks. "Where's Alvin? Someone get Alvin. He needs to handle this."

Ragan wanted to scream. Didn't anyone care about Jo? What if the men hurt her? What if they did the unspeakable? She couldn't bear to think about the horrifying possibilities.

"Now, see here. It's foolish to just ride out of here not knowing where we're going. No telling where they've gone with her." Hubie avoided Ragan's eyes. "Thank goodness, here's Alvin. Sheriff, what do you think we should do?"

"Eh?" Sheriff Lutz approached, cupping his ear. "Somethin' goin' on?"

Hubie leaned closer and held his hand to his mouth. "What do you think we should do about this?"

"About what? What's happened?"

Johnny struck off for the stable. "I'm going after Jo. Anyone who wants to come with me had better find a horse."

"Now, son, don't do anything rash," Mayor Rayles cautioned. "We're all worried about Jo, but we've got to think this thing through and not go off half-cocked and get ourselves killed. Why, you don't even have a gun."

Jesse Rehop unbuckled his holster. "He does now."

Carl frowned. "What are you doing with a gun?"

"I wear it while I'm working, in case I meet up with a rattler." Jesse met Johnny's eyes. "You take it, son, and good luck to you."

Julia wrung her hands. "Jonathan isn't

supposed to have a gun. Don't you men get him in more trouble!"

Rudolph Miller settled the matter. "For heaven's sake, Julia, if this situation doesn't warrant a gun, I don't know what does." He looked to Sheriff Lutz. "Don't you agree, Alvin?"

The old man cupped his ear. "Eh?"

"IT'S ALL RIGHT FOR MCALLISTER TO HAVE A GUN. HE'S GONNA NEED ONE IF HE GOES AFTER JO."

"Snow? You outta your mind?"

"JO, ALVIN!"

Shorty intervened. "Deputize McAllister, Sheriff."

"Why, he's a criminal . . ."

"Deputize him!"

The elderly lawman stepped forward. "Johnny McAllister, I hereby deputize you — now it's a temporary thing, you understand. It don't set aside your sentence in any way. And it don't give you the right to risk your life, but it'll allow you to carry Jesse's gun." He paused, glanced at Ragan, and then frowned. "Which one of the Ramsey girls did you say was missin'?"

"*Jo!*" a chorus of voices yelled.

Alvin gave them a sour look. "Don't have to yell. Raise your right hand, sonny."

Julia clapped her hands at the completion

382

of the brief ceremony. "I'm so proud. Jonathan will make a wonderful sheriff."

"Deputy, Julia," Carl Rayles corrected impatiently.

Johnny turned to Rudy Miller. "I'll need a horse."

"You got it."

"Now, son." Lowell Homer put his hand on Johnny's shoulder. "I can't let you ride out of here by yourself. Jest wouldn't feel right."

"I'm going after her, Lowell, with or without the town's help."

Ragan's heart pounded so hard in her ears she could only catch snatches of the men's conversation. Why didn't someone offer to go with him? Why couldn't this town, just once, stand up and fight! She reached out and caught Johnny's shirtsleeve. "I'm going with you."

"You're staying here." Strapping the leather holster around his waist, he searched the crowd. "Anyone coming with me?"

The men hung their heads, shuffling their feet.

Johnny turned and strode toward the barn. Jerald Hubbard tried to intercept him. "Be reasonable about this, McAllister. We're all married men. We have families to consider."

"And children to raise." Jim Allen fell into step. "You know we'd help if we could, but who'd look after our womenfolk if something was to happen to us?"

Mayor Rayles hurried to keep pace with the others. "I feel certain they won't harm the girl. The gangs have never actually hurt anyone. Just made a nuisance of themselves."

Johnny shook off his hand. "This is more than a nuisance, Carl."

Ragan's stomach balled into a tight knot. Jo would be frantic, scared out of her wits.

"Rudy, where's that horse?" Johnny shouted as they walked into the livery.

Ragan suddenly realized his danger. What would she do if he didn't come back? What if she lost both Jo and him to the red-bearded stranger? She put her fist to her mouth to keep from screaming. *Why doesn't somebody do something to help him?*

Everett stepped from the barn's shadows, holding the reins of two saddled horses, his gun at his hip. "I'm going with you."

Nodding, Johnny reached for one pair of reins and swung aboard.

"Johnny!" Ragan grabbed his hand, and her eyes beseeched him, so frightened she couldn't think.

His hand tightened on hers. "Go home

and be with your family. I'll find your sister."

"Tom will want to help search for Jo."

"Tom isn't here, Ragan, and time isn't on our side."

"Please, Johnny, be careful." If she were to lose either one of them, she couldn't bear it. "Come back to me," she pleaded.

Gripping her hand, he said quietly, "I'll be back."

The two horses galloped from the livery a moment later and headed out of town.

"Any idea where they might have gone?" Everett called.

"No. What about you?"

"My hunch is Sutter's Ridge. It's an easy ride from there to the border."

"How far to Sutter's Ridge?"

"Two or three miles."

They whipped the horses faster. It was the first time Johnny had been on a horse since the day of the bank robbery. The chestnut gelding was smaller than his sorrel but well muscled, and he caught the horse's rhythm easily. His eyes scoured the road, looking for the gang's tracks.

"Looks like they've been here." Everett pointed to a set of fresh prints leading into the canyon.

Johnny circled the area, studying the

ground. It almost looked as if Puet was marking the way, as if he wanted to be tracked.

Everett followed close behind.

Reining up, Johnny got off his horse. The tracks were too obvious. Something was wrong.

"How far do you think they'll go with her? Across the border?"

"Hard to say." Johnny removed his hat. "They've left a trail obvious enough for a simpleton to follow."

"That's what I was thinking. Why do you think they've done that?"

"I have a hunch they're laying a trap for me."

"You?"

Johnny nodded. "The red-bearded man committed the robbery I'm accused of."

Everett turned to look at him. "Are you sure?"

"Positive."

"What do they want with you?"

"They think I have the money. The day of the robbery, I was standing on the bank porch when Puet and his gang came out with Judge Leonard's daughter as a hostage. I made an attempt to save her, and somewhere in the process I ended up with the bank bag. It was lost a couple of miles down the road. I never saw it again, but Puet believes I have it."

"And that's why they took Jo? They want to use her as a bargaining tool?"

"That's how I have it figured."

Everett studied the ground. "What do you think they'll do to her?"

Johnny didn't want to think about that. "We have to find her."

He didn't want to think about the anguish on Ragan's face when he left her standing in the livery. He knew now that he was in love with her, and everything else had ceased to matter. Not Bledso, not vengeance — nothing but Ragan and her happiness concerned him.

He couldn't go on the way he was anymore, always searching, bitterness eating him alive. He wanted to let go of the past and choose to stay with the woman he loved. He wanted to make a home, start a family, be a part of Ragan's family. And Jo was part of that family.

Everett studied the horizon ahead. "Look over there."

"Smoke?"

A faint breeze caught the scent and carried it in their direction.

"Do you think it's them?"

Johnny mounted and kneed the gelding

forward. "Stay close."

"Don't worry. You couldn't lose me if you tried."

Within a hundred yards of the outlaw's camp, they slid out of their saddles and crouched low. Male voices and laughter carried clearly. The smell of fresh coffee scented the air.

"Don't seem too worried, do they?"

That's what bothered Johnny. They didn't appear worried at all.

Everett dropped to the ground and pulled himself on his belly to peer around a bush. The ring of mesquite surrounding the small clearing provided almost no covering. "That's them, all right. I see Jo."

Johnny eased closer. Puet and two other men stood around the campfire, eating and drinking coffee from tin cups. Jo, her hands and feet bound by thick rope, sat at the edge of the clearing.

"What do we do now?" Everett whispered.

"Why, come in and join us, gentlemen. We've been expectin' you."

Johnny glanced behind to see a fourth outlaw with a gun trained on him. His hand automatically dropped to his holster.

"Don't try it, McAllister. One shot, and the girl's a goner."

Johnny and Everett stepped into the clearing a moment later, hands above their heads.

Jo's eyes widened when she saw them, and she struggled against the heavy ropes.

"Well, well, well." Puet stepped away from the fire. "You took the bait. Had you figured to be smarter than that, McAllister."

Jo whimpered, her fingers trying to work free of the ropes. One of the gang members leaned over and smacked her hand. She gave him a withering look, and he backhanded her. Tears welled in her eyes.

"Stay where you are, McAllister." A hammer clicked, and Johnny froze. He couldn't help Jo with a bullet in his chest.

"Let the girl go."

Puet laughed, and his eyes fixed coldly on Johnny. "I want my money."

If they knew it'd been returned to the bank, he'd have nothing to bargain with. "Let Everett take the girl and you can take me. I'll lead you to the money."

The outlaw's eyes blackened with fury. "I'm tired of your games. You're a burr under my saddle, McAllister. If Pete hadn't been so stupid that day, he wouldn't have mistaken you for me; that money would be in my saddlebags, and I'd be long gone from here."

Pete took the slur personally. His lower lip jutted out. "I told you, I was jest tryin' to get out of there —"

"Shut up!"

"You fellas will never get away with —"
Grunting, Everett toppled to the ground
when Pete struck him from behind with a
rifle butt.

Johnny's eyes locked with Puet. "Let the
girl go." They'd kill him when they discovered he'd lied, but at least no one innocent
would die.

"You're giving me orders? You're not in
any position to give orders."

A fist slammed into his gut, and Johnny
doubled over.

"Let the girl go," he repeated tightly. "She
doesn't have anything to do with this."

He saw the next blow coming. *Ironic. I'm
going to die by an outlaw's hand after all.*

"Where are your people, McAllister? That
gutless town that refuses to help their own?"
Pain coursed in black waves, and Johnny realized he was losing consciousness. He
couldn't . . . had to rescue Jo . . .

"Come on, Puet. He ain't got the money.
Let's kill him and the girl and git outta
here."

"Not yet, boys. He's kept me around these
parts far too long." Puet laughed. "First
he'll tell me where that money is."

Johnny moaned in pain. "Touch the girl

and you're a dead man, Puet . . ."

The outlaw jerked him by the hair of the head and yanked him upright. "Fun's over. Where's the money?" A vein bulged in the side of the Puet's neck.

"If you kill me you'll never find it."

Puet shoved him down, and the kick connected solidly. "You like this, boy? I can keep it up all day without killin' you."

The air filled with the sound of triggers clicking into place.

Puet glanced up. The men of Barren Flats pointed double-barrel shotguns, Winchesters, and pistols straight at him. A fraction of a second later, an egg splatted in the middle of his forehead. He blinked, raising his hand to the sticky yolk. "What the —"

A row of wagons rolled from the line of mesquite as women and children, toting large pans, buckets, and slingshots, advanced on the campsite.

"Uh-oh." Pete's hand dropped to his holster.

The other outlaws moved in closer. Squinting, the youngest one stretched to study Puet. "That *egg* on yore face?"

Chaos broke loose.

Gunshots pinged, wounding one of the bandits in the leg. The outlaw dropped to the ground, holding the wound. The citizens of Barren Flats stood up in their buck-boards, defending their positions. Bullets flew, some missing the mark, but others severely wounding. Arms flailed the air as the outlaws tried to shield themselves from the onslaught.

Then the women took over. Eggs with yolks as thick and sticky as gelatinous glue flew through the air. Rolling on the ground, the gang shouted obscenities as the unrelenting attack kept up.

"Make 'em stop, Puet!"

"Shut up! Ouch!"

"Shoot 'em!"

"*You* shoot 'em!" Puet shielded his head with both arms. "I cain't get to my . . . *ouch!* . . . gun!"

Mazilea and Minnie crawled into the campsite on their hands and knees, scooping up the men's weapons, swiping pistols from holsters, and utilizing their bargain day shopping skills to disarm the hoodlums.

Ragan dashed toward Johnny, dropping to her knees to check his injuries. When he opened his eyes, she smiled. "Hello, darling."

He struggled to focus. "Are you wearing a bridal gown?"

"I didn't have time to change."

Struggling to sit up, he fell back. "What is

392

going on?"

"The town is ready to defend you." She leaned down, about to kiss his bloody forehead, but she gave him a loving pat instead. "Lie still. I need to see about Jo." She rose, gathered the folds of Mary's lovely satin and lace skirt in a wad, and bolted off to untie her sister.

"Mess with my Jonathan, and you mess with *me,* misters!" Julia Curbow stood up in her surrey, loaded another egg in her slingshot, and then hauled back and let fly.

Martha, perched daintily on the seat beside her, clapped with delight. "Atta girl, honey. Let 'em have it!"

Shorty Lynch and Carl Rayles galloped by on horseback, balancing a hornet's nest on a long pole between them. As they reached the floundering outlaws, Carl dropped one end of the pole, Shorty leaned over, pulled the rag out of the hole, and tossed the nest. Angry hornets boiled from the paper womb and Carl and Shorty grinned as they galloped off.

The outlaws hammered their heads, batting at the stinging insects.

The youngest one's high-pitched wails troubled Blanche Payton.

"Poor child," she tsked. "Poor, poor child!"

"Don't feel sorry for that boy," Martha admonished. She loaded a slingshot with a rutabaga. "His mama's prayers are the only thing that's kept him alive so far."

In the midst of the pandemonium, Jo and Ragan lifted Johnny to his feet. Clifford Kincaid and Austin dragged Everett to a nearby wagon. The telegraph clerk opened his eyes long enough to grin before passing out cold again.

A wagon wheeled by carrying Jim Allen and his sons. Ragan heard the unmistakable sounds of "oinks" and whirled to see the wagon rattle to a halt beside the writhing outlaws. Jim's two oldest boys sprang from the bed, dragging a barrel between them.

The gang's eyes widened when they spotted two curly-headed boys racing toward them. Flinging their arms over their heads, they shouted curses as slop rained down on them.

"You little hoodlums!" Puet bellowed. "We'll get you for this!"

Then the boys dropped the gate on the wagon, adjusted a wide plank, and hogs poured out.

The pigs squealed, making a beeline for the dinner table. The men's screams equaled the rooting sows'.

As Ragan and Jo supported Johnny past

Judge McMann's wagon, they paused briefly.

"Jo, you all right, girl?"

"I'm fine, Judge. Just a little shaken."

"Johnny?"

"Fine, Judge." He grinned, trying to focus with eyes that were swelling shut. "Glad to see the town's decided to stand up for themselves."

"Me too." The old judge beamed. "You look a sight, boy. You sure you're all right?"

Ragan smiled. "He just needs a little tender loving care."

"Which you'll be only too delighted to provide."

Ragan smiled from ear to ear. "Only too happy."

"Well, don't just stand there, woman. Get your man home, and see to his wounds. Then take Mary's dress off." He looked at the soiled gown, shaking his head. "Pitiful."

Ragan blew him a kiss, and the three hobbled on.

The judge sat back, drawing on his pipe. "Well, Alvin, I have to say it does my heart good to see the town finally take a stand."

Alvin cupped his ear.

"Stand up for — never mind, Alvin. Let's go home. I'm getting too old for this kind of excitement."

Alvin flipped the reins on the horse's rump. "Cold? In this part of the country? You losing your mind, Judge?"

# CHAPTER
# FIFTY-TWO

"My, my." Estelle stepped back, taking stock of the damage the next morning. The townswomen stared at Mary's soiled wedding gown, woefully shaking their heads.

Ragan frowned. "It's bad, isn't it?"

Minnie nodded. "Curdles the blood."

"Mary will be devastated."

"Oh, my, yes . . . and with her weddin' only a few days off."

Minnie dipped a cloth in a pan of wood ash, lye, and water and dabbed at a splotch of yellow egg yolk. "Estelle, I hope you can sew fast."

"I don't like the thought of it, but I can make a dress in three days if I set my mind to it. I'm just thankful the men let us let off a little steam toward those hoodlums. Land knows, we've had to clean up after 'em for years."

The seamstress fussed about at her sewing table. "Never saw such foolish goings-on. Why didn't someone think to defend the town with guns alone? Eggs? Rutabagas? Pigs? And a *hornet's nest!* Never saw the likes. It's a wonder they didn't get their own fool heads stung off. What's this world coming to?" She measured off a length of fabric and carefully stretched it out on the table.

Ragan didn't know what the world was coming to either, but she sure was proud of the citizens of Barren Flats. They'd stood up to Puet and his no-good gang in a remarkable show of solidarity. But best of all, they'd stood up for Jo and Johnny. Their loyalty made her heart sing!

Fireworks went off outside, and a cheer went up. Barren Flats was in a festive mood this morning. Puet and his gang were prominently displayed in a large jail cage in the middle of Main Street. The four men sat in the bottom of their wagon, reeking of pig slop and muck, and nursing some pretty ugly welts.

"How's your young man this morning, Ragan?" Estelle cut into a length of silk, critically eyeing the measure.

"Johnny's fine. He has some cuts and bruises, but he'll heal."

The way he'd responded when she'd gently kissed each abrasion before applying salve assured her he was none the worse for wear. He'd insisted his injuries were well worth the trouble, considering all the attention she gave them.

"Good heavens, will you look at that? Those outlaws are carrying on something awful," Minnie exclaimed.

"What's going on now?" Ragan moved to join her at the window.

Below in the street, Puet let out a string of curses that fouled the air. Julia Curbow calmly walked over to the water barrel, dipped up a bucket, and doused the salty-talking outlaw. The women at the window cheered.

Stumbling backward, the dripping victim sat down hard on the floor of the wagon. His cohorts doubled over laughing and then shrieked when Julia dipped a second bucket and doused them.

Ragan shook her head at the commotion. "I guess Alvin's not going to do anything to stop this public debacle."

Minnie giggled.

"Minnie!" Ragan scolded.

"They're only gettin' what they got comin'."

"Julia's not about to give up her post anytime soon, either." Ragan frowned as the judge's elderly neighbor dipped yet another bucket of water and stood waiting to administer punishment to the next prisoner who acted up.

The band below struck up a merry tune. Warren lugged his tuba across Main Street to join in, and Hubie Banks and Austin Plummer locked arms, breaking into a merry jig.

Toward the end of Main Street, Shorty Lynch held a ladder while Rudy Miller nailed up a crudely lettered sign. It read: AIN'T GONNA TAKE IT ANYMORE! ENTER AT YOUR OWN RISK.

Ragan anxiously scanned the area. Where was Johnny? He was already gone when she arrived at the judge's this morning. She wanted to celebrate Barren Flats' unqualified acceptance of him.

Minnie let the lace curtain drop back in place. "I think we finally have our town back — thanks to Johnny."

Estelle turned to look over her shoulder. "Hand me that thimble, will you, dear?"

"Ragan Ramsey!" Johnny's voice roared from the street below.

Ragan whirled and hurried back to the window to see him striding toward the building. Behind him, Everett and a contingent of male supporters urged him on.

Estelle left the sewing table, frowning. "Who's doing that caterwauling?"

Ragan grinned, so proud she thought she just might burst. "That's my man." She watched behind the curtain as Johnny paused before Estelle's stairway, looking up at the second floor. "Ragan? Are you up there?"

Ducking back with a teasing gleam in her eyes, Ragan motioned for Estelle and Minnie to keep quiet. "Shhhhhhh."

"Why? What's goin' on? Is he angry with you?" Minnie whispered.

If he was, he hadn't mentioned it while she nursed his injuries last night.

"Ragan Ramsey!"

Everett, Shorty, Austin, and Rudy cheered Johnny on from the street.

"Go after her, McAllister!"

"Show her who's boss!"

Estelle frowned. "Oh, my. There's gonna be trouble. I can feel it." She gathered the cut material and scooped scissors and spools from the table in the center of the room.

"Law, now he's taking the stairs two at a time." Minnie backed to the wall.

The door burst open, and Minnie's hands flew up to cover her mouth. Johnny towered in the doorway, his bruised and battered face a mask of determination.

Ragan slowly backed up.

Covering the distance between them, McAllister scooped her off her feet and kissed her, a long, red-blooded, totally improper kiss that made Estelle drop into a nearby chair, looking faint.

When their lips finally parted, Ragan sucked in her breath, staring back at him wide-eyed. "Were you calling me?"

He set her down and gave her a stern look. "You could have been killed out there."

"So could you — and I wouldn't have wanted to go on living without you."

His eyes softened. "And I wouldn't want to go on without you."

"Honest?"

"Honest."

Tittering, Minnie returned to lean out the window. The men below were hooting and catcalling, making a royal nuisance of themselves. "Stop all that racket, Carl Rayles! Have you lost your mind?"

Carl waved a flag in the air, grinning up at his spouse. "Come on down here and join us, Minnie Winnie."

"Minnie Winnie!" She slammed the window shut. "That old fool's been in the spirits again."

Estelle fanned her face with a hanky.

Ragan was oblivious to the commotion.

Johnny's gaze held hers. "There was so

much going on yesterday, I think I forgot to mention how pretty you looked in that wedding gown."

She blushed. "Oh, that. Mary wasn't feeling well, and Estelle knows we're about the same size, so she asked me to put on the dress while she pinned the final fitting. I didn't have time to change back into my clothing when the trouble started."

"Humph." Estelle had recovered enough to return to the sewing table. "Seems to me there's a lot of yakking going on. Seems a certain young man around here ought to ask for a certain young woman's hand in marriage. Then, that certain young woman could have her own bridal gown — providin' I ever find the time to make it."

A slow grin started at Johnny's eyes and moved to the corners of his mouth. "Well, Miss Ramsey? What do you think about me staying on in Barren Flats and making the town my home?"

Ragan caught her breath. "Oh, Johnny! Are you serious?"

"They tell me I'll be a free man in a few days. Sheriff Lutz says Everett is eager to testify that Puet confessed to robbing the bank and that I had nothing to do with it. There's a sizeable reward on the outlaws' heads. Seems the bank at Canyon City was only one of many they hit. Everett and I are going to split the money." His voice softened. "My share will be enough to buy a small spread and get a new start."

Ragan sighed. A new start. That sounded so nice. She affectionately traced his nose with a fingertip. "What about Bledso?"

"There's only one thing I want in my life. And I'm holding her in my arms." He caught her closer to him and held her tightly. "You're the only thing that matters to me."

"Oh, darling, how I've longed to hear you say those words."

They hugged, and Ragan thought she might burst with happiness. Johnny was staying, and Bledso was finally in the past.

"Oh, there's something else you should know. Alvin wants me take his badge."

"His badge? Why?"

"Says he thinks it's about time to step aside. Seems he's just discovered he doesn't hear that well."

She grinned. "Outlaw to sheriff. That's rather sudden, isn't it?"

"I'm getting used to the unexpected."

"Will you take the job?"

"I can always earn a wage building things, but I would like to build lives — like you and Procky." He kissed her and then whispered against her lips, "Not all lives can be changed, but if I can change one, then I've made a difference."

"You can handle those hoodlums?"

"I've handled you, haven't I?"

She playfully boxed his chin.

"Well? What about it? Ready to make this permanent?"

"You and me?"

"You and me."

"Is this a marriage proposal?"

He kissed her again. "If you want, I'll get down on my knees and beg you to marry me."

"Oh, dear. And I've promised myself I'd never entertain the idea of marriage to a man who has two black eyes and a split lip," she teased.

He shrugged. "Life's little problems."

She nodded solemnly. "In that case, I accept."

He lifted a skeptical brow. "Just like that? What about your schooling? Your plans?"

"I've decided that I don't want to go to school. I want to write."

"Write? Books?"

"Novels. I enjoyed doing research for Procky, but I've discovered what I really love is the writing part. Putting words on paper, writing what's in my heart." She hugged him tightly. "And there's no reason I can't do that right here in Barren Flats."

He smiled, touching his nose to hers. "Barren Flats is my home, isn't it? And the judge needs looking after. Then there's the cat to consider."

Minnie and Estelle pretended unusual interest in a spool of thread, allowing the young folks their privacy.

"Until you came along, I hadn't let myself think about marriage, family, and home," he whispered. "All I could think about was killing Bledso. But you — and the Good Lord — changed that. I guess he's been working on me all along, but until I met you I didn't know that family and the love of a good woman were better than bitterness and anger. You thought all those nights you read the Bible aloud that I wasn't listening."

"But you were."

"I was. I'd heard it all before, but after I met you, and witnessed your faith, I began to accept that God judges, not me. I can put the problem in his hand."

She tucked her head beneath his chin. "It's hard, I know, but it's the only way we can live with real peace. God will judge evil."

"I love you, Ragan. I'm sorry it took me so long to admit it." Lifting her off her feet, he swung her around, laughing. "I love you, woman!"

"My, my," Estelle mumbled, stuffing another pin in the corner of her mouth. "This is goin' to be a headache. I suppose now you'll be wanting *your* wedding gown yesterday."

# EPILOGUE

Proctor McMann's parlor was overflowing late Saturday afternoon, the twenty-eighth day of October.

Ragan had insisted the wedding ceremony be limited to immediate family, but that didn't keep Minnie and Mazilea from filling the sitting room with baskets of mums and baking for two days straight prior to the service.

All of Barren Flats was invited to share the joyous occasion of Johnny McAllister and Ragan Ramsey's nuptials with a celebration immediately following the ceremony. A large picnic and street square dance were planned and predicted to go on until the wee hours of the morning.

Fulton Ramsey sat on the bride's right. Holly, Jo, and Rebecca wore their Sunday best, with flowers in their hair. Mary had graciously offered Ragan her wedding dress. Ragan had always thought the girl a bit spoiled, but when she had protested, Mary had said that a gown that pretty needed to be worn more than once. So, today Ragan had it all. The gown of her dreams and the man of her heart.

The best man, Kitty, sat on her haunches to the right of Johnny, a blue ribbon around her neck. Everett, Carl Rayles, and Rudy Miller served as groomsmen.

Judge McMann beamed on the gathering with a grandfatherly smile.

"Do you, John Franklin McAllister, take Ragan Judith Ramsey to be your lawfully wedded wife? Will you love her, honor her, keeping her only to yourself, as long as you both shall live?"

When Johnny turned to Ragan, she saw his promise clearly written in his eyes. "I do."

"Do you, Ragan Judith Ramsey, take John Franklin McAllister to be your lawfully wedded husband? Will you love him, honor him, keeping him only to yourself, as long as you both shall live?"

"I do."

The wedding party laughed when Kitty batted her paw at the judge's shin, adding a resounding "Meeeow."

Judge McMann closed the Bible. "Then it is my great and personal honor to pronounce you man and wife. May God's love shine on you and your marriage. May your days be long upon this earth and your blessings too numerous to count. And, I will personally add, may you be as happy fifty years from today as you are at this very moment. Now, come here and give this old man a kiss from the prettiest bride Barren Flats ever produced."

Smiling, Ragan handed her bouquet to Holly, pecked the judge on the cheek, and then turned into the waiting arms of her husband.

Gold-and-brown banners proclaiming the McAllister/Ramsey marriage lined Main Street. The smell of beef roasting over an open pit filled the air. The women were turned out in their Sunday best, and fiddles tuned up near the bandstand.

Beneath a beautiful star-studded night, Johnny McAllister stepped onto the floor of a gaily decorated gazebo and claimed a waltz with his bride.

Shorty Lynch good-naturedly handed Ragan over with a knowing wink. "Take care of her, son."

Johnny's eyes locked with his bride's. "I will, Shorty." *Thank you, Father.*

Ragan settled into her new husband's arms, marveling at life. Not long ago she had believed she would never find true love and that Johnny would drift through life, never knowing love or family ties. Tonight, he was here in her arms, and her joy was immeasurable.

Johnny gazed down at her, his love openly displayed. "Hello, Mrs. McAllister."

"Hello, Mr. McAllister."

He chuckled, pulling her closer. "Happy?"

"Very happy."

Closing his eyes, Johnny drank in the nectar of forgiveness. Of grace, as Grandpa's words played through his mind. *Johnny boy, the Lord will avenge your enemies.*

For a while he'd forgotten that bit of wisdom, but no more. He would take care of the blessings God allotted him, and let God be God.

"And now, my dear husband, I have a wedding gift for you."

"You do?" His face sobered. "Ragan, I didn't buy you anything —"

"Pffff. Things don't matter. I have everything I've ever wanted. Wait here."

She felt his gaze follow her as she stepped off the dance platform and reached for a package the judge held out to her. Returning, she smiled. "Happy Wedding Day, Johnny McAllister."

Johnny took the package and unwrapped

it. Inside the box lay his grandfather's pistol. Wetness stung his eyes, and he quickly blinked it back.

Gently wiping the lone tear that escaped him, Ragan whispered, "I was afraid it wouldn't get here in time, but it came on the stage yesterday afternoon."

Johnny's voice was thick as he pulled her close and held her. "Thank you, sweetheart. Besides the shirts, it's the best gift I've ever had."

Ragan smiled as her husband held her in his arms. Johnny McAllister wasn't going to feel unwanted or unloved ever again. She would make sure of that.

# ABOUT THE AUTHOR

**Lori Copeland** is the author of more than ninety titles, both historical and contemporary fiction. With more than 3 million copies of her books in print, she has developed a loyal following among her rapidly growing fans in the inspirational market. She has been honored with the Romantic Times Reviewers Choice Award, The Holt Medallion, and Walden Books Best Seller award. In 2000, Lori was inducted into the Missouri Writers Hall of Fame.

Lori lives in the beautiful Ozarks with her husband, Lance, their three children, and five grandchildren.

The employees of Thorndike Press hope you have enjoyed this Large Print book. All our Thorndike, Wheeler, and Kennebec Large Print titles are designed for easy reading, and all our books are made to last. Other Thorndike Press Large Print books are available at your library, through selected bookstores, or directly from us.

For information about titles, please call:
  (800) 223-1244

or visit our Web site at:
  http://gale.cengage.com/thorndike

To share your comments, please write:
Publisher
Thorndike Press
295 Kennedy Memorial Drive
Waterville, ME 04901